Marheh of the Silberay, Book 6.

Harbour Master for the Water Road

By

Rosalind Kentwell

L'Optimisme

Melbourne

Marheh of the Silberay Series

Book 1. Water Road Apprentice

Book 2. Apprentice Still

Book 3. Apprentice in Clanning

Book 4. Water Road Challenge

Book 5. Water Road and River

Book 6. Harbour Master for the Water Road

ISBN: 0-9874868-7-X
ISBN-13: 978-0-9874868-7-5

DEDICATION

For those kind friends who enjoy Marheh's adventures and encourage the writer to continue.

ACKNOWLEDGMENTS

Sally and Elwin – you are such good friends and helpers.
Thank you.

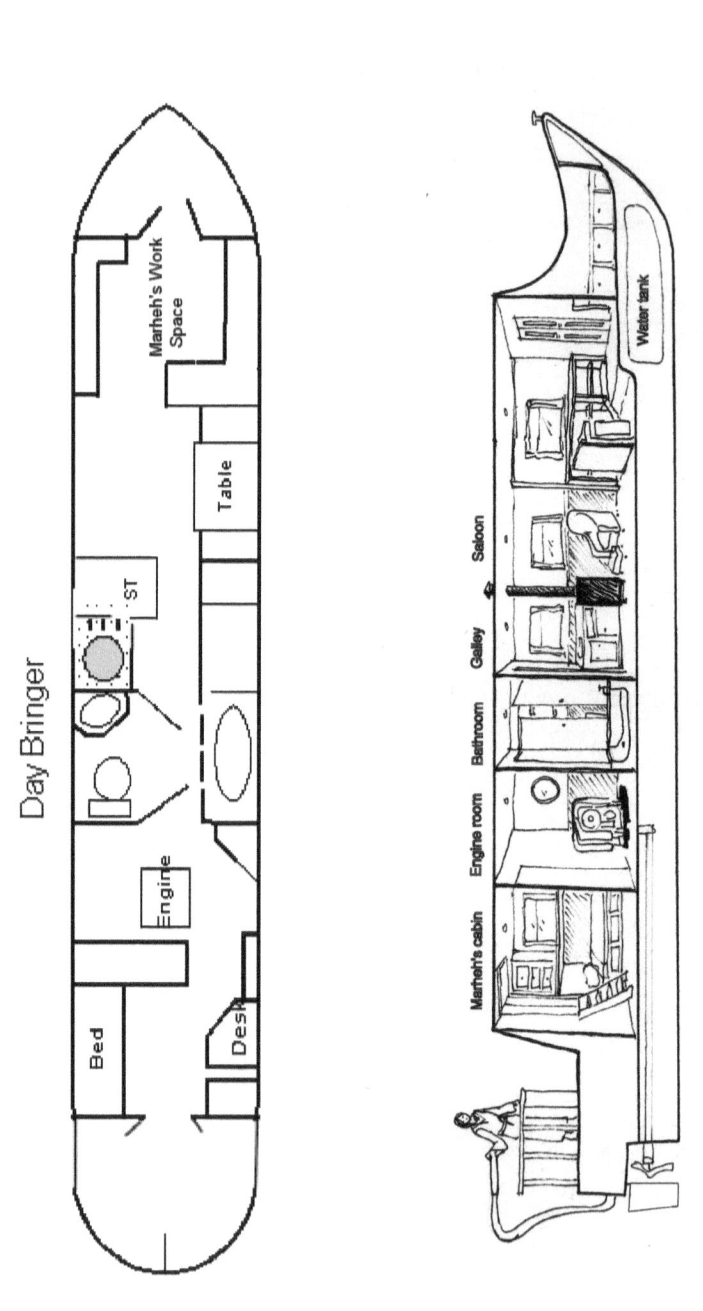

Day Bringer

Bed
Engine
ST
Table
Desk
Marheh's Work Space

Marheh's cabin
Engine room
Bathroom
Galley
Saloon
Water tank

Accounts

Chapter One

Marheh stared down at the ledger.

Diesel	£57.17s.3d
Bituminous paint	£32
Porridge oats	£11.10s,

and so on.

Gilt had assured her that standing in for him as Harbour Master would not be too taxing and would be only for six weeks or so while he went home to care for his father who was critically ill and she made a complete recovery from her injuries. She put her elbows on the desk and let her head sink into her hands, then winced as a twinge from her left collar bone warned her that she still needed to take care.

It was just over three weeks ago that disaster struck. She had been travelling on the section of the water road they called the WEG, the Western Edgerington and Gracedale being rather a mouthful, and her practice of the discipline of the soul had revealed considerable darkness around the town of Edgerington.

It had long been a troubled place. More than twenty years ago she and Nemle had been attacked there by a gang of young men and they had avoided the place after that.

On this occasion however Marheh found that she could not ignore the darkness and pain that she sensed there. Nemle used to speak of listening with her heart and taught Marheh to do the same. What she heard when she listened to Edgerington, was aching misery and despair that called to the Silberay she had become and refused to allow her to pass by.

She had moored on the outskirts of the town and set out, quite late in the afternoon, just to look around and perhaps buy something to add to her evening meal. She did not appear as different as she had those years ago with Nemle. Nowadays it was not uncommon for women to wear trousers. Her uniform still marked her out for those with eyes to see, but she was used to being a stranger where ever she went and confident of her skill with the discipline of the mind to keep her safe in most situations.

The town had expanded since last she visited and only one rather weedy and uncared for field separated the water road from the first of the houses. Tenements, really, she thought as she approached. They looked as if they had never been new, and certainly never cared for. She continued on, feeling sad for the inhabitants of this sorry place, but not concerned for her own safety.

What she had not realised and perhaps would not have recognised as a threat if she had, was that the town football team had just lost an important match and the team and its fans had been drowning their sorrows for the past hour. A mob of large, angry, drunken men were spilling out of the pub as she reached it.

Perhaps any stranger would have served for them to vent their spleen, but Marheh was not just any stranger. Although she no longer had the startling beauty of her youth, at fifty-one she was still an attractive woman and she had about her an indefinable something that marked her as different. It did not take much for catcalls and a couple of lewd invitations to escalate into violence.

She was able to use the discipline of the mind to control the first few who reached for her and this caused a degree of confusion, but there were too many for her to manage and while they were falling over each other she turned and ran, heading across the field to *Day Bringer* and the safety of the water dimension.

She didn't quite make it.

A footballer's tackle brought her to the ground and they were on her. She fought them off as best she could, scratching and biting as well as striking with her mind, clawing her way towards *Day Bringer* while they kicked and hit, sometimes turning on each other in order to get to her. She was crawling when one lusty, footballer's kick lifted her, propelled her the last few feet, to crash into *Day Bringer*'s side and disappear into the water dimension.

The contact with *Day Bringer*'s steel hull had stunned her and the kick in her side added to the hurts already inflicted so she lay huddled against *Day Bringer* in a kind of daze, scarcely conscious that they had sought her for a little before turning their energies to fighting each other.

When she finally emerged to realise her situation it was quite dark and she was alone. She lay still for a while aware of pain and cold. Every breath hurt and she believed she was injured beyond her capacity to deal with alone, but she would have to try to get onto *Day Bringer*. Her attempt at movement cost her so much pain that she lost consciousness. It was not for long, but it left her fearful of trying again. She felt *Day Bringer*'s hull against her, a consolation and a kind of safety, closed her eyes and tried to enter the soul song.

Her soul friend, the Silberay Kel, had heard her moment of anguish. It rang and reverberated like a deep toned gong in his mind. The sound was not something he had ever experienced but he recognised its call immediately. He had been washing his supper dishes but he did not hesitate. Leaving everything he ran to the engine room. Five minutes later he was under way.

Darkness and speed restrictions did not matter. He knew, more or less, where she should be and it was not very near. At least he was pointing in the right direction and did not need to waste time finding a turning place. *Storm Cloud*'s headlamp shone on the water and showed him the banks of the water road. He had never travelled so fast, heedless of the wash he was creating, caring for nothing except the urgent need to reach her.

It was about two hours past dawn when he saw *Day Bringer* moored at the bottom of the weedy field. He eased *Storm Cloud* in behind her, careful now not to make her rock too much in case Marheh was onboard and injured. The small movement she did make was enough to draw Marheh back from the soul song and cause a small, involuntary, quickly bitten back, cry of pain.

Kel heard her even above the sound of *Storm Cloud*'s engine, idling now as he prepared to step off and moor, but did not see her until he stood on the bank with *Storm Cloud*'s centre line in his hand. He spent a moment hammering in a mooring pin and tying his centre line in cursory fashion just so he could keep hold of his boat when he needed, then he ran to crouch down beside her.

There was blood on her face and her clothes were torn and dirty. She looked grey and she took only shallow breaths. He saw her shiver and wince and shiver again. She could barely speak and when he tried to lift her she cried out and fainted.

When she came back to herself there was sky above her, she was wrapped in something warm and lying flat on her back. It took some minutes before she realised she was lying on *Storm Cloud*'s roof. The noise of *Storm Cloud*'s engine was beneath her and she was moving fast. The few clouds she could see were still. She was being carried beneath them. Breathing still hurt and her whole body ached, particularly the side where the last kick had landed, but she could trust Kel. She closed her eyes and went inwards again.

It was not until later when she had been in hospital for twenty-four hours that Kel was permitted to visit and help her to make sense of the rescue that she remembered only as confusion and pain with occasional moments of respite when she saw the sky, blue and limitless, above her.

She had a broken collar bone and two broken ribs as well as massive bruising and was fairly heavily sedated, but she was able to smile and whisper his name and curl her fingers around his hand when he took hers. He understood what she wanted to know and told her how he had been fearful of injuring her further if he carried her down stairs to his bunk and that he would have been unable to check on her there. So he had laid her on the roof and set off immediately for the Harbour. It had seemed best to go there where there would be no need for explanations about the water dimension. Gracedale might have been a possibility but the Harbour was not much further. Her breathing had been shallow and he had been very anxious, but Gilt had swung into action as soon as he arrived, an ambulance had come quickly and now all she had to do was heal.

After a couple more days in hospital while they made sure she did not have a collapsed lung she was transferred back to the Harbour, to the house where the old ones, the Silberay who had retired, were cared for, with many instructions about how she was to behave.

She was not a good patient and instructions had never been welcome. She tried to do as she was asked but with indifferent success and even the news that her Silberay uncle, her father's brother Jik, had brought *Day Bringer* back to the Harbour for her could not persuade her to obedience and appropriate patient behaviour.

It was Jik and Gilt together who had come up with the idea that she might replace Gilt so he could go to his father. She had been doubtful at first, but when she understood that Gilt had a real need and when Jik told her he would confiscate *Day Bringer*'s keys if she tried to go boating she agreed to try to make a good substitute Harbour Master.

She had expected it to be only for six weeks while she was convalescent, but yesterday Gilt had telephoned and explained that it was now understood that his father would not recover. If she would continue to do his job he could stay as long as he was needed to support his mother and care for his father.

Marheh could only agree, but it meant more of a challenge than she had expected. The next Gathering was only three months away and it would be her job to plan and prepare for this time of ceremony and celebration as well as for restocking boats, scheduling repairs and refurbishments and arranging for suppliers of all kinds to be available for consultation. The Silberay expected to use these three weeks for much more than just catching up with friends. Without even thinking about how the goods had been provided she herself had, purchased cheap fuel and coal, ordered new boots and new uniforms and enjoyed a welcome breakfast and a farewell feast. How could she possibly manage all that?

She looked again at the ledger in front of her. Perhaps if she looked back at the account books from the last Gathering two years ago it might help, but it was so much outside the scope of her own skills. She was used to doing only what she was good at. Even if she gave this job all her attention she doubted she could make a success of it and she didn't want to give it all her attention. Damn Jik. How dare he get her into this!

She closed the ledger and stood up. One thing she could do was go across to visit the old ones. Fylan, their carer, would no doubt scold her for moving onto *Day Bringer*, but she would feed her too and the four retired Silberay in residence were always glad to see her. Perhaps one of them would have some advice for her. Hadn't Teg been Harbour Master for a few years? She might try to talk with him on his own. If she consulted all four, Blin would out talk the others even if he had nothing to say.

Fylan met her at the door of the house.

"I've kept you some lunch but you don't deserve it."

Marheh grinned at her.

"What have I done now?"

"You are not taking proper care of yourself. Lunch time was nearly three hours ago and you didn't eat then, did you?"

"Please Ma'am, I wasn't hungry then. I'm not getting enough exercise to get hungry."

Fylan laughed.

"I suppose you're old enough to know your own mind about eating, but I'm concerned that you'll be cold on *Day Bringer* and coughing will not do your ribs any good."

"I've plenty of coal and I can always pick up more, it's part of my salary."

She looked sideways at Fylan waiting for the explosion.

"Marheh Carron, if you think you can lift a bag of coal anytime soon you'll find yourself back in hospital in a straight jacket."

Marheh laughed.

"I thought that might get a bite. I'm being careful, I promise. Jik put a couple of bags on the back deck and I have a little bucket that I take in and out."

"No more than ten pieces per trip," Fylan said severely, then laughed. "What am I doing telling you what to do? I ought to know better. I'm probably putting ideas into your head."

"I'll build up gradually and stop if it hurts. Will that pass?"

"It will have to won't it? I doubt that anything I can say will stop you doing more than you should."

She moved aside to let Marheh enter.

"You'll be best eating in the kitchen. Blin is in full flight in the sitting room."

She followed her into the kitchen, put a loaf on the table and ladled soup into a bowl from a large pot on the stove. Marheh smiled her thanks.

"You spoil me. I don't deserve it."

"Neither you do, but it doesn't seem to make any difference. I still think of you as my patient I suppose."

It was good soup and Marheh accepted a second helping when it was offered, realising that she was quite hungry.

"Do you think you could ask Teg to come and talk to me here? I'm a bit out of my depth with this job, especially now that Gilt doesn't expect to be back for the Gathering."

"Of course I could. I'll tell him I want his help, that way Blin won't think of joining us."

Off she went and came back a few minutes later with a very old man. He walked slowly, leaning heavily on his stick and he looked frail, but his eyes were bright and interested and he greeted Marheh cheerfully.

"Here's an honour, the Harbour Master visiting. How are you lass?"

"Struggling!" She made a face. "I've just learned that Gilt won't be back before the Gathering and I need some advice."

Teg sat down opposite her at the table. Fylan offered him sperit and slid a steaming mug in front of him without waiting for an answer.

"Of course I'll help if I can lass, but anything I know will be very out of date. It's twenty five years or more since I was in the position. You were still an apprentice."

"As long ago as that! But you'll know the kinds of things that need to be done before a Gathering. I don't even know where to start and I'm horribly afraid of running us into debt. I've not had the responsibility for this kind of spending before."

Teg gave a little chuckle.

"You stay afraid of debt and you'll do alright, better than me at any rate. My first Gathering nearly bankrupted us. The next two years were very lean."

"Nemle and I often had lean years, but I thought that was just us. I never noticed what was happening here."

"I expect you've noticed more than you think. Most of it is commonsense really."

Marheh gave a short laugh.

"My closest friend, you know Kel, he tells me I'm not sensible. He even claims that it is one of my strengths."

Teg laughed.

"I do seem to remember you pushing a few boundaries in your youth."

He paused for a moment of thought.

"Why don't you think about the expectations you've had of past Harbour Masters. The Gathering is not the whole of the job. Make a list of priorities for yourself. Come and show it to me if you want and I'll tell you what I think."

He reached across the table to put a hand over hers.

"Your Uncle Jik was a fine Harbour Master. I'll do what I can, but why don't you ask him?"

Why don't I, she thought, walking slowly back to the Harbour Master's office. Her office. She couldn't get her head around that notion. She had spent half an hour with the old ones in the sitting room, knowing they appreciated her visits. Blin was not someone she could ever feel comfortable with but the others were kind and wise.

She suspected her reluctance to ask Jik for help was mostly about pride. She had never liked to admit there was anything she couldn't do. She would ask him, she resolved, but not yet. Teg's suggestion appealed to her. She would go back and tackle the accounts now because she was expected to be in the office in case any Silberay needed to be in touch, but when office hours were over and she was back on *Day Bringer* she would take out her journal and write down the good things she remembered and the less good too and try to see where she might contribute to the position.

In the office

Chapter Two

Next morning she went across to the office feeling much more positive. She had considered the Harbour Masters she had admired and tried to articulate the reasons why. She had also considered those she had ignored or even resented, which was more difficult, and tried to be just in her assessment of their efforts.

Communication was really important. She had always been critical when decisions were made without consulting those most affected. Of course, she had to acknowledge that she was not without fault in that direction. It was hard to find a balance between independence and collaboration and collaboration always seemed to take up too much time when she knew exactly what she wanted to achieve.

She needed to make more effort to get to know all the Silberay too, not just her particular friends. She remembered how impressed she had been when Bixa, the Harbour Master before Gilt, had seemed to know all about her and been able to respond suitably when she needed help with a job she had been given.

She sat down at her desk full of good intentions. Two things were immediately important. How many Silberay were there really and how much money was there. She took out first the latest roll listing each individual, their status, apprentice or mentor or neither, and the name of their boat. As she began to read she realised she really only knew about half of them, despite there being so few. Of course they only met as a whole group every two years, but that was no excuse. She just had not been very interested except in her particular friends. She thought about that for a while, feeling a bit ashamed that it was so.

She was still considering the roll and trying to put names and faces together in her mind when the telephone on her desk began to ring. She looked at it for a moment with disfavour before reaching to answer it.

"Silberay Harbour."

"Who's that? I need to speak to Gilt."

It was a woman's voice, a little agitated. Marheh thought she knew who it was but was not prepared to guess.

"I'm sorry, Gilt is not here. It's Marheh speaking."

"What are you doing answering the phone?"

"I'm standing in for him for the next little while."

"You are! Why you?"

It had to be Tippa, Marheh thought. She had been apprenticed at the same time as Marheh and had become a rather forthright friendly adversary over the years they had known each other.

"I was on the spot and without a job when Gilt needed to leave," she said. "Is there something I can do for you?"

"I need a tow back to the Harbour and I'll need to book the dry dock. My prop has gone, just disappeared."

"Disappeared?"

"That's what I said. I lost way, managed to get in to moor, looked through the weed hatch and nothing there."

Marheh raised her eyebrows at this evidence of poor maintenance but did not comment.

"Where are you exactly?" she asked instead.

"Great Northern, just south of Fairdale. That's where I'm ringing from."

"There's no one here who can come for you," Marheh said carefully. "But I will have the next person who rings from that direction go and find you. Will you be alright for supplies for a few days?"

"Why can't you come? I don't need to hang around here."

"I'm sorry but I'm not allowed to take the boat out at the moment."

"Why? Have you been breaking rules again?"

"No, just bones."

Tippa's half teasing interrogation changed to concern.

"Really. Are you alright?"

"Yes, I'm fine, but the doctors don't want me to do too much in the way of pulling and working locks for another couple of weeks."

"Fair enough. I'll ring back in a couple of days and see what you have been able to arrange."

"That will be best, oh, and Tippa, if you need any immediate help there is a friend at Fairdale Lading. Her name is Kithla. She lives in a cottage on the main street. She'll be known as Kathleen if you need to ask."

The pips went at Tippa's end of the line. Marheh hung up and spent a moment remembering how she had met Kithla in the first few months of her apprenticeship. After an inauspicious beginning when she had been sulky and rude they had become friends and remained so even though a year or more might pass between meetings. Kithla would be happy to help Tippa if she was able.

She stood up and went to look at the big chart on the wall that showed the bookings for the dry dock. If she could get Tippa back within the next ten days there would be no difficulty in booking her a couple of days but soon after that the boats belonging to those mentors who were due to retire at the Gathering would be coming for refitting for the apprentices who would be taking them over. Then the boats belonging to those Silberay who were about to become mentors would need refitting too.

Fortunately a lot of the work could be done in the wet dock, but she would need to organise tradesmen so that it would all be done in time for the various ceremonies at the Gathering. Perhaps she should order a new propeller for Tippa too, but if the propeller had gone, what did that say about the condition of the shaft.

She sighed. So much for planning her morning. She had best see what she could find out about the local tradesmen the Silberay usually used and book them up. She would not be popular if the boats were not ready for the Consigning Ceremony. She went back to look at the bookings for refits. *Evening Star* and *Cloudburst* were there, but surely there were more than that. *Cloudburst* she knew belonged to Whin. He was to have an apprentice, so as well as a thorough overhaul of the engine and an inspection of the hull before it was blacked, the mentor's cabin would need to be fitted. He at least was organised and had made his bookings in good time.

Surely there were three Silberay retiring though, and another apprentice. Was *Evening Star* being prepared for an apprentice and mentor or a full working Silberay? Who else would need to come in for a refit? She went back to the rolls, this time looking for dates and ages. Was she expected to contact those who had not made their booking yet?

It was not difficult to find *Evening Star* and discover that Zinda was about to retire and leave her boat to her apprentice Lidy, but what kind of work did Lidy do to support herself? What did she require in the way of workspace once the mentor's cabin was dismantled? Since Zinda had booked time there should be some record somewhere of the work to be done. But what about the others? Who were they and what did they need? Where were they and how could she contact them?

The telephone rang. It was the boot maker who usually attended at the Gathering. Thank you for getting in touch but he had retired since the last Gathering and was about to move to the seaside and no, he couldn't recommend anyone else, most people bought shoes ready made nowadays.

Marheh put the phone down very carefully having wished him well in his retirement. Then she took a deep breath. Before she could let it out and express her frustration verbally the telephone rang again.

"Silberay Harbour," she said, struggling to maintain at least a semblance of

13

patience.

"That's not Gilt," a woman's voice said.

"No it isn't," Marheh snapped. "Sorry, I wish it was."

The woman laughed.

"Marheh, what are you doing in the Harbour Master's office?"

"Oh my goodness, Bixa! Where are you?"

"Just north of Highington, why?"

"I was hoping you might be able to help me, but you're too far away."

"Why do you need help? That's not like you." Bixa still sounded amused.

"I've been landed with doing the Harbour Master's job for the next several months and I'm no good at it, but you were a great Harbour Master."

"There's obviously a story in there somewhere, but I'll have to wait to hear it, or my pennies will run out before I've made my booking. I'll need to bring *Spring Song* in for a refit. I'm to have an apprentice this Gathering."

The booking was made and Bixa agreed to come in four weeks before the Gathering and told Marheh where she could find the records of what work needed doing. The pips went and the call ended before Marheh could get out any more questions but she did fell a little more positive. Bixa had promised to ring again in a few days.

By the end of the week Marheh was beginning to feel as if she might be getting on top of the job. She realised that she had not really taken it seriously while she expected Gilt to come back before the Gathering. Bixa had been as good as her word and rung again, with enough pennies for a follow on so that Marheh could ask all her questions. She was determined to do the best she could, anything less would be letting herself down as well as the Silberay. She didn't have to like it though. She had not touched her clay since her injury. At first the doctor had advised against it, but now she came back to *Day Bringer* too tired to focus. Some days she did not even sing and that worried her. The soul song was the most important work of the Silberay and she was good at it, but it too required more of her than she had to give after a day of problems to solve.

It was not quite a month since the attack and she was aware that she had not yet completely healed. Odd twinges caught her when she tried to do things that normally would have been easy. There were nightmares too, not every night, but often enough for her to recognise there was more than bodily healing required. Singing would help with that too if she practised it as she should.

Her duties were a bit lighter at the weekend. She needed to be in the office on Saturday for a couple of hours only, between nine and eleven, after that her time was her own. She would go and have lunch with Fylan and the old ones but then she could be beautifully solitary on *Day Bringer* where there was no telephone and no demands except the ones she made on herself.

Practising the disciplines had to be a priority, not just the discipline of the soul, but also the discipline of the mind. Both were an essential part of her life as Silberay and she knew she could never be whole without them. She went across to the office resolving to spend the afternoon with the disciplines. With any luck she would have a quiet morning too and be able to concentrate on the accounts.

The only calls she had came towards the end of the morning and she was grateful for them both. Jik rang first, anxious for her and glad to know she was recovering. He was not too far from Tippa so she was able to ask him to help her, which would bring him back to the Harbour too. Now that she felt more in control she would not mind asking for his advice.

Then Kel rang. He too wanted reassurance that she was healing. He had gone back to his assigned route. It would take him in a wide circle through Deerford and beyond and he was unlikely to be back before the Gathering. It was good to hear his voice even though, as soul friends, they could also communicate mind to mind. She explained her need to practise and knew he would be ready for her that afternoon.

She packed up her papers and the account books, wanting to leave her desk clear for Monday. The morning of study had given her a better picture of the financial position and she could see that solvency was a question of balance, not much different, except in scale, from her personal finances. The main exception was the ordering. If she ordered unwisely the Harbour would be left with unwanted goods, but if she didn't order enough the Silberay would be put out. She would put it out of her mind now though and concentrate on her own needs.

Fylan welcomed her warmly and accepted her offer to set the table.

"You're looking a bit more like yourself now, I'm glad to see."

"Who did I look like before," Marheh asked with a grin.

"Not a who at all, more of a what. Six pennyworth of God help us, my mother would have said."

Marheh laughed.

"Well any improvement is largely down to you, thank you very much."

She put the last of the side plates at each place and the butter dish in the centre of the table beside Fylan's newly baked loaf.

"How are your charges today?"

"As well as can be expected at their age, I think. Mieka is just gently fading away now, but very peaceful. She likes to spend most of the day in bed, but always wants to get up for lunch. I think she is just waiting for the Gathering so she can see Ofta again."

Marheh nodded. The bond between mentor and apprentice was a strong one and usually continued past the mentor's retirement. There were times when she still missed Nemle's physical presence. It was nearly twelve years now since she had retired and she had been dead for five years.

"Blin does a good job of driving us all mad," Fylan went on. "But the others are very patient with him." She turned off the gas under her saucepan and turned to look at Marheh. "He seems quite … obsessed really, with you. Has he always been like that?"

Marheh nodded.

"It used to upset me when I was younger. I think I was even a little afraid of him, but now it's just, just sad really."

Fylan gave a brief nod then left for the sitting room. Mieka would need her help to get to the table.

Lunch passed fairly comfortably. Teg, Mieka and Sula as well as Fylan, seemed pleased to have her there and were kind and clever at turning Blin's more personal remarks. He referred to her always as the Harbour Master, but he managed to make it a term of derision, a means of mocking her.

"We are all friends here Blin," she had said at last. "There is no need to be formal."

But he only smirked at her, obviously pleased to have provoked even that response.

Back on *Day Bringer* it was not as easy as she had expected to put aside her new responsibilities and Blin's antagonism continued to disturb her. His obsession dated from the early years of her apprenticeship and she should be used to it by now, but, despite her words to Fylan, she was not as unaffected as she had implied. Singing was what was important now however and she did succeed in giving it all her attention.

A candle flame was always her portal to the soul song, something she built in her mind's eye that would let her through to the place where she became the song. Almost always there were other singers making melody around her or providing a rich pad of harmony to let her soar. As she became more practised over the years she had come to understand the song was never silent, even when she thought she was singing alone, because the song was what continued even beyond death. If she had been able to enter the song at the times in her life when her need was greatest she had found love there and support. She had to give all she was to the song though and not merely seek to shelter in it. There were times when the song became light in dark places and spinning a golden thread of sound was all consuming work.

Here at the Harbour where so many Silberay had sung to sustain the life around them she expected the singing to be all light, but when she returned to herself she realised that even here there were undercurrents, dark patches that smudged the edges of the song.

She reached her mind to Kel then, putting aside all other concerns for the moment. He had been waiting for her and greeted her with the image of his hug and his smile. She responded gratefully and they spent a few moments giving each other images of their recent activities. Communication mind to mind tended to be in pictures rather than words, at least that was how Marheh had always experienced it and she was aware that it had been that way for Nemle and was now for Kel. She showed him her labours over the accounts, mocking herself a little with the gloomy portrait she sent. He showed her that he had sandpaper and an almost completed wooden box in his hands. She showed him lunch with the old ones and he showed her his apple core and the bread crumbs on his plate. All that was the easy part. The real challenge was in attack and defence. They needed that practice and rather enjoyed it, teasing each other with subtle tricks and stratagems designed to sneak under the opponent's guard and register a hit.

Marheh's talent with the discipline of the mind was almost legendary amongst the Silberay and normally Kel could not hope to get near her, but they had long since worked out a way that she could handicap herself so that combat was more equal. Even so he did not often defeat her, but today he managed to land the equivalent of a good smack on her rear so that she yelped and conceded.

Their goodbye was always another hug so that there would be no hard feelings no matter who had won. She returned to herself smiling a little, conscious of his care for her. Mentally tired but physically restless she couldn't seem to settle to anything. It would be light for another half hour, she decided, looking out at the wintery sky. A walk was what she needed. She had not had any real exercise since the attack and walking had always been important to her peace of mind.

It was cold out. Up to now the winter had been quite mild but that seemed to be changing. She rugged up well, conscious that she still needed to be careful, but determined to have some real exercise and not just a stroll around the Harbour. A drive of perhaps one hundred yards led out to the lane. It was looking a bit the worse for wear and she wondered whether it was her job to see to it, perhaps ordering some gravel to spread over the worst places. It was not very urgent though, and she would wait until closer to the Gathering before making any decisions about it.

She had not walked the lanes around the Harbour since Nemle died and that was five and a half years ago. She had driven herself hard trying to deaden her feelings of sadness and loss and not really paid much attention to the landscape, but it had not been the one she saw now. Then the fields and hedges that marked two farms had abutted the Harbour property and given her peace and solitude for her walks. Now, as she turned out of the drive, she saw that the lane had turned into a road and both farms had been replaced by houses. How had it happened so quickly? Why had she not noticed before?

She stood for a moment wondering which way to turn, then set off in the direction of Sefton Middle. Thirty years ago when she was first apprenticed to the Silberay it had been a small town about two miles from the Harbour. Now it seemed to have reached out and joined it.

The Silberay were largely independent, but they had always dealt with the local tradesmen when they could and made a point of being on good terms with their neighbours. They were not often at the Harbour though. The Gathering only took place every second year, just for three weeks in early spring and she was aware that she had not left the Harbour during the two Gatherings since Nemle's death. There was always plenty to do, friends to greet, boat maintenance, ceremonies, classes and discussion and the Harbour Master had always arranged for everything they needed to be delivered to them. Perhaps it was time to change that, but it did save time. Anyway, it was not up to her to change anything, she was just a temporary substitute for the real Harbour Master.

She continued to walk, hugging her coat around her as the wind freshened. She was conscious that she was still not fully fit. Walking was not as easy as it should be and the chilly air seemed bent on persuading her to retreat to *Day Bringer*'s nice warm fire. Not yet, she told herself, stepping a little faster in the hope of warming up.

There was not much sign of life about the houses she was passing but perhaps she could not expect that. A chilly winter Saturday evening invited indoor pursuits sitting snugly around a fire and she could see smoke from several chimneys. The boundary fence of the Harbour ended and now the houses extended on both sides of the road. She had not noticed any of this coming back from the hospital, but she had probably had her eyes closed. She knew she had been very dopey from the pain relief medicine she had been given.

What did these neighbours think about the enclosed land opposite? They could be forgiven for believing the owners to be arrogant and uncaring since they never saw them and they looked to have so much. The new houses were quite pleasant to look at, but they were terraces, with common walls and not much land, not in front where she could see at any rate. From windows on the first floor some of them would have a view of the Harbour buildings. What did they think about them? How could they understand their purpose if they couldn't see the water and the boats?

She continued to puzzle over this as she went, forgetting that she was not to go too far. She remembered there had been a footpath over the fields that gave access to the Harbour and she wondered what had happened to it. Perhaps she could find signs of it, a space between the houses or even a road.

A little further on there was an alley way with the high blank walls of the houses on either side. There had been a stile there once, she remembered, looking down the shadowy path. It was very dark between the houses and for a moment she thought about just retracing her steps, but the realisation that she was a bit fearful was enough to have her lift her chin and start down the alley.

She could see the path was lighter after the houses, but it was still narrow with high fences on either side. It seemed that the new houses did at least have some land at the back.

She came to another road, a cul de sac, just giving access to some more houses. The alley continued however and so she kept going, wondering whether it still gave access to the Harbour. It was nearly dark now. She had been out longer than she planned and she was uncomfortably aware that the pride that had made her tackle the alley had not demonstrated her courage, but her folly. She was tired, aching and cold despite her exercise.

The next section gave onto another cul de sac and as she entered it she saw that some of these houses backed onto Silberay land. At the furthest end she recognised the Harbour fence and the gate that would give her access. Thankfully she walked towards it, only to find when she reached it that it was firmly locked.

It was never locked, she thought, pushing at it in vain. It shouldn't be locked, was her next thought. Who are we keeping out?

There was no help for it. She had to retrace her steps if she wanted to get back to *Day Bringer*. It was her own silly fault if she ached all over. Lights were going on in the houses now and she could smell the smoke of the fires that warmed them. At least *Day Bringer* would be nice and warm when she reached her. She met no one in the alley, but when she reached the road she saw that a bus had just deposited two passengers who were about to cross towards her.

It was too dark to see more than that they were both women. Hats and scarves as well as heavy coats made them bulky shapes. She hesitated. These were her neighbours. They seemed to know each other. They were chatting together as they walked. As they got nearer they stopped talking and looked at Marheh curiously. One of them just nodded as she passed, but the other stopped.

"Are you alright lass?" she asked. "Not lost your way?"

"I'm fine. Just walked a bit further than I meant to," Marheh said. "But thank you for asking."

The first woman turned back to look at her.

"You came out of the alley."

It was an accusation, not a comment.

"Yes."

"I've not seen you about before. What did you want with the alley?"

"I was just exploring," Marheh said mildly, wondering at the need for this inquisition. Was it just curiosity or something more?

"Funny time to explore. Up to no good I shouldn't wonder."

"Don't be silly Belinda." The second woman smiled at Marheh.

"Don't let us hold you up." She paused then continued. "But I wouldn't explore the alley if I were you, not in the dark."

Post

Chapter Three

By the time she got back to *Day Bringer* Marheh was tired, cold and very conscious that she had been foolish to push herself as far as she had. There had been no need for it and the way she ached suggested that she had set back her recovery. At least she had got in before the rain that was just beginning to be heard on *Day Bringer*'s roof.

She hung her outdoor clothes in the engine room and made her way through to the saloon. Her fire was still glowing and the boat felt very snug after the bleak outside. She knew she should eat, but preparing something seemed too much effort. She put a few more pieces of coal on the fire, sank into the armchair and closed her eyes. Her walk had given her things to think about and she would in a minute, but not just yet.

She woke some hours later. It was still raining, her lamp had gone out and the fire was very low. Stupid, stupid, stupid, she kept castigating herself as she stumbled through to her cabin, shrugged off her clothes and put herself to bed, shivering a little and aching all over.

The next morning she slept late, allowing herself to drowse even longer, knowing she had no responsibilities and aware that she would be very cold out of bed. She had been too dopey to do anything about the fire when she woke from the armchair and the tip of her nose, emerging from the bedclothes, was telling her it had gone out. She snuggled into the covers and let her mind drift. The aches she had awakened yesterday seemed to have eased and she could turn her thought to the fruits of her exploration, all those houses surrounding the Harbour, people who had no idea who their neighbours were or what they did. The locked gate was a problem too. It seemed to her that it sent the wrong message. Keep out! We don't want to know you. But if the alley was not a place to explore at night perhaps there was safety in the locked gate.

She tried to let sleep take her again but her thoughts would not let go. The day was not going to get any warmer. She would have to face the cold some time and it might as well be sooner than later. She flung back the covers in a rush and scrambled into her clothes. No one would know or care that she had not washed, not today. The movement caused a few twinges but nothing too bad and she acknowledged briefly that she had got off lightly after her exertions the previous day.

Fire first, not just for her comfort but for *Day Bringer* too. If she let the water in the pipes freeze it could start a whole chain of disasters. Once she saw the flames take hold she turned the tap on over the kettle and was relieved to see the water running freely. It would be a while before she could have anything hot though. Well, it served her right. Practising the disciplines had to include being disciplined about her everyday life and she had ignored the voice of commonsense.

She moved about the boat, making her bed, doing a bit of tidying, bringing in a bit more coal. It was even colder out on the back deck and grey clouds seemed almost low enough to touch. One of the bags of coal was half empty now and she lifted it experimentally. Perhaps she could carry it down to the engine room without injuring herself. That way she would not have to go out in the weather when she wanted fuel. She would not be surprised if they had snow. She was not the weather prophet that Nemle had been, but her years of boating in all sorts of conditions had given her a reasonable accuracy. She stood for a moment longer then went down for her coat. It was her day off. She would give herself a holiday.

One of the few advantages of her hew responsibilities was the library. It was not a very big selection, perhaps as many as a thousand titles, available to all the Silberay to select from and take on their travels and for now she had the run of it, not limited by the lack of space that usually restricted her selection to two or three titles.

By the time she got back with half a dozen hastily chosen books *Day Bringer* was beginning to warm up and her kettle had nearly boiled. Porridge followed by bacon and eggs would combine breakfast and lunch and then she would read.

Indulgence was all very well, she thought, as she closed the novel she had just finished, but it did leave you feeling a bit dissatisfied. There had to be a balance. She stood up and stretched and discovered that it was tea time already. Out the window the gantries had a dusting of snow and she thought there was more to come. It was nearly dark. No exploring today. She would sing though, but today she would be sensible and prepare her evening meal first.

Next morning she woke to a world of white. Making her way to the office was a challenge. She was conscious that a fall would not be an occasion for laughter as it might have been in the past. The administration building was bitterly cold. She would not be taking her coat off any time soon. Most of the rooms were empty, just waiting for the Silberay to return for the Gathering. For the first time she thought about the waste that was. There were several small meeting rooms as well as the large hall where they held the ceremonies and celebrations. An annex held a small dormitory, some bathrooms and a laundry. Upstairs, as well as the library, there was a small flat for the Harbour Master should he or she choose to use it. Gilt had made her free of it, but she preferred the familiarity of *Day Bringer*. She had used his bathroom though, indulging in the luxury of a full size bath.

When she was first apprenticed there was an Apprentice Master as well as the Harbour Master, but now most of that job was done by the Harbour Master since there were so few apprentices. At least the mentors would look after the necessary classes at the Gathering. All she would need to do was timetable the rooms and that could wait until Bixa came in. She thought she might take a walk around the whole complex at lunchtime and just see exactly what there was.

Her first phone call of the day was from Tippa, wanting to know when help was coming. She had just hung up when the coal supplier arrived with a delivery for the house. She wanted to ask him about a bulk order for the Gathering so she put on her coat and went out to meet him.

The house, she discovered, had a coal cellar, and loose coal was being tipped carefully down the chute. Lose coal was no use to the boaters though. She watched for a few moments, not wanting to interrupt the unloading, but when it was done she approached the driver.

"Do you supply bags of coal as well?"

"Can do."

"I'll be needing to order some for when the boats come back, but I'm new to the job and I'm not quite sure how to go about it."

The man looked at her with compassion.

"Boats is it love? Well you just tell me what you want and I'll pass it on to the office."

She began to calculate then realised that he was just humouring her.

"You go in out of the cold love, the boats will be a long time coming." He reached into his pocket and pulled out a grubby piece of paper. "I've got to give this to the lady of the house," he said. "You come along with me. She'll be missing you I expect. Don't you fret about the coal."

"But…" she began, then realised she would be wasting her breath.

She allowed him to usher her to the kitchen door where Fylan was waiting. He handed over the invoice he carried and nodded towards Marheh.

"This one must have got out."

"She will do it," Fylan said gravely, not looking at Marheh. "She's quite harmless, just deluded, poor pet. Thank you for looking out for her."

The man nodded.

"That lot should do you for three months or so. You'll let the office know when you need more."

"I will," Fylan said and turned to Marheh, still hovering near the door. "In you go."

By the time she had closed the door Marheh could see the laughter barely contained. She put her thumbs to her ears, waggled her fingers and pulled her best hideous face.

"Harmless and deluded am I?"

"Absolutely."

They both began to laugh until Marheh had to hug her ribs and sit down.

"Oh dear, it was stupid of me not to realise."

"What did you do, tell him about the water?"

Fylan sat down opposite.

"I said something about the boats coming back. I suppose I thought that if he'd been supplying the Harbour for sometime he would know a bit about us."

Fylan shook her head.

"I doubt there's one person in twenty, or even more, who have ever heard of Silberay, and of those who have, most think you're just a myth."

"So what do the neighbours think goes on here? Do you know?"

"Not really. No one comes to call except for deliveries and most of them don't speculate. They know I care for the old ones. Probably most of them think like the coal man."

Marheh sighed.

"I've been thinking we should be more communicative, share what we have, tell people who we are, but it isn't as easy as that is it?"

Fylan shook her head and Marheh could feel her sympathy.

"Some of the tradesmen who come to work on the boats are aware. They know you and one or two even talk about you. Perhaps you can build on that."

"I'll keep that in mind." She stood up. "I'd best get back to the office. The post will be here before long, if it isn't already."

Fylan stood up and gave her a hug.

"Come back for lunch, alright? 12.30 not 3 o'clock this time."

As she made her way back to the administration building Marheh saw the postman, on his bicycle, pedalling away down the drive.

There was usually more mail on a Monday and it was all for her to deal with. Sometimes it was just a question of distributing it to the appropriate pigeon hole, but if the recipient was not expecting to return for some months she might need to forward it to another address, usually a post office, for collection. That was just the easy part. There were other letters which she had actively to follow up. Bills needed paying and had to be entered in her account book, receipts needed to be filed. There was no income at this time of year when the Silberay had all paid their dues. Fortunately the half yearly bank interest would have come in last month, but it was not very much. If she had understood what her study of the ledgers had revealed it appeared that the Silberay had been drawing on capital over the last few years.

The bills were easily spotted amongst the pile of letters because they tended to be addressed in odd ways; The Manager, The Chief Accountant, The Owner, The Business Manager, The Accounts Department. She represented them all. No one addressed mail to the Harbour Master. So far there had not been anything too unsettling this morning. Two letters, addressed to The Owner, had offered to buy the property and she had filed these in the waste paper basket. There had been a couple of these each week from different estate agents. Obviously someone thought they could profit from the land now it was so much part of Sefton Middle.

She picked up the second to last envelope and slid her little paper knife under the flap. It was just a single sheet, typed, on printed letterhead from the Sefton Middle town council informing her that the property had been re-zoned, no longer agricultural but residential. She studied it for a few minutes wondering how this would affect the Silberay and who should be informed. Probably she could leave it until the Gathering and then tell the mentors. They might know what it meant. Obviously that was why the estate agents were interested.

The last letter was the bank statement advising her that the account balance as at December 31st was £527.13s.6d. She stared at it, trying to calculate what it meant in terms of the next couple of months. The Silberay would begin paying their annual dues at the Gathering, but until then there would be nothing coming in. She had sent off cheques to the value of at least £100 since this statement but of course some of that would be recouped at the Gathering when the Silberay bought diesel. Perhaps some would contribute to the cost of blacking the hulls of their boats, but it was not compulsory. The other costs were mostly associated with maintaining the house for the old ones. Sometimes some of them were able to contribute but of the ones there now she thought only Teg had the means.

She sighed. She could not really count on more than £400 to cover the necessities of the next two months until the Gathering, as well as provide food for the two big feasts, wages for the helpers and tradesmen she would need to employ and materials for the five refits. She wasn't an accountant. How could she work out how to manage? The first thing that would have to go was her own bit of a salary. She didn't really need money, not when she could have food and coal. Of course she did not have time to practise her craft, but a couple more months wouldn't matter.

The telephone interrupted these gloomy thoughts. To Marheh's surprise it was her mother Greya, wanting to hear from her that she was alright. Only last week she had written a carefully worded letter home explaining that she had had a small accident, was perfectly fine now, but would be working at the Harbour until the Gathering.

"Your father and I thought we might come and visit you. We know you won't have told us the whole truth about what happened."

"But I'm perfectly alright, just filling in for the Harbour Master." She was nearly 52 for goodness sake, not a child. "I don't think you and father should be travelling in this weather. The roads are icy."

"That's alright. Sef doesn't want to drive but Mek will bring us. Is there somewhere at the Harbour where we can stay or should we look for a room in the village?"

"I'm not using the Harbour Master's flat," Marheh said slowly. "You could stay there, but you don't need to come."

"We want to," Greya said firmly. "We'll arrive in time for supper on Wednesday."

Marheh put the phone down with very mixed feelings. Of course it would be nice to see them, but she was so busy and preoccupied with this new job and it meant she would have to buy food and cook it. She could hardly expect Fylan to feed her parents as well. That meant a trip into town. Maybe that would not be such a bad thing. She could see for herself how the place had grown and perhaps even put out feelers to try to get a sense of how the Silberay and the Harbour were viewed by the local people. If she went in her lunchtime tomorrow that would give her time to plan a menu and make a shopping list. She had better pack up all the work she had ready for firing too. Mek could take it back to the pottery with him. She had been exploring ideas for her next signature piece before the attack and there were a dozen or more little figures that would do for the markets and a new doll's head for her sister-in-law Fali to play with. She had been earning her salary from the pottery up until now and perhaps she would be justified in asking her father to continue paying it even if she couldn't work as much for the next couple of months.

With a short break for lunch with Fylan and the old ones, she spent the rest of the day trying to arrange for tradesmen to come to attend to the boats that would need refitting. The usual carpenter had been an apprentice when he first came with his father and now he had an apprentice of his own. He, at least, knew the Silberay and understood the water dimension even if he couldn't see it. Better than that, he had offered to recruit another two workers who would be able to help him with the interiors.

The exterior work for Whin on *Cloudburst* was more of a problem. He had requested a hull inspection because he thought there were some thin places that would need reinforcing. She had written to the welder who had come last Gathering, but had not had a reply as yet. Whin would do the blacking himself, but the engine overhaul needed an expert too.

Even when she got home to *Day Bringer* that evening she could feel her mind still busy with the worries of the day. She knew she should sing, but entering the song was impossible unless she could quiet her mind's activity. In the end she managed it and the song took her so that she soared within it.

Singing at the Harbour was usually a gift, music and light supported by a chorus of voices that held her, encouraged and enabled her, so that her own song reached and danced, striving up ward and outward, filling her surroundings with a bright joyfulness. At first everything seemed as usual, but the progression moved her, not to joy, but to regret, and she emerged at last to a feeling of aching sadness.

It was so unexpected that she found herself weeping, silent tears that she could not explain or understand. It was several minutes before she could gather herself and get up to begin her evening meal. Even as she ate the feeling lingered along with a confused sense of mission, as if she were being called to some action not yet clear to her. Whatever it was, she didn't want it, but it would not leave her alone. In the end, when she had eaten and cleared up, built the fire and damped it to last until morning and even changed into her nightclothes, she did not go immediately to bed, but sat with her journal to try to make sense of it.

Is there something wrong here at the Harbour, she wrote, *or is it the town pressing in? I wish I was out on the water road, not here with all the worries of the Harbour Master. I suppose it is selfish of me really, because I can see that the job has to be done, but I just don't feel that it is my job.* She paused then, staring at the fire, glowing softly through the glass door. *Except, even while I'm writing that, I know there is something here that is my job, whether I want it or not. Now I have to find it.*

She sat a while longer, her journal lying closed on her lap, then she got up and went to bed.

Autumn Wind

Chapter Four

Next morning's mail brought her a nasty shock. Paying the town rates was not something she had factored into her financial calculations, but here was the bill, addressed to Mr Silberay, The Harbour, Durand Road, Sefton Middle. £400 seemed an enormous sum. It did not need to be paid all at once, but £100 was due at the end of the month. Was it always as much as that? Perhaps she could find out from the record of last year's payments. No wonder Gilt had needed to use some capital to keep on top of things, but it was not only Gilt, as far as she could tell the practice had begun with Leura although it did not seem as if Bixa had needed to resort to it.

She spent half an hour going back through old ledgers, but could only find payments totalling £173 for the previous year. Had the Silberay failed to pay or was there some mistake? Perhaps she should visit the town hall as well as shopping for food. Gilt had given her a telephone number where she could try to contact him in an emergency. Was this an emergency?

It would be easy enough to enquire at the town hall, she decided, reluctant as always to ask for help. It might mean being away from the office a bit longer, but that couldn't be helped.

There had not been any more snow, but it was cold enough that it was still lying and the grey sky and the low clouds suggested that more would come. She shivered a little, despite her warm coat and scarf. Walking down the drive had not prepared her for the chilly wait for the bus.

It was only a short ride to the town centre. She would have walked it if she had time. She hardly recognised the place when she alighted and needed to stand for a few moments to orient herself. It was the church that helped her the most. It as least was unchanged although buildings pressed around it, shops and houses, that had not been there five years ago.

At the town hall she found a helpful clerk who explained the rate notice and pointed out the land value.

"The rates are based on the value of your land," the woman said. "Obviously you and Mr Silberay have a valuable property. Durand Road is a nice part of town isn't it?"

Marheh could only nod her acknowledgement of this comment.

"I wondered," she began. "As far as I can see, the cost is much higher than last year. Why would that be?"

The woman turned to a large filing cabinet behind her, thought for a moment then pulled out a drawer and a file. Spreading it out on the counter, she nodded sagely.

"I thought I remembered. Parts of Durand Road have been re-zoned. You would have had a letter. Residential land is much more valuable than agricultural."

"But…" Marheh began, wanting to protest.

"You're lucky really," the woman went on. "The property has increased in value. You'd get a nice sum if you sold. Properly invested you could probably live comfortably without needing to work."

"I see," Marheh said, aware that her response was inadequate but too taken aback to do any better. "Thank you for your help." She turned to go then turned back again. "Have you never heard of the Silberay?"

The woman smiled at her kindly.

"No love. Your husband's family is it? What does he do then, that I might have heard of him?"

"I just wondered," Marheh said, making for the door.

Out on the pavement she stood for a moment trying to collect herself and remember what else she had to do. It was worse than she thought. Mr Silberay, valuable property, sell and get a nice sum. Without the Harbour the water road would die. Selling was not an option, but how could they manage to pay more? More important, how could they share who they were and persuade people of the value of what they did? She shivered and drew her coat more tightly around her. Perhaps she should have worn her cloak, the lovely ceremonial garment that had marked her graduation and was part of her uniform, but while it might have marked her as different there was not much point if no one recognised her because of it.

She pulled herself together enough to find the butcher and the green grocer and purchase her ingredients but the bus ride back to the Harbour was not long enough for her to even approach a solution to the problems she faced. Well, the Silberay faced really, but she seemed to be in the firing line at the moment.

The bus was quite full and a couple of other women got out when she did. They seemed to know each other and looked at Marheh curiously.

"It isn't you that's bought number seventy is it?" one of them asked. "I'm two doors up at number seventy-four."

"No," Marheh smiled. "But we must be neighbours I think." She indicated the entrance to the Harbour. "I'm living here at the moment."

"You a nurse then?"

"No I'm in the office."

"It's a funny name, the Harbour, no sea around here. We've often wondered what goes on there. The kids call it the loony bin. Are they dangerous, the patients?"

"No, just old." She smiled again, struck by an idea. "They can't get about much, but if you cared to visit I'm sure they would appreciate it."

The two women looked at each other.

"We could, I suppose," the spokeswoman said. "Sometime, if you're sure it isn't dangerous."

"Quite sure," Marheh said, hitching her bag more securely on her good shoulder and preparing to cross the road. "You would be very welcome."

She looked both ways for traffic then turned back for a moment to say goodbye before she crossed. Dangerous, she thought as she walked down the drive. Teg, Mieka and Sula dangerous! She had better tell Fylan what she had done, just in case the women's curiosity brought them. It might be the beginning of something useful if they did come, something that might change the way the neighbours saw the Harbour.

The warmth of the kitchen was very welcome after the chill of the outside and Fylan insisted on giving her soup and a crumpet. She was very pleased by the possibility of visitors, not just from the neighbourhood but also Marheh's parents.

"There's likely to be a bit of coming and going from now till the Gathering," Marheh said. "I wouldn't be surprised if Jik gets here tomorrow. He's bringing *Sunrise* in for Tippa. After that Bixa will be coming in and Whin, Zinda and Lidy."

"Well make use of Jik and Bixa, don't feel you have to do everything yourself," Fylan said.

Marheh made a face.

"I'll have to. I don't like admitting it, but there are more issues than I can handle."

Fylan laughed. "Admitting it is a good start."

The rest of the afternoon was spent at her desk, but the routine work could not hold her attention for long and she kept returning to the worry of financial difficulties and the problem of recognition. At least there were to be two new apprentices this Gathering. There had not been any at the last Gathering. Should she be contacting them, letting them know how welcome they were, or was that the job of the prospective mentor? How did they come to know of the Silberay?

She was very glad when it was five o'clock and she could return to the familiar comfort and warmth of *Day Bringer*. She had a small radiator in the office, but the rest of the building was so cold that its small warmth struggled to make any progress against the chill. The flat would be cold too and she made a note to herself to be sure to put some heating on next morning to welcome her parents.

Supper, singing and sleep and Wednesday arrived before she knew it. More snow had fallen overnight, but the sky was clear and held the promise of sunshine and a fine day. It would have been good to be out on the water road although standing at the tiller would have been chilly. She made her way to the office carrying one of the boxes she had packed with her work. It would be no good asking Mek to get it from *Day Bringer*. This brother was uncomfortable with the idea of the water dimension and tried to ignore Marheh's different life. Of her three younger brothers, he was the closest to her in age and their relationship had become adversarial, largely, she thought now, because she had tried to tell him what to do. Being the oldest, her mother had expected her to look after the boys, but it was hardly surprising that Mek had resented his bossy big sister.

There had been a time when relations had become very strained between them and even now she was careful in her dealings with him, but she had been of service to his daughter Wilda and that had helped to mend fences.

As usual her office was very cold. She put the radiator on then carried her box to the table by the front door and went upstairs to the flat. It too was cold and she put the heater on first before looking around to see what was needed to welcome her parents.

She had only just got back to the office, still with her coat on, when the telephone rang, then the post arrived and she was absorbed into the day's routine. No major shocks today, just bits and pieces that seemed to need her attention when what she really wanted was thinking time. Her two or three hours each day at the tiller had been thinking time and she missed it. Thinking time was necessary to her well being and her understanding of the world around her.

Her desk faced a window which looked out over the Harbour. It meant she could keep an eye on any comings and goings, but for days now all she had seen were the snow covered gantries and *Day Bringer*, looking lonely in the almost empty Harbour. This morning though, she found herself glancing up quite often. Jik could perhaps arrive today with *Sunrise*. Helping with the dry dock would be a welcome change from the uncongenial paperwork.

Silberay had to learn to be independent and apprentice classes during the Gathering had involved the operation and use of the dry dock. It was not something that could be managed alone however so the Harbour Master was often called upon to assist. Of course Jik and his apprentice Dom would be here to help Tippa, but like it or not, she was going to be there too. There had to be some pleasures to be had in this job.

She was just thinking about lunch when she saw a prow appear under the bridge at the entrance to the Harbour. In another moment she identified it as *Autumn Wind*. Grabbing her coat she headed for the loading bay and stood watching as *Autumn Wind* made her slow way through the basin with *Sunrise* closely tied behind her. Dom was just making his way to *Autumn Wind*'s prow as she watched. He saw her and waved then looked back at Jik who was calling to Tippa, at *Sunrise*'s tiller. She waved a hand in acknowledgement then Jik bent to release the strap that held the two boats together. Nicely done, Marheh thought, as Jik throttled back and allowed *Sunrise* to glide towards the loading bay ahead of him.

There was just enough forward movement for Tippa to steer neatly into place and step off with her centre line. Marheh went forward to help her, but Tippa waved her back.

"Don't even think of it! From what Jik told me you won't be up to pulling yet."

Marheh made a face.

"He's probably right. I hate him."

Tippa gave a short laugh.

"Still the same old Marheh. The Silberay are living dangerously making you Harbour Master. How many boats have you rocked already?"

Marheh laughed but did not otherwise respond. She was probably going to disturb the still waters that surrounded the Silberay, but the discoveries she had been making were not her fault nor hers to disclose.

Jik and Dom were mooring up behind *Day Bringer* on the nearest gantry. She watched as they finished tying off. Jik strolled towards the loading bay while Dom disappeared below. He was so reliable, Marheh thought. He would listen to her concerns and advise. He had always taken her seriously, even when she was a child. A smile lit her face as he reached her. He winked at her and sketched a salute.

"Mission accomplished Harbour Master."

"It's good to see you."

She might have said more, but Tippa broke in.

"You'll stay to help with the dry dock though, won't you?"

"Of course, but I fancy a bit of lunch first."

"Fair enough. I'll go up with Marheh and get on the telephone to the chandler to organise what I need."

"Wouldn't it be better to have a proper look first?" Marheh said.

"I know what I need, a new propeller. I don't want to wait around any longer than I have to."

"It's been a while since *Sunrise* was docked," Marheh said carefully. "I thought perhaps you might want to black the hull while she is there."

"How do you know when she was docked?"

"It's part of the job," Marheh said lightly.

Tippa opened her mouth to respond but Jik got in first.

"Why don't we meet back here in an hour? We'll need Dom's help and he is busy with lunch right now." He turned to Marheh. "Harbour Master, we were hoping you would eat with us today."

"I'd love to." She tried to match his formality. "I'll just need to pop over and tell Fylan not to expect me. Shall I join you in ten minutes?"

It was beautifully warm on *Autumn Wind* and Dom had baked as well as making a thick pea and ham soup for their lunch so the saloon smelt very welcoming. Dom grinned at her and Jik stood up to give her a careful hug when she appeared.

"Thank goodness," she said when he released her. "The formality was beginning to worry me."

He smiled.

"I thought Tippa was being a bit cavalier. You're doing an important job."

"Even if I'm only an unworthy substitute for the real thing." She raised her eyebrows. "Tippa is never going to take me seriously. We've too much history."

"How is it going?"

"Problems, stuff I need to talk about with you, but I don't feel quite as helpless as I did in the beginning."

"You, helpless!" Dom said. "I don't believe it."

Marheh grinned at him.

"It's true. I took one look at all that paperwork and would have run away if I could."

Dom shook his head.

"Lunch is ready when you are."

Talk of problems was put aside while they ate, but when they had finished Dom stood up.

"I'm happy to clear up here, if you need to talk business with Jik."

Marheh shook her head.

"Jik might be prepared to exploit his apprentice, but I'm not going to." She looked from him to Jik. "There are things that need to be discussed. I do need advice, but…" It took her a few moments to find the right words. "Dom, you represent the future and it's the future that is at stake." She hesitated again then spoke quickly. "I want to tell you both what has happened and what I think, but it is not something we can fix in an hour and it is not something that should be generally known at this stage."

The two men looked at her, curiosity and concern on their faces.

"Then we will not speak of it until we have time enough," Jik said gravely. "How urgent is it?"

Marheh shook her head.

"Not immediately urgent but very troubling in the long term. I believe we need to bring the problem to the Gathering and at least suggest some ways forward."

The early part of the afternoon was spent getting *Sunrise* into the dry dock. It all went very smoothly though Marheh was not allowed to help as much as she would have liked and had to content herself with holding one of the ropes that kept her in place as the water drained out around her. She could pretend she was needed however and so neglect the office for the hour or so. Just watching it all happening as it had done for over one hundred years was interesting even though she had seen it often.

Sunrise was bow hauled into the dock and Jik and Dom began to slot the heavy timbers that would hold back the water into place across the entrance. Then, once the sluices in the dock were opened and the water could run out, they stood with shovels full of light gravel, ash and sand and fed these down so that the pressure of water trying to enter forced them into any gaps.

That had usually been her job when *Day Bringer* was docked, but she could see that it would not be sensible for her to do it now.

When *Sunrise* was resting comfortably on the blocks on the floor of the dock Marheh and Tippa both pulled on rubber boots and climbed down into the last foot of water, anxious to see the extent of the problem and too impatient to wait until the floor was completely dry.

As they waded around to the stern Marheh could see plenty of evidence of neglect, but for the moment she held her tongue, knowing that any comment from her would not be welcome. Tippa too was silent. Marheh held back as she reached the stern and bent to examine the shaft. When she finally straightened again she looked at Marheh.

"It's a mess! Go on, say it, I told you so."

Marheh shook her head but said nothing. Tippa sighed.

"She'll need more than just a new prop and a coat of black won't she?"

"I think so," Marheh said carefully. "But I'm no expert."

"How bad is it?" Jik called from above them.

"Come and see," Tippa said. "Bring your apprentice for a lesson in how not to look after a boat."

Impulsively Marheh put her arms around her, shocked to see a couple of tears escape with Tippa's bitter words.

"We'll get her right again."

"Will we? Can we? At what cost?"

Marheh did not reply. She knew Tippa earned her living making things from wool and fabric and selling them at markets. Her own experience told her it was not likely to provide for much in the way of extras. She and Nemle had often had lean times when all they had to rely on were the markets. It was just lucky that the family pottery paid her a wage now since her signature pieces had proved so successful.

"There will be a way," she said at last, wondering whether she was holding out false hope."

Jik and Dom, having pulled on their own rubber boots, made their way down the ladder to join the women.

"Let it be a lesson," Tippa said to Dom, as they came up to look at the stern, the edge of the counter, the missing propeller and the hull, bare and rusting in places where the protective coat of black bituminous paint had been scraped away by the rigors of travel.

"I kept putting off docking her, telling myself she'd had a good going over when Bildu retired."

"But that's nearly twelve years!" Jik said.

"Yes."

Jik put a hand on *Sunrise*'s hull, patting her reassuringly.

"Well, she's here now. Dom and I will give you a hand getting the rust off and doing the blacking." He bent to tap the bottom of the counter and pick at a bit of rust. "I think you'll need a bit of welding here though. I expect Marheh can organise that, and the new propeller."

"I can't pay," Tippa said bluntly. "I thought I could just about manage a new prop but that will clean me out."

"Payment is not a priority, getting *Sunrise* right again is," Marheh said, wondering what she was promising.

The Silberay were going to have to find money somewhere if individuals were to continue with the work that was the reason for their life on the water road.

The last foot of water had disappeared as they were speaking. Jik looked around.

"We'll put a gangplank across from the edge so you can get on board," he said to Tippa. "Then there will be an hour or so of daylight still and we can get started."

The others disappeared to change into their oldest clothes and Marheh drifted reluctantly back towards the office. She still had not heard back from the welder, and that was obviously a priority now. She had not quite reached the building when she was startled by a couple of loud toots from around the front.

They came again and she began to run. The afternoon's event had completely erased the arrival of her parents but this must be them. Mek would be impatient to be away again. He would not be home before dark as it was.

When she reached them her father was just opening the car door for her mother and Mek was taking a suitcase from the boot.

"Not much of a welcome," Mek said, depositing the suitcase at her feet.

"Sorry, I didn't hear you arrive."

It was no use trying to placate Mek but her parents would understand. She turned to greet them, wincing a little at her father's bear hug.

"Careful Sef," her mother said. "How are you really daughter?"

"I'm fine, truly, it's just my ribs are not quite mended yet."

"I'll be away then," Mek said, slamming the boot. "I'll be back to pick you up again Sunday unless I hear from you."

"I've a box for the pottery," Marheh said quickly. "It's just inside the door."

Mek shrugged and opened the boot again while Marheh hurried to open the door and pick up her box.

"I haven't been able to work much the last few weeks but I'd be grateful for some more clay when you come back if you've time to collect it."

Mek gave a grunt that might have been assent, took the box from her and thrust it into the boot and under the elasticised webbing that would keep it from bouncing around. Mek's business involved the transport of fragile goods and Marheh knew she could trust him with her pieces whatever he might think of her.

"I wish you and Mek got on better," her mother said when they had watched him drive away.

"We do get on better than we did," Marheh said. "But he still doesn't approve of what I do and I can't change who I am."

She turned to lead the way inside. Sef and Greya followed, but once in the hall they stopped to look around curiously.

"It's a bit Spartan," Sef said. "I hope your office is a bit warmer."

"Yes it is, and I've had the heater on in the flat since this morning so you should be quite snug."

She took them upstairs to the flat and left them in the bedroom to unpack while she went to put the kettle on in the little kitchen.

The living room in the flat had a window with the same outlook as the one in her office. When she came out of the kitchen her parents were standing there looking out.

"A field of snowy white," Greya said, turning to smile at her. "But sometimes, just for an instant we catch a glimpse of something else."

"Tell us about it, daughter," Sef said. "Make us see what you see."

She walked across to stand between them. The extra height from the first floor gave her a wider view and she took a moment to take in what she was seeing then she began.

"You can see the edge of the house to the left," she began, knowing this would be visible to them. "That's where the old ones live out their last days. Beyond it is a glimpse of the hard standing where boats are stored if there is no one to take them over. It is happening more often now because the number of apprentices has been dwindling for years."

"Out of the water?" Sef asked.

Marheh nodded.

"There is a winch and rollers. It is quite a ceremony at the Gathering, with everyone helping. The boats deserve our respect."

She was silent for a moment, thinking of the last Gathering when Blin had retired and *Westerly* had been winched carefully out.

"The trees beyond that shelter a little arm of the water road where the private part of the graduation ceremony is held, just the mentor and the apprentice in the place where the Harbour began. Right in front of us is the main pool. There is a bridge over the entrance and gantries for mooring along the left side. Below us is the loading dock and to the right the dry dock and the wet dock, but you can see those. *Day Bringer* is moored just beyond the wet dock with *Autumn Wind* behind her."

She turned to her father.

"I didn't tell you that Jik is here. He came in this morning. I didn't tell him you were coming."

Sef smiled.

"It will be a surprise for him."

"Could you see any of what I described?" Marheh asked, knowing her parents believed in the truth of what she was telling them even if they did not see it.

"The bridge," Sef said. "I saw it as you spoke and if I half close my eyes I think I can see it still, but mostly it is, as Greya said, a field covered lightly with snow."

The whistle of the kettle interrupted then and Marheh hurried back to the kitchen. She made sperit for them all and sat with them to drink it.

"I'll have to go back to the office now," she said, setting down her mug. "I've planned supper on *Day Bringer* though, so I'll come for you about six o'clock."

She bent to kiss them goodbye, but Sef stood up.

"I'll come along with you so we know where to find you."

Towards the front door

Chapter Five

It was hard to settle to office work after the various other activities of the day, but she managed to deal with the afternoon post and was there to answer the telephone call from Lidy, who was calling to ask when *Evening Star* was expected back for her refit. Like the other callers, she had been surprised to find Marheh answering her call, but not amused, as those who had known Marheh as a young woman had been.

"Zinda is getting a bit forgetful," she explained as Marheh read her the dates from the chart. "She was anxious about it, so I said I would confirm."

"Sensible," Marheh agreed. "And it means I can ask you what you need in the work area, so as to prepare the carpenter."

That was one thing to tick off her list, she thought as she hung up, but she still had not heard from the welder and now it was critical. Perhaps she should try to telephone. She thought she had the number, but she hated doing it, even when it was to someone she knew. She could never be sure she was not interrupting something important.

Her first call was not answered though she listened to it ringing more than a dozen times. What would she do if he was no longer in business? She would be expected to find someone else. She finished her filing and was tempted to go and see how the work on *Sunrise* was progressing, but without any news for them she knew she had no excuse to leave the office. She stood up to pace restlessly around the little space, looking at the chart for the dry dock bookings, opening the filing cabinet drawers, even turning over the calendar on the wall to see if Gilt had written anything important that she should know about.

The next time she rang she heard the engaged signal which encouraged her and five minutes later she was successful in connecting.

"Sefton Welding," said a woman's voice.

Marheh explained who she was and why she was calling, mentioning her letter.

"He isn't interested," the woman said.

"Oh."

"He has enough work without having to deal with disappearing boats and all the other weird stuff that goes on there."

Marheh opened her mouth to protest but the woman had already hung up. Disappearing boats, weird stuff, the woman's words echoed in her mind as she stared out her window at the Harbour. Now what? She could look in the telephone book and see if she could find someone else or she could go to the address in Sefton Middle and try to persuade them that the Silberay were harmless. The telephone book was handy but the entries under welders were few and no other close by. It might be better anyway to go in person and see whether she could promote greater understanding. It was too late to do anything about it now, she needed to be getting on with preparing the meal for her parents, but she could talk it over with them and with Jik too.

Her mind was busy with this problem all the time she was assembling her ingredients and preparing the meal. Fortunately Wakefield Steak was a dish she had cooked successfully many times. She had chosen it for that reason. Cooking was not her forte although she liked to be hospitable.

Once the savoury smell of the dish had begun to waft through *Day Bringer* she set the table and went to get her parents. It would have been nice to invite Jik too, but then she would need to include Dom and Tippa and the meal would not stretch so far. Work in the dry dock was finished for the day however, so she called in to *Autumn Wind* and issued an invitation for the two men to visit after supper, and please bring a stool each.

Sef and Greya were used to being guided onto *Day Bringer*. They closed their eyes and allowed Marheh's description and her touch to show them where to step as they went along the gantry and onboard. Then they could follow her down into her cabin and through to the saloon. It was already dark, so their view from *Day Bringer* was limited, but now, from within the water dimension, they could see reflections, the moon as it came and went behind the moving clouds and the cabin lights from *Autumn Wind* and *Day Bringer* glimmering on the dark water.

"I'll bring you on board in daylight too," she said, watching their rapt faces as they gazed out of *Day Bringer*'s uncurtained windows. "Then you can see it all for yourselves."

She settled them in the fixed seats at the table and took a stool for herself. Cooking for her parents was a rare occurrence and Wakefield Steak was one of Nemle's recipes so she was confident that the meal would be a treat for them. Conversation during dinner was limited to pleasant subjects, the latest news of her brothers and their families, the successes of the pottery and, from Marheh, little jokes against herself in her new role. She knew there would be an accounting though. They were concerned about her and would quiz her until they were confident that she was recovering from her injuries and not just the physical ones either. It was the price of being loved, so she would be grateful.

Fortunately the inquisition was over by the time Jik and Dom arrived. She had been able to skate over the actual attack by explaining that it had all happened too fast.

"And once I was in the water dimension and they couldn't find me it was just a question of enduring until help came."

She did not speak of the pain, the cold and the fear and made light of the broken bones that had been the catalyst for her present role.

"I'm healing well," she told them. "All but the worst bruises have gone completely and I can laugh without hurting and carry a bit of shopping, just can't wear my back pack yet."

She was making sperit for them when Jik and Dom arrived. It was a simple matter to set out a couple more mugs, and Dom, whose cooking skills contributed to the common purse on *Autumn Wind*, had brought some of his biscuits to share.

Once everyone was comfortably provided for and the first greetings were over Marheh broached the subject that was most on her mind.

"The Silberay don't exist here any more," she began. "Our neighbours don't know us. If they think about the Harbour at all they believe it is an old people's home or even an asylum. The welder doesn't want to deal with 'weird stuff' like disappearing boats and the rate notice was addressed to Mr Silberay."

She wouldn't speak of the financial crisis yet, though her father might have ideas about that too.

"It's no wonder we have so few apprentices if even our own neighbours don't know who we are. It seems to me to be important that we at least try to share ourselves here."

Jik looked at her affectionately.

"A new crusade, niece?"

"Don't patronise me Jik."

He held up his hands in protest.

"I'm not, truly, we've often needed you to awaken us to uncomfortable realities."

She looked at him suspiciously for a moment then realized he was sincere.

"All those new houses, people live so close to us now. What do they think when they look out over our land. They only see empty fields, not even any crops or animals. There was a notice from the town council explaining that this area has been re-zoned from agricultural to residential and lots of letters from real estate agents asking for first refusal, or offering to do a valuation. Owning the land was enough once when we were in the midst of a farming community but I don't think it is now."

"But we do own it," Jik said. "It can't be taken away from us."

"Can't it?" She looked around at them all. "This had better be just between us at the moment, but both Gilt and Leura have drawn on capital to pay for upkeep. Our finances are not getting any better. Our income is less and our expenses are higher. Our rates have tripled and when I went to the town hall to inquire I was told it was because of the re-zoning. The woman I spoke to told me I was lucky because the value of my property had increased to such an extent."

She stopped speaking abruptly as if she had suddenly run out of steam. The others seemed a bit taken aback by her revelations.

"Are you sure they were using capital?" Jik said at last.

"I'm not really sure of anything," Marheh said. "I'm no accountant, but I've really tried to get on top of the job you've forced on me and I can't see where else the money came from, and the capital has decreased. If I pay the rates, even just the first instalment, there will be very little left to pay Fylan, or to provide for the Gathering. I don't know what to do."

That was not something any of her listeners had ever heard her say before and it shocked them into silence for a few minutes. It was her father who responded first.

"I'm not an accountant either," he said slowly. "But I have balanced the books for the pottery for many years, and Jik, you have held the position that is now Marheh's. Could I suggest that the three of us spend tomorrow morning going over the figures just to confirm Marheh's suspicious, which will at least show us where we stand. Then we can consider some strategies."

Jik nodded.

"I will, of course. Dom won't mind if I leave off work on *Sunrise*'s hull. It is good of you to consider yourself as one of us Sef."

Marheh did not speak, but reached out a hand to each of them gratefully.

"I don't think we should say anything to Tippa at this stage," Jik continued.

"Better to say nothing until we have something concrete to tell all the Silberay."

"If you all have a job for tomorrow, I will put my mind to the other problem," Greya said. "I see what the neighbours see, so perhaps that will help me to understand what they feel about what they see and how that might be enlarged to include the truth of the Silberay."

Marheh smiled at her mother.

"I did have one or two ideas about that. I met a couple of women off the bus and invited them to visit the old ones. I doubt they will, but perhaps it might be a start."

"A good start," Jik said. "If we can make it happen."

Dom, who had been listening intently to the conversation, cleared his throat hesitantly.

"Perhaps…" he said and stopped as the others turned to him.

Marheh smiled and he took courage.

"We do have quite a lot of space between the buildings and the road. Could we perhaps make it available for our neighbours to use?"

"I wondered about that," Marheh said. "We might even open the buildings. After all we only use all of them every two years. It seems a waste to have them standing empty the rest of the time."

"You might find there are groups who would pay something to have the use of a meeting room," Sef said. "It would add to the Harbour Master's job though."

"I don't think that would matter," Marheh said. "But I do think the routes should be rearranged. We've actually neglected this area it seems to me, just relying on the song of the old ones to shield it. That was enough when there were fewer people around us, but I don't think it is now."

Marheh went to bed with her mind still buzzing with ideas and possibilities. It took her a while to get to sleep, but she slept well and woke feeling full of purpose. Breakfast was soon over and after she had washed up and banked her fire she hurried across to the Harbour Master's office, anxious to be there and organised when Sef and Jik arrived. There were account books and some files of bank statements that they would need to look at together, and it would be nice if she could warm the office a little too.

They were not long after her and the three of them were soon poring over the records, Marheh pointing out her concerns and the other two nodding and frowning as the poor state of the finances was confirmed. By lunchtime they had seen enough to establish the truth of Marheh's discoveries and get a clear picture of what seemed like disaster.

"We've been a bit complacent, haven't we?" Jik said, pushing back his chair.

"And perhaps a bit naive," Marheh said. "We've thought things could continue forever the way they were and taken the Harbour for granted."

Sef looked from one to the other. Both of them lived largely in another dimension, working to support themselves in a simple lifestyle, but giving as much of themselves as they could to the song that was their true calling. He supposed that to be true of most of the Silberay. They were innocents really when it came to the workings of commerce and economics.

"It's easy to understand why one or two of your Harbour Master's have drawn on capital," he said. "There have been times when interest rates have been very low, and most of your income has come from interest, but it was not very wise."

"We do pay dues," Marheh said.

"But we've tended to be generous if people say they can't afford them," Jik added.

"I've more or less told Tippa the Silberay would pay for her welding," Marheh said. "And I believe we've always paid for the changes when an apprentice graduates or a Silberay becomes a mentor."

"And ideally that's how it should be," Sef said slowly. "Your work is what is important. I'm guessing that the administration of the Silberay was originally structured to free you from financial distractions and enable you to concentrate most of your attention on the song."

Jik nodded.

"I'm sure you're right, though I doubt many of the younger Silberay could articulate it as clearly as that."

Sef laughed.

"When you have a daughter like Marheh it forces you to learn about things you might otherwise never have known."

Marheh gave a little snort of protest. Her father and Jik were brothers, contemporaries and she loved them dearly but sometimes they did make her feel as if she was still a child.

"Well things will have to change now whether we like it or not," she said. "And maybe it will be for the best. We might be able to understand other people's problems better if we have similar ones ourselves."

"Out of the mouths of babes!" Jik said, teasing her.

She rounded on him, ready to snap, then saw the twinkle in his eyes and drew herself up with great dignity, lifting her chin and looking severely from one to the other.

"Be sensible you two. We've identified the problem. I was not imagining things. Now we need to look for a solution."

Sef smiled at her.

"Don't scold. You're quite right. It was just a momentary lapse."

She laughed then and put Marheh the Great back in her box. She didn't need her very often these days.

"Perhaps we should look at immediate priorities first, Sef went on. "And then think about the longer term."

. . . . .

While the others were closeted in the office Greya was considering her own offer of assistance.

She pottered around in the flat for a half hour or so, doing a bit of tidying, making the bed and looking out of each window as she moved from room to room. It was a nice bright morning. The cold would not matter if she dressed warmly and a walk around would help her to understand.

Well wrapped up, she made her way to the front door and helped herself to a walking stick from a stand beside the door. There was still snow lying about and she didn't want to slip. Stepping outside, she stood for a moment to get her bearings. She knew this front space did not conceal anything. It was just what it appeared, an expanse of snow covered land bordered by a row of trees and a fence along the road at its edge. It would be quite big enough for youngsters to chase about kicking a ball, or to give over to allotments if that was something the neighbourhood needed. She set off down the drive, stepping carefully over the ruts their arrival had made in the snow.

At the road she stopped again to look across at the houses on the other side. Pleasant enough homes, she thought, but not large, and not much space in front where she could see. Turning back, she studied the landscape of the Harbour. These neighbours would be seeing what she saw.

There were the two houses, the small one where Marheh had explained that the old ones lived, and the big house that Marheh called the administration building. Both were old, at least one hundred years old, perhaps more in the case of the big house. She could just pick out the original farm house that had obviously been added to extensively from time to time. They looked prosperous, even privileged, standing alone in the wide white fields. It was difficult to believe in that other dimension where Marheh dwelt, even though she had seen it herself from *Day Bringer*.

Half hidden by the big house were two more, barn-like buildings that she knew were the dry dock and the wet dock. Could the neighbours ever understand their purpose though? She began to walk back down the drive, thinking to visit the old ones before returning to the flat. If the Silberay wanted to become more visible, more understood and accepted in their neighbourhood, they had quite a challenge ahead. It was something the old ones could be part of too. She didn't know them, but she thought some of them would welcome the opportunity to contribute.

She took the left hand fork of the drive and knocked at the door of the house. Fylan opened it and smiled a greeting.

"I'm Greya, Marheh's mother," she said. "I believe you helped nurse my difficult daughter. I wanted to meet you and say thank you. Marheh thought the old ones might enjoy a visitor too."

"Indeed they will," Fylan said. "Especially one like you who is sympathetic to the water road."

She ushered Greya inside, closed the door and led her into the sitting room where Teg, Blin and Sula were comfortably ensconced by a cheerful coal fire. Teg was reading, Sula was knitting and Blin was dozing, but they all looked up as she entered.

"This is Greya, our Harbour Master's mother come to visit," Fylan said.

"How nice." Teg struggled to his feet. "You are very welcome. Come in, sit down."

Once she was comfortably seated, Fylan said. "It's almost time for elevenses. Have you time to join us?"

"That would be lovely. Marheh is busy with Jik and my husband in the office. They won't miss me."

"Good. You stay and chat and I'll go and get organised."

She smiled at Teg.

"Will you introduce yourselves? I'll just check and see if Mieka would like to get up and join us."

She disappeared and Teg began the introductions with quiet grace. He had barely finished when Blin took over.

"The Harbour Master's mother, fancy." He eyed her intently. "You do have a look of her, I suppose."

Greya smiled politely, not quite liking the intensity of his gaze.

"I doubt she would be flattered to hear you say so," she said, then turned to Sula. "That's lovely work. Is it something for yourself?"

Sula was about to reply, smiling and spreading out her knitting, but Blin spoke again.

"The Silberay spoil her you know, overlook her behaviour and flatter her into thinking she is special."

"Blin!"

Teg and Sula spoke together.

"That is rude and untrue," Sula continued. "If anything the Silberay have been hard on Marheh and asked a lot of her because she is special."

"I was just saying," Blin grumbled. "Her mother ought to know."

"I do know my daughter," Greya said quietly. "I know her and love her and have no intention of talking about her." She looked to Teg and Sula. "I would much rather talk about you. I've no doubt your lives have been interesting and challenging. You must have seen many changes."

Teg and Sula responded warmly and the conversation became general. Blin said little more but glowered from his chair and, when Fylan brought in a loaded tray, fed himself biscuits in a continuous stream.

Greya was very thoughtful as she walked back to the big house. Obviously Marheh's life as Silberay was not without its difficulties. She had not been able to raise the subject of the neighbours when it was clear that Blin would be antagonistic to any idea that came from Marheh.

She let herself in through the front door and stood a moment looking around. It was almost as cold here in the hall as it was outside. The place looked rather drab and tired, she thought, taking time now to consider what she was seeing.

She didn't expect housework to be part of the Harbour Master's duties, but the place needed someone to care for it. The Silberay would need to factor that into their planning, especially if they decided to extend the use of their buildings. Marheh, she knew, would not think about that possibility. She would probably not even notice the dust and cobwebs, the lack of polish or even the remnants of muddy footprints on the parquetry at the entrance.

She returned her walking stick to its place by the door and continued along the passage towards the Harbour Master's office, opening doors as she passed them, trying to get a feel for the place. She found a couple of small rooms fitted out like classrooms with a blackboard and a dozen desks. The kitchen was off to the side, quite a large space, but very old fashioned, with only a wood burning stove. A sturdy wooden table stood in the centre of the room and a dresser held crockery that would all need washing before it was next used. There was a big sink on one wall with a wooden draining rack above it. Saucepans of various sizes hung from the rafters. She could not see any sign of a refrigerator. Who on earth would they find to cook in here, she wondered, picturing her own comfortable home? Its fabric was old too, but it was well maintained and up to date where it needed to be.

She made her way back to the passage and along to the Harbour Master's office feeling rather sad. Her family and Sef's had supported the Silberay and valued their contribution to the world around them as long as she could remember. One of Sef's uncles, his brother and their own much loved daughter had all chosen to dedicate themselves to the Silberay, but it almost seemed as if it was a way of life that was dying.

She was warmly welcomed into the Harbour Master's office but understood that here too the news was not good.

"I've had elevenses with Fylan and the old ones," she said. "But you must be getting thirsty. Why don't we adjourn to the flat? It will be more comfortable and I can make sperit for you."

Sef put his arm around her.

"That will be nice. I think we need it now."

"I shouldn't leave the office really," Marheh said. "What if the telephone rings?"

"It will ring in the flat too," Jik told her. "You won't have discovered that since you're not using it, but it is useful if you need a break from the office."

"I hate telephones," she grumbled. "Why would you want one where you live? It's bad enough in the office. They never bring good news."

Greya laughed and turned to Sef.

"Obviously we were not good news. Perhaps we should have just arrived unannounced."

Marheh reddened.

"I didn't mean that."

She began to fumble with the papers on her desk.

"You go on up. I'll just tidy these and join you in a few minutes."

Greya and Sef exchanged glances then Sef stood back to let Greya go before him.

"Don't be long," Greya said as she led the way.

When they were out of sight Marheh slammed the papers down and took a deep breath. What was it about parents that made her feel like a child? Not just a child, she supposed in one sense she would always be a child to her parents, but a difficult child who needed special handling. She knew they loved her, that was the important thing to focus on. She picked up the papers again. Some needed to be re-filed, but the two pages of notes and priorities she had made with Sef and Jik she would take upstairs so they could continue to work on them.

Walking in Sefton Middle

Chapter Six

At lunch Dom suggested he might provide their evening meal, but he would cook in the flat so that everyone could be comfortable. It was an offer too good to refuse. Jik took his place in the dry dock working beside Tippa for the afternoon while Dom took the bus into town for supplies and returned to commandeer the flat's small kitchen.

Marheh spent the early part of the afternoon in the office, but later she redeemed her promise to take Sef and Greya onto *Day Bringer* so they could see the extent of the Harbour in daylight.

"It's a shame you don't have more visitors," Greya said, after gazing for sometime in silent contemplation. "Seeing it all would help them to understand."

"There are some who don't want to understand," Marheh said. "The welder doesn't want anything to do with us. If I'm honest there are also Silberay who don't want to be understood. I thought perhaps we could have an open day during the Gathering when there are lots of people here to share the work of host, but they would think I was out of line if I arranged it without consultation with the mentors. I can hear the tut-tutting already, but consulting the mentors would mean leaving any action until the next Gathering and in two years it might all be too late."

"You could at least talk it over with Jik," Sef said. "He's a mentor, and what about consulting the old ones. It seems like a good idea to me."

"The old ones would enjoy visitors too," Greya said. "Although I'm not sure Blin is quite the advocate you need."

"He's not so bad if I'm out of the picture," Marheh said. "But he has the idea that Nemle spoiled me and the Silberay allowed it. He was not given an apprentice, there were not enough that year, and he has never forgiven the Silberay for that."

She moved to stand between them.

"Have you seen enough? You're welcome to stay as long as you like. I can come back for you in an hour or so if you want, but I think I'd better go and see how the work in the dry dock is progressing and then try to track down another welder. I haven't ordered Tippa's new propeller either, so I need to talk to her about what she needs."

"Perhaps you could come back for us once you have been to the dry dock," Sef said. "I'd like to look a while longer so as to fix it in my memory."

"I'm trying to imagine it filled with boats like *Day Bringer*," Greya added.

Marheh smiled and gave them both a hug.

"I won't be long."

It was quite gloomy in the dry dock although the lights were on. She peered in from the edge and used the sounds of scraping to direct her gaze towards the two workers, then she made her way down into the depths. *Sunrise*'s hull looked nearly ready for the blacking paint. She could see where patches of rust had been scraped away and anti-rust paint applied. Tippa and Jik were both working on the other side of the boat. She thought they had not heard her arrive.

"How is it going?" she asked, moving around to them.

"Marheh!" Jik greeted her with a smile. "We should be finished with the scrapers in an hour or so. The anti-rust can go on and dry overnight and we should be ready to start blacking tomorrow. There's just the one spot below the counter that needs some plate welded over it."

Tippa looked up from the patch of rust she was attacking.

"Jik and Dom have been fantastic. The whole job has been so much easier than if I'd been doing it alone."

She and Jik were both rather grubby and Marheh thought Tippa looked tired. It would have been dreary on her own on *Sunrise* last night and she was probably worried about the work and how to pay for it.

"Dom is cooking supper in the flat. My parents are visiting. Will you join us?"

"You won't want an extra in a family party."

"Yes we will," Jik said. "You will keep us on our best behaviour. Marheh can be very provoking at times."

"See what I have to put up with! Please come."

"Thanks, I'd like that. What time?"

They settled on a time and began a discussion about suitable propellers. Jik reminded Marheh that there was a big catalogue of boating supplies in the office and suggested he and Tippa call in to look at it on the way to supper. She explained her problem with the welder and Jik agreed that a visit might be helpful.

"You might consider asking Sef to go with you," he said. "Not because he is a man," he added quickly when Marheh frowned and seemed to protest. "But because he is not Silberay."

She screwed up her face.

"It makes sense I suppose but I know what will happen. Father will get into conversation with him and I will be told to go away and play."

Jik laughed.

"Will that really matter if Sef can persuade him to reconsider?"

"I suppose not. Alright I'll go and break it to him that he has a mission for tomorrow. See you both at supper."

She made her way back to *Day Bringer* and guided her parents off and out of the water dimension.

Leaving Tippa on her own this evening when the rest of them would be together would be hurtful, she thought, when she was back in her office, but did it mean that they could not discuss the financial troubles of the Silberay? It would be common knowledge soon enough and surely now the more ideas the better. There were priorities. The morning's discussion had been helpful in working out the essentials that needed to be paid for before the Gathering as well as the minimum required to enable the Gathering to proceed more or less as usual.

Sef and Jik had offered to finance the welcome breakfast that was so important in establishing a happy atmosphere. It didn't seem fair to accept really, but she knew they could afford it and it would help enormously.

She realised suddenly, rather appalled by the thought, that she would be expected to make the speech of welcome. It would be an opportunity, if she could manage to use it, to challenge the Silberay to make positive changes, but was she capable of it.

What she needed to do now was make some kind of time line, otherwise the Gathering would be upon her before she knew it. Already she was behind because of the welder and she would need to remind herself when Bixa was coming in, and Whin and Zinda.

The whole job, the planning and the detail, was so foreign to her, and the older Silberay especially would not forget the troublesome apprentice she had been, always questioning the way things were done. She put her head in her hands for a moment then looked up and out the window to the quiet water, *Day Bringer* and *Autumn Wind*, and the grey wintry sky.

It they lost the Harbour the water road would cease to exist. There was no possibility of rebuilding somewhere else. This was their inheritance from Sila and just now it was her job to keep it, to maintain it and plan for its continuance. There would always be some who would shoot the messenger when the news was bad, and the news she would bring was very bad, but this was not about her. She had dealt with disapproval before and she could again.

Marheh was already in the flat with Dom and her parents when Jik arrived with Tippa. After the introductions Tippa looked around curiously.

"I've not been in here before," she said. "I always imagined it to be a bit more luxurious." She looked sideways at Marheh. "But then I always imagined that the position of Harbour Master was an important one."

Marheh laughed.

"The position might be important, but the present incumbent isn't."

Jik looked at her and winked, but said nothing.

"Tippa and I began our apprenticeship at the same Gathering," Marheh explained to her parents. "She remembers what a know-all trouble maker I was then."

Greya smiled.

"Too much Marheh the Great was there?" Sef said.

Marheh lifted her chin for a moment, mocking herself, then headed for the kitchen to help Dom.

Ten minutes later they were all sitting around the table enjoying the onion soup Dom had prepared to begin the meal. It was quite a tight fit with six of them but there were no complaints. Indeed the four Silberay found it quite spacious. Tippa was loud in praise of Jik and Dom and the help they had given her and Sef and Greya were happy to encourage her to speak of *Sunrise* and the work that needed to be done. Marheh, sitting between Jik and Sef, was quite silent. Listening to Tippa now it was difficult to remember her distress when the extent of the deterioration was revealed.

She had appointed herself assistant to the cook and was quite glad to be able to escape to the kitchen to give herself a talking to. Tippa had always been able to rub her up the wrong way. She thought it dated from the time when she had been accused of lying and only promoted on probation. Tippa had snubbed her then, unlike Pon, the other apprentice at their level. Tippa was the oldest of the three as well and obviously thought Marheh, the youngest, was too forward with her opinions.

The meal was delicious and Dom was suitably complimented as they lingered around the table with chocolates and port provided by Sef and Greya.

There would be no point in raising her problems now, Marheh thought. Why spoil the evening? Then Jik spoke, quite formally, almost as if making a speech.

"We've had a most enjoyable meal, thank you Dom, and, sensibly, we have kept our conversation away from serious subjects. There is, however, a very serious subject that has come to light as Marheh has been studying the ramifications of her new job. I think she is to be complimented on her diligence. I'm going to ask her to outline her discoveries and some of the ideas she has had for addressing the issues and invite discussion and suggestions."

He stopped speaking to smile at Marheh.

"I know you were thinking that talk of problems might spoil our pleasant evening, but let's focus on solutions."

Marheh looked around at them all. Jik had been very tactful and paved the way for her beautifully. There was no need for Tippa to know that she was the only one for whom the news would be a complete surprise.

"It's money," she said bluntly. "Our income has gone down and our expenses have gone up."

She paused and looked at them again. Sef and Greya looked sympathetic, Dom looked interested, Jik thoughtful and Tippa troubled, perhaps even angry.

"And it's recognition too," she went on. "Our neighbours don't know who we are or why we are here. I don't think we can address one without addressing the other."

"Trust you to rock the boat," Tippa said. "Does that mean you won't pay for my welding?"

Marheh shook her head.

"No it doesn't. Helping our own is important, but if we don't change some of the things we do the Silberay will die."

"For goodness sake, that's a bit of an exaggeration isn't it? Surely it's just a question of tightening our belts for a bit?"

"No," Marheh said. "Tightening our belts would just be a very short term solution, a patch, when what we need is a re-make."

Tippa still looked angry but did not protest any further. Marheh recognised that her reaction would be echoed by many of the Silberay and realised the sense in including her now. If she could be persuaded of the need for change she would be a formidable ally just because she was not one of Marheh's particular friends.

"Jik, Sef and I went over the accounts this morning," she continued. "I didn't trust my own understanding. What they found more than confirmed what I believed. If we continue the way we have been, in less than ten years we will be bankrupt."

"But you've had some ideas," Jik prompted as she paused again.

"Some," she agreed. "But not enough and some need to be put in place quickly, to be acted on this Gathering. Next Gathering might be too late."

"Well go on then, unveil the grand plan. Are we to name it after you?"

Greya gave a little gasp at this but Marheh just laughed. She was used to Tippa's bluntness.

"Only if it fails," she said. "I want us really to focus on getting to know our neighbours, have an open day during the Gathering, talk to the council about letting our grounds be used for a children's playground or allotments, if there is a need. Perhaps they might adjust the rates if we do.

"It would be good to encourage the neighbours to visit the old ones. They could share their life as Silberay too. Then, if people began to feel more comfortable with us, they might be prepared to rent our buildings for events or classes, after all we only use them every two years. I think the routes should be adjusted too so that there are more Silberay coming and going. We need to be a presence all the time."

"You've really thought about it, haven't you?" Tippa said. "I'm not sure I really want the effort and I don't know that it will do us much good financially, but I can see your reasoning I think."

"I think it's a good idea," Dom said. "If we become better known we might get more apprentices and that's our future."

"The way things are now it's to easy to forget that the Harbour needs our support," Marheh said. "Mostly we only think of it supporting us. I know I hardly ever give it a thought when I'm out on the water road."

"It seems to me," Sef said. "That your Harbour Masters need more support and some training in financial matters before taking on the job. There have been costly mistakes made through ignorance."

"This is not about blame," Jik said. "I think it is important to emphasise that, but it is clear that we have to change. It's getting late and we all have work to do tomorrow, but could we put our minds to the problem."

"And our hearts and souls," Marheh said softly.

"Those too," Jik agreed, giving her a little smile.

Marheh lingered in the flat to help clear up and say goodnight to her parents before heading back to *Day Bringer*. She changed into her nightdress, but her mind was buzzing still and she knew she would not sleep yet. The evening had not gone too badly, better than she expected really. Of course Jik had been a great help and, since Tippa was disposed to be an admirer, his words carried more weight with her than Marheh's would ever do.

She put on dressing gown and slippers and went through to the saloon to build the fire and curl up in the armchair. For a little while she watched the flickering flames through the glass, their light her only illumination, then she lit her candle knowing it would help her enter the soul song.

It was difficult to discipline her mind to focus even with the candle, but at last she managed to let go of all the busyness that distracted her. The song took her then. A simple tune came first, her own little melody, tucked into the larger music that was usually present when she sang. She was not allowed to rest there for long however, more kept being asked of her. The music was not all light and the sombre tones beneath her demanded new harmonies that would modify the aching sadness, pushing her to new heights until her song became a sparkling cadenza that exploded in a shower of golden rain.

Day Bringer's comfortable darkness, the gentle lapping of the fire, the soft glow of the candle were all there when she returned. The memory of the song held her for a moment before she slept, still curled up in the armchair.

By morning she was back in her bed. Sometime in the night she had woken and taken herself there although she had no memory of it now. Memory was all of the song. As she dressed and breakfasted she kept returning there to puzzle over what it might be asking of her. Her sense that there was something she needed to understand was stronger than ever now.

She went early to the office, hoping to make an appointment to visit the welder, before he got too involved in what ever his workday held. It was the same woman who answered the telephone. Marheh did not introduce herself in the way she had previously however, instead giving her name as Mary Carron and explaining that she was hoping to meet the welder to discuss the feasibility of some work she needed done.

This, it seemed, was perfectly possible and she could visit the workshop any time after midday. She went upstairs to tell Sef before returning to tackle the morning post. Jik and Dom would be helping Tippa with the blacking today and she promised herself a mid morning break to go and check on their progress and tell them what she had arranged. With any luck Tippa's new propeller would be delivered today too, although perhaps they should not expect it until tomorrow.

She still had not heard from the other two retiring Silberay and she was beginning to be concerned that any necessary refits could not be done in time. She did not know either Juni or Vey very well and could not seem to associate them with anyone younger. Looking up the rolls again she found that neither of them had an apprentice now, although Juni had begun with one who had decided, after five years, that the life was not for her.

She looked up and out through the window at the almost empty Harbour. That meant two more boats would come out of the water this Gathering. It was unlikely they would be used again. Perhaps she should have taken Tippa's propeller from one of the boats already on the hard standing but it seemed somehow disrespectful. She made a note to go and check on the winch and the rollers that would be needed for that particular ceremony then headed out to visit the dry dock.

Later, as she and Sef waited for the bus to town, she began to tell him about the boats coming out of the water.

"I keep turning over ways they could be used again," she finished. "But it could only happen if we had more wanting to be apprentices than we had

Silberay turning seventy, and that doesn't seem very likely."

"How would work if it did happen?" Sef asked. "It must have in the past when numbers were building."

"I think perhaps an older apprentice might move onto another boat so the mentor could take another apprentice. It would have to be carefully managed though. It wouldn't work if the mentor was too old, or the apprentice too immature."

"Well, if it happens, I'm sure you'll find a way."

The bus came then. It was quite full so the short journey was spent in separate seats. Marheh used the time trying to plan what she would say to the welder to persuade him to return to the Harbour, but she did not come to any decisions except to tell him the truth, that he was very much needed, and to offer to take him on board *Day Bringer* so that he could see the Harbour and any other boats that were there.

The welder's workshop was tucked away in an alley in a rather run down part of town. It was perhaps ten minutes walk from the nearest bus stop by streets and lanes that were new to Marheh. They passed a garage with a car raised on a hoist and a couple more standing inside. A pair of legs was visible at the side of one of these. A shop selling bicycles, new and second hand, and a very tired looking charity shop led up to the alley which was mostly lined with blank brick walls although there were a couple of doors giving access to somewhere unnamed.

Sefton Welding was at the furthest end. There was a neat, rather weathered, sign above two large open doors. An array of tools lined one wall and, at the very back of the space, a small lighted window revealed a sort of cubby hole office. As they approached they saw a man stand up inside it and a moment later he was coming towards them.

"The wife telephoned," he said, looking at Marheh. "You must be Mrs Carron."

She smiled and held out her hand.

"Mary, how do you do?"

He was not a very big man, but lean and wiry. The hand he gave Marheh was a bit grimy but his handshake was firm. Sef introduced himself, explaining that he was Marheh's father, and, as she had predicted, her presence immediately became unimportant.

She let them talk, looking curiously around the big, empty workshop. If he did, indeed, have enough work to be able to refuse hers it was not going on here. Then she heard Sef say something that linked her with the Silberay. She looked up to see the man pale and step back from her as if she was to be feared. She made a little, inarticulate sound of protest and took a step back herself. Sef looked from one to the other. The welder's fear was showing as anger now.

"Get her away," he shouted to Sef. "Get her away. I won't have anything to do with their magic."

"It isn't magic," she tried to tell him, but he continued to back away, still shouting at Sef to get her away.

She went. Sef would have no chance of changing his ideas if she was still present. The rejection hurt, but his reaction made her even more convinced that the Silberay as a whole were not doing enough to make themselves known amongst their neighbours. She walked slowly down the alley, hugging her coat around her. Her father could be very persuasive but she would need to give him plenty of time if he was to succeed with the welder. What could have happened to him at the last Gathering to have caused his present reaction?

She turned the corner and stood in front of the charity shop, looking at, but not seeing, the dusty window display. Surely the Silberay had not treated him badly. He would have seen the boats he had worked on disappear into the water dimension as they left the dry dock, but someone would have explained that, wouldn't they? She sighed and drew her coat closer around her. Perhaps not. Everyone was always busy and preoccupied at the Gathering. She walked on a little, unwilling to believe that the Silberay, and she included herself, had been so uncaring.

She stopped again, looking at the bicycles and wondering, for a brief moment, whether she could make use of one. It might be handy for getting about, but walking suited her. Perhaps she thought suddenly, perhaps it was not the Silberay. Perhaps he had spoken of his experiences at the Harbour and someone had persuaded him there had been magic involved, and not good magic either.

In a way she would rather believe that, except it might mean the Yareblis, traditional enemies of the Silberay, were practising in Sefton Middle. She wandered on a little, past the garage, where legs no longer showed from beneath the car, but a torso disappeared under the bonnet. She remembered a time when cars were a novelty, but now they were everywhere. Could Yareblis be at work here? Surely the song of the old ones at the Harbour would be enough to make them feel ill at ease.

After the garage she came to an intersection. She could walk back towards the bus stop or turn the other way and explore further. Either way, she decided, she must focus herself to listen with her heart, and perhaps, if she could find somewhere to sit quietly, she might even sing.

She chose to turn back towards the bus stop closer to the centre of town. Carefully she began to build the candle flame that was her portal to the soul song. She would not enter, not yet anyway, but carry it ahead of her to illuminate the places where she walked, allowing her to listen to their health. It worked best when there were living, growing things to call to her. Here were only streets and pavements, but even here she could catch a feeling, sadness or joy, contentment or the malaise of indifference.

She walked on, not really seeing the appearance of the streets she trod, but giving herself to understanding the reality beneath the bricks and mortar, the concrete and macadam.

Her steps slowed as she neared the bus stop. There on the main road listening became confused so that she relinquished the candle and just stood looking. There had been some attempt to make the street pleasant, a few trees planted near the bus stop and a seat. The nearby shops were, she had to search for the right word, pretentious, she decided, very different from those closer to the welder. There, even the tired charity shop had been more real.

It began to feel imperative that she sing, but not just here. There were too many people passing and nowhere she could be inconspicuous. Not that anyone was taking notice of her now, all the passers by kept strictly to themselves, but the trancelike state that singing induced would draw attention in this place. She turned back to retrace her steps again. In the quieter streets she might find a place where she could sit and sing for a little time.

A tiny corner with a seat, a stunted tree and bits of rubbish amongst the dead leaves on the cobblestones seemed the best she could find so she settled herself there. Even now, in the early afternoon, the winter sun did not reach it so it was cold and dank, but it was out of the way. The chill would prevent her staying too long in the song.

Although her portal was close it cost her a small struggle to enter. The necessary relinquishing of self was always more difficult if she felt herself physically vulnerable. Lifting the song was hard too. There was no joy in the music that she joined and spinning her own song to modulate the drab tones around her was a challenge to her passion and determination.

She did not remain there long, but long enough to sense something of the grey dreariness that enveloped Sefton Middle and to sing a little light to push it back. She rested for a few minutes before walking on, thinking about what she had experienced. There were other towns she had encountered like this one. In the past it had meant work for her against the Yareblis. She had never thought to find Yareblis influence so close to the Harbour though. Were other Silberay aware, or did no one spend enough time at the Harbour to discover it? She would not have, she knew, if circumstances had not thrust her into the Harbour Master job. The song of the old ones perhaps disguised the malaise that pushed from Sefton Middle.

She had just arrived at the corner by the garage when she was surprised to see Sef and the welder coming towards her. She hesitated. What did it mean? Had Sef persuaded the man to give the Harbour another chance?

Her father smiled when he saw her and turned to his companion. The welder hesitated in his turn but seemed to make up his mind to courage for he continued on with Sef until they reached her.

"Toby," Sef said. "I'd like you to meet my daughter Marheh. She is Silberay, which can be a bit of a trial to both of us and I can't actually tell you that she is harmless, but I can swear to her passion for justice and her championing of those less fortunate."

"Father!" Marheh protested, a little embarrassed by this introduction, though it was delivered in a half teasing manner.

"I can't honestly say I'm pleased to meet you," Toby said. "But your dad has spoken up for you and I'm prepared to consider giving you, you Sil… Silberay another chance."

"That's very good of you," Marheh said. "I hope we can make you more welcome than before, and explain things properly so the boats won't seem so strange."

"Toby has agreed to come back with us and visit the Harbour," Sef said. "So you can turn around and head back to the bus stop."

Tippa's surprise

Chapter Seven

During the bus ride Marheh thought very hard about the best approach to take when they reached the Harbour, but as they walked together along the drive towards the administration building she realised that Sef was doing a far better job of explaining then she could ever do because he saw as the welder did.

"Do you have children?" she heard Sef ask.

"Aye, we've three kids, two sons and a daughter."

"Then you will be able to imagine how difficult it was for my wife and me when Marheh's first word was boat, and we couldn't even see it. She was a real handful too. I remember standing in the back garden and suddenly she disappeared. The water road runs along our boundary and a boat had arrived and she had invited herself on board. Imagine a three year old suddenly vanishing into a different dimension! Luckily my brother can see the water. He was a great help in explaining things."

"But you said you've seen it?"

"Yes, Marheh showed us. She invited us onto her boat, my wife and I both and I know she will invite you too."

"Of course," Marheh said.

Toby looked a bit doubtful at this offer, but said nothing and Marheh did not press. As they continued along the drive she could hear Sef expanding on what a handful she had been to bring up and asking Toby more about his own family. Greya came to the front door when Sef rang and Marheh could see Toby responding to her warmth.

"Will you all come with me to *Day Bringer*?" she invited, turning to Toby to explain that was the name of her boat.

"You needn't worry about coming on board," she joked to Toby. "I'm much too scared of the hiding father would give me if I let anything happen to you."

He managed a smile at that and nodded.

"I'll come if your Mum and Dad are coming too."

She led the way around the building to the loading dock. It was the last place they could all see and she knew it appeared to the others like a paved terrace. Leading Toby along the gantries with his eyes closed she thought would ask him to trust her beyond what was reasonable so she planned to bring *Day Bringer* to the dock instead. She explained that she would disappear to them and be gone for ten minutes or so, but she heard Toby's gasp when she stepped into the water dimension and, as she moved away, heard Greya and Sef reassuring him. She jogged along the gantry to *Day Bringer* recognising that it was important to be as quick as she could, not giving Toby too much time to think. This would be the first time she had boated since the attack too and she realised she was looking forward even to this tiny journey.

It might have been a little over ten minutes by the time she eased *Day Bringer* up to the loading dock and stepped off, centre line in hand. Toby took a step back when she appeared, but then seemed to gather himself.

She smiled at him.

"I'll take mother on board first," she said. "That way you can see what happens. Then you and father can come together. Do you think you can trust me now?"

She wound the centre line around a bollard and took her mother's hand, talking through the steps although she knew Greya did not really need instruction.

A few minutes later she was back for Sef and Toby. A little hesitation and a little encouragement from Sef and Toby closed his eyes and allowed himself to be led on board and down the back steps to her cabin.

"Thank you for trusting me," she said, when he was standing at the foot of the steps. "You can open your eyes now."

He followed her through the boat looking a bit dazed. Greya was already in the saloon, but Sef kept close to Toby in case he needed reassurance. It was clear that he was gaining in confidence though and when Marheh offered to take *Day Bringer* on a lap of the Harbour he was eager to accept.

"I can't take you out of the Harbour," she explained. "Because there is no turning place nearer than an hour away in either direction, but if you would like we could make a time for you to bring your family and spend an afternoon."

She left him to think about that and went out to untie the centre line and move *Day Bringer* slowly around the basin, knowing that Greya and Sef would be able to answer any questions he might have.

She would have loved to keep going, out onto the water road. This little taste made her realise just how much she missed it. What she was doing was worthwhile though, especially if it meant that he would return to work on the boats.

She took *Day Bringer* back to the loading dock and helped the others disembark. Taking *Day Bringer* back to her mooring could be left for a solitary pleasure later on. Now it was important to take Toby along to the dry dock to look at what was needed for *Sunrise*. He was very quiet, but not antagonistic or fearful now, just trying to absorb and make sense of his experience.

The dry dock was where he had worked before and he walked around *Sunrise* examining the hull and explaining what he would do as if there had never been a problem. When he was finally ready to go he took his leave of Marheh, Sef and Greya gratefully and as if they were old friends.

"I'll be back with my tools and the plate that's needed come Monday. I've taken measurements," he said. "It was good of you to take so much trouble over me and if you really meant it, about bringing the wife and kids, well I reckon we'd be mad not to take you up on it."

"Of course I meant it," Marheh said. "Check with your family what day would suit and we can fix a date when you come on Monday."

That night, as she reviewed her day before going to bed, she couldn't help feeling pleased. The welder had become a friend, in large part because of Sef, she had taken a little jaunt on *Day Bringer* without hurting herself, and she had sung in Sefton Middle and so learned something of the lives there. Her journal received a few little comments and some questions for the future before she sang again, just briefly, wanting to connect for a few moments with those other singers who always seemed to be there offering love and support.

Next day she spent the morning in the office with Jik, going over plans and possibilities, testing her ideas against his experience and commonsense. Tippa's blacking was finished and he and Dom were going back to their assigned route. She would miss them, but he had promised to return a fortnight before the Gathering to give her a hand with last minute preparations. Mek was to come for Sef and Greya that afternoon too. She was glad now that they had not let her dissuade them from coming.

Tippa's new propeller had come and Toby had promised to help fit that too since it seemed the shaft might need some attention. Tippa would probably remain at the Harbour for at least the next week for the work to be done. It must be rather gloomy living on board *Sunrise* while she was in the dry dock, and cold too, since she couldn't have much of a fire. Perhaps she should offer her the flat once her parents had gone, or she might like to sleep in the annex where the two new apprentices would stay until they were inducted at the end of the Gathering.

Mek arrived mid afternoon. He had brought her the clay she had asked for and she was suitably grateful. Jik had delayed his departure in order to great his nephew and say goodbye to his brother and sister-in-law, but he left as soon as they had gone.

Marheh spent the rest of the afternoon on *Day Bringer*. She couldn't seem to settle to anything useful, but the walk that would have helped was not really practical given the approach of evening and her memory of her previous weekend's folly. She did visit the dry dock and Tippa and offer her the flat, but she said she would feel happier in the annex.

"Just as long as you're warm enough," Marheh said. "There is a big bank of black clouds on their way here."

"The annex will be fine," Tippa said. "I'll feel like an apprentice again."

She climbed over the side of *Sunrise* and down into the dock and invited Marheh to join her.

"The blacking looks good, doesn't it?" Marheh said.

Tippa nodded.

"And the welder took a good look at the counter and the prop shaft and says he can deal with it all." She hesitated and kicked at some invisible object on the floor of the dock. "He said you'd offered to take him and his family out on *Day Bringer*."

Marheh nodded.

"You're really keen on this get to know the neighbours idea, aren't you?"

"Yes, I am. It seems to me the first step. If our neighbours don't know who we are, how can we expect anyone else to?"

"Well, it certainly worked with the welder, and I'm grateful." She looked at Marheh. "If you want to encourage it at the Gathering, I'll support you."

Marheh smiled.

"Great! That means a lot. Everyone knows … "

She stopped abruptly.

Tippa laughed.

"Go on, say it. Everyone knows that I've never been one of your admirers. Well, that might just be changing."

Marheh shook her head.

"An honest, critical friend is much more use to me than an admirer." She paused and grinned. "Do you need a hand taking stuff across to the annex?"

The short encounter encouraged her and she returned to *Day Bringer* feeling positive enough to take out some clay to work while her evening meal was cooking.

The work on *Sunrise* took the whole of the following week. There was not much Tippa could do to help it along but instead she surprised Marheh by offering to spring clean the annex ready for the Gathering.

"You know I can't pay the cost of the welding," she said. "But I can save you the cost of cleaning."

Marheh, never very observant about housework, had not even thought about the need, but there were obvious signs of neglect when she actually looked. It was not just the new apprentices who would need the accommodation either. Bixa and Whin would both need to move off their boats while the refits were done, Lidy too perhaps. Zinda would be more likely to move into the house. There was always a demand for the bathrooms too. Baths, full size baths, were a great luxury if most of your days were spent without one.

She made sure Tippa knew how grateful she was not just for the offer but also for alerting her to the need. Tippa laughed when she thanked her and teased her for having a mind above housework. Marheh was surprised to find the beginnings of a friendship developing and hastened to cement it with an invitation to share an evening meal on *Day Bringer*.

Tippa reciprocated after she had spent a day cleaning the big kitchen.

"What have you done? It looks lovely."

Marheh stood and gazed. The room was warm from the oven, all the dishes and pots sparkled and shone, the table was set with a pretty cloth patterned with yellow daisies, there were candles on the table and an appetising smell welcomed her.

Tippa laughed.

"Scrubbed and polished mostly. I quite enjoyed it once I got started. It's nice to see a result."

Impulsively Marheh gave her a hug.

"It's wonderful. I wouldn't have known where to start. I think mother implied that something needed to be done about the kitchen, but it just looked like a kitchen to me."

Tippa laughed again.

"Nemle must have despaired of you sometimes. Come and eat."

The week went past quickly and happily and Marheh realised, as she waved Tippa goodbye, that she would miss the company. She had not neglected the old ones and Fylan, but Tippa was her contemporary and knew her in a different way. She had not neglected Toby either and now she put her mind to planning the excursion they had fixed for the next weekend.

The family came out in their little car on Saturday afternoon. They were lucky with the weather and although it was very cold the sun shone in a clear blue sky. Marheh had moved *Day Bringer* to the loading dock again, but she greeted them at the front door of the administration building so that she could introduce them carefully to what would happen.

Toby's wife was Susan. She was obviously still uncertain, and a bit abrupt because of it. The three children were on their best behaviour and stood solemnly beside their parents. The youngest looked to Marheh to be about four or five years old. She had tight hold of Susan's hand, while the two boys stood one on each side of Toby. Marheh learned their names. The little girl was Emily, the older boy Jack and the younger Rob. She greeted them with a smile and a word of welcome before turning to Toby.

"Did you explain your experience?" she asked, then to the children. "Did Dad tell you about his boat ride?"

"He said he had to shut his eyes," Jack said. "Then he held hands with you and your Dad."

"That's right. Then, when I say open your eyes you will be on a boat. Do you think you can do that?"

"Where's your Dad then?"

"He had to go home, but we'll manage alright without him." She turned to

Susan. "Will you follow me and we'll go around to the loading dock?"

"How do I know that what you did with Toby wasn't just a trick to get us all, and this time you won't let us come back?"

"You don't really, I suppose," Marheh said after a moment of thought. "But if Toby told you about the boat you will understand that it would be uncomfortably crowded for us all to live on."

"You might not want us to live."

"Susan!" Toby said.

"Well, how do I know?"

Marheh could see that she was frightened and belligerent because of it.

"I promise not to ask you to do anything you don't want to," she said. "If you decide not to come onto the boat I'll show you around the buildings that are not in the water dimension and take you to meet the old ones, or just give you tea and go back with you to your car if that is what you would prefer."

"Come on Mum. Dad said we would be going on a boat. I want to do that. You do too, don't you Rob?"

The younger boy nodded.

"Emily wants to go on a boat," the little girl said.

"Why don't we just go closer to where the boat is moored and then talk about it again?" Marheh said, wondering where Susan's fears had come from. Did she just have a vivid imagination or had she been told stories that fed her fear?

She led the way along the building, the little family following, not too closely behind. She thought she could hear Toby trying to reassure Susan. Then they rounded the corner to where there was a view of the Harbour and she heard Susan exclaim.

"Toby, you mean thing! Why did you make up that story to frighten me?"

Marheh swung around to them.

"What story?" Toby said, plainly puzzled by her accusation.

"You told me the water was invisible."

"So it is."

"Don't be silly. There's a whole big lake, and I suppose that must be the boat we're going on."

"Can you see it?" Toby said.

"Of course I can. It's there. You might as well stop this nonsense."

"It isn't nonsense," Marheh said quietly. "Not everyone can see it. Most people can't. Seeing is a privilege."

"But it's there," Susan protested.

"You and I know that," Marheh said. "But I don't believe your children do and Toby only knows because I took him into the water dimension."

Susan glared at Marheh for a moment or two then turned to Jack.

"Tell me what you see," she said. "What's there?"

Jack seemed a bit disconcerted by her question, but he answered easily enough.

"It's a big field Mum, just like Dad told us."

Rob, what's there?"

The younger boy looked at her and away, disturbed by her distress.

"What's there?" she said again.

"A field Mum," he said at last.

Susan looked at her family standing uncertainly before her and began to cry, soundlessly, tears trickling. Toby sprang to put his arms around her and for a moment Marheh thought she might reject him but then she let herself be held and comforted.

Marheh turned away, tears pricking her own eyes. What should she do to retrieve the situation? She could feel Susan's confusion and longed to help her but in a way she had been the cause. She turned back to see all the family hugging her. Then she saw her gather herself and reassure her children before looking over their heads to Marheh.

"I'm sorry. It's been a bit of a shock," she said. "Will you help me understand?"

"I'll do my best," Marheh said. "Are you alright? Would you like to go inside and sit for a bit, or have a cup of tea?"

"I'm alright. The children are looking forward to the boat. Can we go onboard?"

"Of course. Let's all go down to the landing."

Three hours later Marheh sank, exhausted, into her armchair. She had seen the family back to their car after their outing, the children relaxed and chattering happily, Toby and Susan comfortable with her and the idea of the water dimension. She was glad she had made the effort to invite them, particularly since she had helped Susan to make a discovery about herself, but it had been a tiring day and she had found herself not quite as fit as she expected. Now she ached. All she really wanted was to be tucked up, warm and snug, in bed, but she took up her journal, thinking it was important to clarify for herself what had happened. She needed to have it clear if she wanted to encourage others to do as she had done.

It was such a surprise to find that Susan could see, she began. *I couldn't understand how she could get to thirty five and not have discovered already, but when we talked about it I could see that it was not so strange. She only came to Sefton Middle after she and Toby married and her life focused around him and his work and the children. It makes me think that there must be others, perhaps many others, in the same position, with a gift they don't know they have. She has promised to come back and visit the old ones. They will enjoy that, and she can ask them questions and listen to their stories.*

I took them north to the first turning place. Once they were used to the water dimension the children could explore Day Bringer and even sit in the well deck with Susan. It was more difficult for Toby and he was happier looking out from the saloon with Day Bringer's hull keeping him enclosed.

I moored for a bit while we had tea. My scones were rock hard. I'm never confident that they will turn out well. They were eaten, however, and Susan brought biscuits she had made so we had plenty.

I think Susan was reconciled to her different viewpoint by the time she left, but it obviously disturbed and challenged her at first. Children adjust to new ideas so much more easily it seems. The day has shown me how important it is to be known.

Her pen paused for a moment then continued.

The day has been very hard work and it would be easy to stop there. I really prefer solitude, my song and my clay, but I think if I don't act when it matters then I'm really denying my song.

She closed the journal then and tucked it away. Now, of course, she should sing. Because she had acted she needed to restore herself and reinforce the action she had taken, but she was so tired. Tired was irrelevant, she told herself, and reached for her portal.

The next two weeks passed fairly quietly. Her office hours were spent dealing with the post, the bills and invoices, the letters to be answered or forwarded, and going over the arrangements for the Gathering. She was confident now of being able to manage the important things. The real test would come next month when the boats began to come in for the refits they needed and then it would be a race towards the welcome breakfast and the demands and expectations of the Silberay.

Susan visited with Emily and Marheh introduced her to Fylan and the old ones, who enjoyed the novelty of the child's presence as well as Susan's obvious interest in their lives and their philosophy. She talked with Marheh too about the gift she had discovered in herself and how best she might use it. The children had loved the boat and the excitement of disappearing into the water dimension, but it had led to problems for the boys when they spoke of it at school. Jack had been angry and upset when he was accused of lying. It had not been as difficult for Rob who was young enough to be excused what was seen as his too vivid imagination and had not understood that his story had not been believed.

Hiding her initial reluctance, Marheh issued another invitation, this time for the children each to bring one friend. She couldn't manage more, but perhaps having one witness to the truth of their adventures would be enough. It was what she wanted, wasn't it, for the Silberay to become better known?

The three extra children were from three different families and Marheh realised that there might be repercussions when they went home to tell of their afternoon. She mentioned it to Susan before they departed and made sure she knew how to contact the Harbour if she needed to. Susan had been careful in her wording of the invitations to the children's friends, but was aware that one set of parents could be difficult and may not be easily reconciled to the story their son would take home from his adventure in the disappearing boat on the invisible water.

The ripples from her initial act of kindness were spreading in ways she had not imagined and not all of them easy to deal with.

Susan rang, rather apologetic, the Monday after their excursion. The parents of Jack's friend had not been as difficult as she had expected, after all, their son had come home having enjoyed his afternoon and seemingly none the worse for his adventure. She had had no trouble with that conversation. The parents of Rob's friend, on the other hand, belonged to some kind of strict religious cult. His father had been extremely angry at the idea that his son had been exposed to magic. There was no good magic. It was, by definition, evil, and his boy was bewitched. Susan had had to tell him how to contact Marheh when her attempts at explanation and appeasement failed. She was ringing to warn Marheh.

After Susan's final, apologetic goodbye Marheh put the phone down very carefully, controlling herself with difficulty and managing to bite back the expletive that threatened to emerge. This was all her doing. Perhaps there were good reasons why the Silberay kept themselves to themselves. She stood up and walked back and forth across the floor in front of her desk. She had issued her invitations in the hope that the Silberay would be understood. She had relieved Toby's initial fear of her and that had to be good, but otherwise the revelation of the water dimension had caused trouble for Susan and her boys and looked as if it would cause trouble for the Silberay too.

She spun around as the phone rang and composed herself in order to answer it calmly. It was only Whin, however, confirming that he would arrive the first week of February. Like the other older Silberay, he was both surprised and amused that she was acting as Harbour Master. It was a reaction she was becoming rather tired of, but she managed to speak politely, thank him, and hang up before letting off steam.

It was difficult to concentrate on the office work with the threat of an irate phone call hanging over her but she managed at least to finish with the post before heading over to Fylan for a bit of friendly company. She would have enjoyed her elevenses with the old ones better if Blin had not been in evidence but Teg and Sula just about had his measure and managed to curb his worst excesses.

As the day wore on without the angry call she was anticipating she began to relax and hope that the child's parents had thought better of complaining.

She was just tidying her desk in preparation for leaving it when she heard loud banging at the front door. She froze for a moment then collected herself and walked quickly to answer it. It sounded urgent and angry as she got nearer and she found she was drawing herself up and lifting her chin in preparation.

A moment's pause with her hand on the door knob then she whisked it open so that the noisy visitor was left with his fist in the air. He was not alone. A man and a woman with a child between them stood behind him.

"Can I help you?" she asked gravely, looking from on to the other.

Perhaps she was not quite what they expected since they seemed to be struck dumb. She waited, deliberately patient, a look of benign interest on her face. She recognised the child as one of her guests and guessed that he stood between his parents. The woman looked a bit uncomfortable she thought, but the man was stoney faced. In front of them, he who had been battering the door, was now preparing to resume his attack.

He was a tall man and gaunt, dressed in an elaborate garment that seemed to have an ecclesiastical flavour.

"Ask him if this is the woman," he snapped at the child's mother.

She bent to whisper and listen then nodded.

"Well, is it?"

"Yes."

The woman's voice was soft and, Marheh thought, perhaps frightened. The man turned back to face her, his eyes glaring and his mouth working. He looked as if he was building up a head of steam, getting ready to boil over and for a moment Marheh wanted to laugh despite the seriousness of the situation. She did her best to maintain the expression of benign interest she had deliberately adopted earlier and waited in silence.

"The face of evil is comely," he said suddenly.

Marheh's expression did not change although she was finding it difficult to maintain.

"Evil," he said again, louder this time.

Then he shouted it.

Marheh stepped back a little as his spittle threatened but stood impassive as he launched into a diatribe that seemed to include identifying her as the devil, a magician and a witch. When he began what sounded like a ritual curse she took another step back and swiftly closed the door against him, thrusting home the bolt that was stiff with disuse.

Holding herself together she walked quickly back to the office the shouting fading as she went. She let herself out the back way and headed for *Day Bringer*, pausing only to switch off the light and lock the door. She would not run. She would not allow herself to run. Then *Day Bringer*'s warmth and safety enfolded her and she found she was shaking. She stood in her cabin fighting for control. How could who she was inspire so much hatred? She tried to empty her mind of the poisonous words he had poured over her, breathing deeply and letting the familiar comfort of her cabin embrace her. Then, as if she had called him, she knew Kel was there in her mind, full of concern for her, holding her in his love. She sank onto her bunk and opened herself to him, then, he lifted her and she found her candle flame beckoning her into the soul song.

Nothing to be afraid of

Chapter Eight

Next morning she woke late. Despite the song and its healing her sleep had been plagued by nightmares, the more disturbing because they came back to her in snatches each time she woke. She was naked and lashed to a wheel, she was drowning, she was burning, and in each vignette there were onlookers who cheered and jeered. The images came from the words of the curse, half heard as she walked away, but lodged somewhere within her to surface when she was most vulnerable.

They were old punishments from a crueller age, they couldn't be applied to her now, she told herself, not even if she had really been the evil creature of his accusation. She didn't believe in curses any more than she believed in magic, yet the knowledge of it continued to torment her as she dressed and breakfasted and made her way to the office to begin the day's work.

It was difficult to concentrate and she had achieved very little by the time the post arrived. She had left the office door open on purpose to listen for the sound of it falling through the mail slot and she went straight away to collect it, wanting a task that would be straightforward but require her attention. There was not much of it, perhaps half a dozen items, but as she bent to pick it up she also gathered something that had not been delivered by the postman. It was a wilting bundle of leaves and stalks. She turned it over in her hand and smiled. If she remembered Nemle's lessons, this was St John's Wort. As well as being very useful medicinally it also offered protection against witches.

Dear Nemle, she had tried hard to interest her apprentice in the work of a herbalist, but the young Marheh had other ideas. Something must have stuck with her though. She carried the plant along with the mail back to the office. She would put it in a glass of water on her desk and hope it might revive a little. Any visitor would see that it held nothing to disturb her.

She had just finished doing this when the telephone rang. She could answer it easily now. The herb which had been intended to unsettle her further had in fact done the opposite. Her caller however was neither threatening nor merely businesslike. It was Kel, concerned for her and wanting to know more detail than their mental communication could manage.

It was not a long call, she wouldn't let him extend his three minutes, but hearing his voice warmed her and she was glad to be able to thank him for his loving response to yesterday's need. He was heading towards the Harbour now, but did not expect to arrive much before the Gathering since his route was quite distant and he had some catching up to do, having taken time away when she had been attacked. She had not expected otherwise, though it would have been nice to have his steady, rocklike support during the hectic month ahead.

After she hung up she bent to her work with new energy. Perhaps there was something to be said for telephones after all.

The next few days went past quietly enough. She had half expected another visit from the man who had cursed her and went so far as to replace the St John's Wort on her desk just in case. The whole incident had made her question her ideas of sharing with the local community but after a day or two of dithering she realised that she could not put off making a decision if she was hoping to enlist the support of the Silberay at the Gathering.

There was always a cost. It was something she should have remembered. The important thing was to recognise the price and decide whether the gain was worth it.

Her journal received quite a lot of attention during this time. It was always helpful to write things down. Yes, no, don't know, could all be dealt with systematically, but underneath she knew that her initial impulse, that the Silberay should promote understanding and share themselves amongst their neighbours was the right one whatever the cost.

At the end of the week Susan came again, partly to visit the old ones, but mostly to apologise to Marheh for the actions of Rob's friend's parents and to warn her of rumblings she had heard about the dark doings of the witch at the Harbour. It seemed that the leader of the cult had begun a hate campaign against her that was gathering momentum.

"He can twist things and make people afraid, like I was, because they don't understand," she said. "You will be careful, won't you?"

Marheh agreed she would be careful, but after Susan had gone she wondered what that actually meant. It would be sensible to lock doors more consistently than usual perhaps, but unless there were Yareblis about, *Day Bringer* was in no danger.

The Yareblis, traditional enemies of the Silberay, had never threatened the Harbour. The song of the old ones made it uncomfortable for them and there were plenty of other places where they could act without Silberay interference. They could see the water road, but were not as dependent on it as the Silberay were. Marheh had suffered in encounters with them and knew from experience the kind of actions they chose. They tended to be cold and controlled in their dealings with others. The kind of passionate hatred the cult leader was showing was quite different.

That did not necessarily make it easier to deal with though. Marheh had skills and techniques, honed and practised, for dealing with the Yareblis. This was something different. She tried to make sense of what she was feeling and realised that Susan had been right to speak of fear. The Yareblis used people and controlled them in order to obtain power. Their hatred of the Silberay was cold and dispassionate. If the Silberay got in their way they would try to squash them in much the same way as they would deal with an annoying fly. People were only objects to serve them.

The cult leader manipulated people by playing on their fears. She considered that for a bit and realised there had been other times in her life when fear had made ordinary people aggressive towards her, sometimes simply because she was a stranger. It made it all the more important that the Silberay share themselves with their neighbours.

She stood up and walked around her desk, once and then again and again. She had not had any real exercise for weeks. How could she think stuck in here? Walking was what oiled thought for her. No wonder she was being so indecisive. If she had been out on the water road she would have walked the landscape listening with her heart, so why not do that here in a limited way?

Her lunch hour would give her time to walk the two and a half miles into town. She could listen as she went, perhaps buy a few necessities and take the bus back. It was too late today and tomorrow, being Saturday, she would not even need to hurry back.

That decided she returned to her desk with new resolution.

Next morning she woke to a grey, blustery day. It was not cold enough for snow, but the sky held the promise of rain. She would not be put off by that however, she decided, as she battled the wind just to get to the office. She was really only there for the telephone. Her work this morning was to sing and to prepare her mind and heart to listen. She had not done enough of that lately. It was too easy to let the tasks of administration take all her time and energy.

Nothing this morning interrupted her solitude so that when midday came she felt herself ready for anything. It was still very windy and spats of rain were blown in her face as she hurried back to *Day Bringer* to get her pack and her waterproof coat. Fylan raised her eyebrows when Marheh called in to ask if she had any commissions in town.

"You're going to walk, in this!"

"It isn't so bad, and I need the exercise and the thinking time. Susan told me there is talk against us. I want to hear it if I can."

Fylan nodded.

"Let me know when you get back, and plan to eat supper with us."

Marheh grinned.

"Thanks, I will."

She pulled on her old knitted hat, settled her pack more comfortably and set off.

Not surprisingly, given the weather, she met no one on her walk into town. She did her best to listen with her heart, holding her candle flame in front of her mind and trying to let it illuminate the places she passed. As usual in a town, what she heard was confused, especially as she came closer to the centre. There was sadness, fear and weariness, but warmth and hope broke through in places.

If it had been a nicer day she might have chosen to sit for a while on one of the seats in the town square. That way she could have absorbed the atmosphere without drawing attention to herself. Instead she strolled between shops, standing under awnings to keep dry, studying the goods in the windows and making tentative conversational approaches to any shoppers sheltering with her. A smile and a comment on the weather sometimes led to a more extended exchange, especially if there was an extra heavy shower, so that shelter was needed for longer.

She did not feel as if she was accomplishing a great deal and the shoppers were disappearing fast since it was early closing. There was still the pub, however. She had passed the Wheatsheaf on her walk into town and the Cock and Hen was just opposite where she stood outside the general store.

She was never very comfortable going into a pub on her own, but today it made sense. There would be others getting out of the rain and enjoying a convivial afternoon. If she wanted to listen to gossip the pub would be the place. Hopefully she could find a quiet corner where she wouldn't be noticed and nurse a half of bitter shandy for twenty minutes or so.

She crossed the road and pushed open the door. A few heads turned as she entered but the buzz of noisy conversation continued unabated. She stood a moment to get her bearings then made her way across to the bar.

It was quite crowded and she could not see a table, but there was an empty stool at one end so she perched there with her drink. At first the bits and pieces of talk swirled around her without making much sense. Comments on the weather, the chances of the local football team and the sloth of the barmaid mingled together. She sipped her shandy and studied the array of sparkling glasses and bottles behind the bar. Then one conversation began to emerge.

"I tell you, it isn't right!"

"What do you mean? I can't see anything wrong with it. We don't want that here."

"I wouldn't believe anything that arrogant so and so said."

"It isn't just him. My next door neighbour knows someone they've bewitched."

"Bewitched! That's a joke, right?"

"Not the way he tells it. Things disappear, and people."

"So? You're going to go with that charlatan and tell them they're not wanted?"

"We'll show them, not tell them."

Marheh did not want to turn around to see the speakers who seemed to be fairly close behind her, but she was curious. There could be other explanations, but what she had heard felt suspiciously like the kind of rumblings Susan had warned her about. She finished her drink, put the glass down and stood up to go, taking the opportunity to look towards where she thought the conversation might have come from. She couldn't be sure, there were a couple of possibilities, but two men sat at the little table directly behind her, both in profile, both casually dressed, with thick jumpers and corduroy trousers.

There was not much room so it was not surprising that she murmured "Excuse me" as she squeezed past them. They both looked at her then, and one of them spoke.

"You're right then lass?"

"Yes thanks."

She knew then. The one who had spoken was the man who had been sceptical. He might even be an ally of sorts. His companion must have been the one talking of action.

It was still raining, but she decided not to take the bus. Rain didn't worry her and she needed to think about what she had heard. Were they, in fact, speaking of the Harbour? There must be other interpretations. She was still turning it over in her mind when she realised that she was approaching the Wheatsheaf. This was close enough to be thought of as her local. If there were rumblings they were likely to be heard here. Another half of bitter shandy wouldn't break the bank though it wasn't really the weather for it. In her mind shandy was a summer drink. Perhaps she would ask for cider this time since she really didn't like beer.

What she had not realised was that she was much more conspicuous here where most of the patrons were neighbours and knew each other. When she walked in there was a moment when heads turned towards her and conversations paused for a couple of seconds. She walked across to the bar feeling her cheeks redden.

"For goodness sake, grow up," she admonished herself inwardly. "This is something adults do all the time. Yes, but I don't."

The conversation with herself continued until she was at the bar and ordering her half of cider.

Looking around, she spotted a small, empty, corner table and made her away towards it, hoping to disappear. One or two of the people she passed nodded a casual greeting and others looked curiously at her. She wondered whether it was expected that she ask to join one of the little groups, but she was not comfortable with doing that and squeezed hastily into her solitary corner.

After a few minutes interest in her seemed to have died down and the hum of conversation that had eased on her arrival began to build again. She took a deep breath, let it out slowly and began to relax then to look around.

The clientele in the Cock and Hen had been mostly men, but here there were couples and mixed groups enjoying themselves in the warmth. In the wall opposite her there was a fireplace with a cheerful wood fire crackling and spluttering. A largish group had pulled a couple of tables together in front of it. Two or three men were playing darts and there was a bit of good humoured barracking going on from another table also near the fire.

These were her neighbours and she didn't know any of them. What would happen if she went across to one of the groups and introduced herself, not just introduced herself but said who she was and what she did? She looked from face to face wondering whether she dared.

Not this time, she decided, but she would come again. If she came fairly often then they might get used to seeing her. That would make it easier to make friends.

A woman looked up and met her eyes, exchanged smiles then looked away again. Marheh sipped at her cider. She couldn't see anyone else who was alone. Perhaps next time Fylan might come with her. That would make it easier to be there, but perhaps not easier to meet the neighbours.

She finished her drink and stood up to go. It was not far to the Harbour but perhaps, after two drinks, it might be sensible to find a toilet. There was a sign over a doorway not far from her corner and she made her way towards it. Two cubicles and one of them occupied. As she came out again the other door opened and a woman joined her at the basins. Their eyes met in the mirror and they smiled at each other then the woman turned to study Marheh.

"Aren't you the woman who works at the old people's home?" she asked. "The one they call the Harbour."

"That's right."

Marheh looked at the woman. Where had they met? Then she remembered.

"You were on the bus," she said. "You live at number seventy four."

"I do," the woman agreed. "You've not been in before, at least not when I've been here."

"No, I'm still getting used to the job really and it isn't easy on my own."

"The place attracts a lot of rumours, you know," the woman said. "Stories about what goes on there."

"What kind of stories?" Marheh asked, masking her concern by pulling down clean towel from the dispenser and drying her hands.

"Black magic, witchcraft, there's folks that say the place is haunted. I don't believe them myself but I've a friend whose bedroom overlooks the grounds and she swears she's seen people appear out of nowhere and disappear again."

"Oh, but..." Marheh's words died on her lips. She could hardly say that it didn't happen but nor could she explain in this casual encounter.

The woman was looking at her, waiting for her to continue.

"I haven't seen anything like that," she said at last. It sounded lame even to her.

"Just telling you," the woman said. "There's talk. You might want to be careful."

"Thank you," Marheh said. "I will."

She turned to go then, leaving the woman, who was taking out her comb, and making her way back through to the main door and out into the rain. Witchcraft, black magic and haunting, it was a lot to take in. It would be very hard to change people's perceptions. People appearing and disappearing did seem like haunting and people were frightened of ghosts.

The rain was coming down harder now and she remembered her hat, thrust into her coat pocket in the pub. She pulled it out and put it on and quickened her steps.

"You might want to be careful," the woman had said.

Careful of what, the ghosts or the people who feared them? If people believed the Harbour was haunted they were not likely to want to use the buildings or the grounds and suggestions of black magic and witchcraft would only attract sensation seekers.

By the time she reached the Harbour she was quite wet. She splashed her way to the house, remembering she had promised to let Fylan know of her return. She went to the kitchen door and found Fylan preparing the evening meal.

"There are some who won't be told," she said, raising her eyebrows at Marheh's state of dampness.

Marheh laughed.

"Reporting my return ma'am," she said. "And I do actually like walking in the rain when I know I'm going to be dry when I get home."

Fylan laughed.

"Off you go then. Supper is at six."

Her evening with the old ones was pleasant despite Blin's thinly veiled antagonism and when she returned to *Day Bringer* there was time to practise with Kel as well as sing before she went to bed.

Next morning she was up early anticipating a day for herself. The sun was shining. Although she was aware that it was very cold outside inside *Day Bringer* was snug and warm. She made herself toast and boiled an egg for her breakfast, tidied up and took out her clay. Three hours later she stepped back from her work, stretched and looked at it critically. She had begun, as she often did, by just playing, allowing the clay to talk to her. What she had ended up with was quite disconcerting. She had built a single, standing figure, a woman, not young. Although she was alone there was a wariness and a watchfulness about her that suggested the presence of danger, perhaps of enemies near at hand. What was really unsettling was that she recognised herself.

After several minutes study she covered it carefully with a damp cloth and went to move the kettle further onto the fire. Sperit would be nice and then she might think about lunch.

She was standing in front of the little counter in the galley, spooning a mixture of spices and dried berries into her favourite mug when movement outside caught her eye and she looked up to see running figures, half a dozen or so, circling the administration building. Without stopping to think she moved the kettle off the stove and hurried outside. There was something furtive about the runners but their attention was all on the building. Obviously they were unaware of *Day Bringer* and could not see her where she stood, still in the water dimension.

She watched and waited for a few minutes, wondering what they were doing. Showing herself might be risky, especially if someone saw her appear from what would seem like nowhere, but she could not hide on Day Bringer if they were intent on causing damage.

She ran lightly along the gantry towards the loading dock, pausing to check she was unobserved before stepping onto the dock.

The nearest figure had his back to her and seemed to be trying to see into her office. She took a few steps towards him then asked quietly

"Can I help you?"

The man jumped and spun around then gave a yell which brought three more men racing around the corner of the building and skidding to a halt at the sight of her. She felt a moment of panic. This was too strong a reminder of the attack at Edgerington. She did not want to use mind control against them either. It would just confirm their fears.

Taking a deep breath she stepped a couple of paces towards them, smiling a greeting.

"We don't often have visitors," she said. "How can I help you?"

The men looked at each other as if to see which of them had words for her. Then, before any of them spoke, two more men came around the corner. One of them was the cult leader who had cursed her.

"The witch!" he shouted. "Take hold of her!"

No one moved.

Marheh held herself steady with difficulty, determined not to show fear or to give them any reason to believe his accusation.

"I don't believe in witches," she said, looking at the other men. "Do you?"

Still no one moved. Marheh realised that she could not return to *Day Bringer* so she took a couple of careful steps towards the group of men. Two of them shuffled backwards, but the others remained where they were. She saw that one of them was Rob's friend's father. He was studying her with such a mixture of fear and hatred that she stepped back involuntarily. It seemed an impasse. She wondered whether she could plant the idea of departure in a couple of minds without them realising it. If there any one of them was uncomfortable here it should not be too difficult to do it so that he did not realise it was not his own idea. Then if one went, others might follow.

She was just beginning to explore the possibility, looking for the least antagonistic face when she heard muttering, a kind of rhythmic pulse of sound that built as one man after another took up the chant their leader had begun.

At first the words were indistinct but as the volume rose the words became clear.

"Burn witch! Burn witch! Burn witch!"

It was an effort to hold herself still, but she knew if she tried to run they would be on her. Six were too many. Controlling them all would take too long and leave her vulnerable.

"Burn witch!"

"Not a witch," she whispered into one mind. "I don't want to be part of this."

Would he take the thought to be his own?

"Burn witch!"

They wouldn't really burn her, would they?

Into another mind, "I don't want to be part of this." She could not afford to stay there to reinforce the thought. She had to see. While they were still she was safe but if one moved towards her it would ignite them all.

"Burn witch, burn witch!"

Back to the first mind, as quick as thought, "There are no such things as witches. I don't want to be part of this."

A moment to look at the faces, then back to the second mind and then a third. Was the chant fading, just a little? Fear was a thing you could put somewhere outside you, but it kept beating on the door and keeping it out needed strength. Don't let them see it. Be brave. Was she telling herself that or had it drifted into the other minds?

One of the men had stopped chanting.

She saw his face clear, saw him see her, really see her for the first time. He touched the man next to him and spoke, so that this man stopped chanting to listen to his words.

It made a difference. The sound faltered. Then it was only the leader and the father of Rob's friend who kept it up, and the chant sounded thin and a trifle foolish. She looked at the other men.

"May I pass," she said. "I'd like to go in."

When nothing happened she moved towards them heading for the back door to the building and hoping with all her heart that she had left it unlocked as usual.

The men hesitated then moved aside so she could pass. It cost her everything she had left to keep going with her back to them, but the hand that reached for the door knob was steady. It turned and the door opened and she was in. Very carefully she closed the door behind her. Still careful she slid the seldom used bolt across. Only then did she begin to shake.

Her knees buckled and she slipped to the floor to sit, her back against the door, arms tight around her trembling legs, trying to hold herself together.

A century or more seemed to pass while she struggled to control her reaction, then, as if she had called him, Kel was there in her mind. She felt the silent tears begin as he held her. Her trembling eased, she could reach for him in her turn and rest in the comfort of his care.

Poster

Chapter Nine

When she had recovered herself enough she went into her office to look out of the window. What if they were still there, still hating and fearing her? But there was no sign of them. Perhaps her subtle suggestions had influenced them, or perhaps just the bitter cold. She sent her mind to Kel to reassure him. She had understood him to be ready to abandon his route if she needed him, but she wouldn't ask that of him.

She stood a little straighter and lifted her chin. She hadn't done so badly on her own.

She ought to go and warn Fylan, she thought next. What if they came back and targeted the house next time. Stepping outside again needed resolution. For a moment she stood in the doorway, ready to retreat, before walking across to the house, forcing herself to go steadily, not running, not anxiously scanning the grounds.

Fylan was at the kitchen door when she arrived, as if she had sensed her coming.

"Marheh, what's happened," she said, drawing her inside and shutting the door behind her.

"Nothing," Marheh said, feeling the tears begin again. "I mean… I mean…"

Fylan led her to a chair and pushed her gently into it.

"You're as pale as a ghost. You can't tell me nothing has happened"

She shook her head, struggling to contain her tears and find words to explain.

"Just sit for a bit," Fylan said. "I'll make sperit."

Five minutes later, a mug of sperit clasped safely in both hands, Marheh was able to begin an explanation. Fylan was suitably concerned and promised to be careful about answering doors and keeping them locked. She would have been happy to provide Marheh's evening meal too, but all Marheh wanted was to be back on *Day Bringer*. She needed to be alone now and *Day Bringer* would keep her safe.

The warmth and familiarity were healing and the small, ordinary tasks, putting coal on the fire, lighting the lamp, helped to steady her. She prepared meat and vegetables for a casserole and put it in the oven to cook slowly while she practised with Kel and sang. Then, after eating, she took out her journal.

Nemle would have asked me what I have learned, she wrote, *so I'm trying to understand. I know I was frightened, terrified would be a better word, and I'm quite proud that I don't think I let them see it. The hard thing is that it was all my own fault. If I had not shared Day Bringer and the water dimension with Toby and Susan it wouldn't have happened, but probably Tippa's welding would not have happened either. Now I'm so confused I don't know what to do for the best. No, that's not true. I do know what to do but I'm frightened to do it. In general it might not matter that most people don't recognise or understand the Silberay, but here at the Harbour it is important that our neighbours know us.*

I hadn't thought about people seeing us enter and leave the water dimension. I suppose I haven't had to before. If they don't know why it happens it isn't surprising that they fear it.

I'm determined to go ahead with planning an open day at the Gathering, but I'm also going to practise using my mind to suggest rather than control. I used to do it with Nemle, but more recently I've been practising combat and control rather than subtleness. I'll ask Fylan and the old ones if they will help. I'm sure the possibility that they can slap me down if they detect me will appeal. (Maybe I won't ask Blin though!)

She closed the journal. She felt a bit better now, but very tired. The last thing to do before bed was to go and look at her morning's work. It was still disconcerting. She wondered what her subconscious had known. It was good enough to fire, perhaps even good enough to be her new signature piece, or at least the beginnings of an idea for it.

She wrapped it carefully again and went to bed. Tomorrow was an office day. She would look again at her work next weekend.

Next morning she took her drawing things with her to the office. If she was going to organise an open day she would need to advertise. When the essentials were accomplished she might have time to design a little leaflet that could be printed and distributed in neighbourhood mail slots and letter boxes. If she kept it simple it might not be too expensive to pay for from her own funds.

She was a bit distracted dealing with the mail but fortunately it was mostly straightforward. There was one unsettling communication from someone signing himself Hemera, the light. It was addressed to *The Witch, Personification of Evil. Fire will purge*, it read, *Evil will be driven out. I, Hemera, curse the day you were born. You will pay for your sin.*

It was very melodramatic, she tried to tell herself, putting it aside, laughable really, the high flown language and the grandiose pseudonym, but it was too close to the fright of yesterday to be completely discounted. Was Hemera, perhaps, the cult leader? For a moment she covered her face with her hands, then sat up straight, crumpled the page and tossed it into the waste basket.

"Best place for it," she said aloud and went resolutely back to her letter opener.

Designing her leaflet would have been fun, was fun, except the threat from the waste basket kept intruding. Still, she managed to draw up something she hoped would be interesting and enticing. Under the heading OPEN DAY she wrote Visit the Harbour, Enter the Water Dimension, then, in smaller letters, below a stylised drawing of *Day Bringer*, Boat Rides, Tours of the Buildings, Afternoon Tea. She decided on a date, the weekend beginning the last week of the Gathering, and drew on Marheh the Great to convince herself that not only was she right to do it, but that, as Harbour Master, she had the right. She knew there were those amongst the mentors who would accuse her of exceeding the mandate of her position, but it was her position, even if only temporarily, and she had to do it to the best of her ability.

She looked in the telephone book to discover that there was a printer in Sefton Middle and rang to explain what she wanted and make an appointment for the next day during her lunch hour. She realised that telephoning was no longer quite as difficult as she had found it at first. You could get used to anything, she thought, as she hung up the receiver.

At the end of the afternoon she went across to the house to visit Fylan and the old ones. She would ask her, Teg and Sula if they would allow her to practise with them. It might be too much for Mieka and she did not want to be beholden to Blin.

Teg and Fylan were interested and amused at the idea that they could help her practise mind control and promised to be very severe if they detected her presence. Sula was interested too, but wanted reassurance that Marheh would not manipulate her thoughts and actions.

"I promise," Marheh said. "I just want to practise being subtle and making suggestions rather than controlling. I used to with Nemle, but not since I graduated, and I think," she paused, looking for words. "Controls are for the Yareblis, but they frighten ordinary people even when they are not used against them."

Sula smiled then and nodded.

"Alright, you can do your worst."

It was all very well to get permission, she thought, returning to *Day Bringer* after the evening meal, but what kind of suggestions could she make that would not manipulate their thoughts to some extent. Perhaps it would be enough initially simply to try to enter a mind without being noticed.

She sat in her armchair and concentrated. Fylan would be resting now after all the meal preparation and the cleaning up. She would be relaxed and perhaps less armoured against her. She wouldn't actually do anything, just visit, hopefully without being notices.

"Ouch!" Noticed and chided! She gave a wry smile and withdrew.

The Silberay were so lucky to have Fylan. Marheh had got to know her story while she had been her patient. She had not discovered the water road until after she had been widowed in her early thirties. She had never been apprenticed, but, having taken the job as assistant to the woman who had been the carer back then, she had learned all she could from the old ones. She was perhaps ten years older than Marheh, who valued the care given her when she was still convalescent and the affectionate support offered now.

The next week went past quickly. She paid her visit to the printer and made arrangements with him. Five hundred copies of the leaflet would stretch her finances a bit but she would not have the Silberay pay. The regular office work continued and she tried not to allow the receipt of a couple more letters from Hemera to unsettle her although she was conscious of being more diligent in locking doors than she had been in the past. Getting home to *Day Bringer* was more of a relief than ever. She was safe there in the water dimension and could relax a bit. Practising with Fylan and Teg had soon revived the skills she had learned with Nemle and she thought she would be able to turn the intent of any would-be assailant without being detected.

The weekend had been quiet, with no return visit from the cult leader and his followers and the following Tuesday she was able to collect her leaflets from the printer. At first she thought she might begin delivering them in her lunch hour but a look at her diary reminded her that Bixa had promised to come in early. She had said a month before the Gathering so Marheh could begin to look for her as soon as next week. She would wait.

Now she had the leaflets another week would not matter and she could talk it over with Bixa before burning her boats. Of course if Bixa did not agree with her – but she would not entertain that possibility.

By next morning she had changed her mind. If she was not going to take Bixa's advice unless she agreed with it then it was hypocritical to ask for it. So, lunchtime saw her walking Durand Road pushing her leaflets into letter boxes and through mail slots. It took her over half an hour just to distribute fifty leaflets, but at least she had made a start. Now it was up to her to persuade the Silberay and make the open day happen.

By dint of extra walking at the weekend she finished distribution of all but a handful of her leaflets. These few she kept to show Bixa, and later the rest of the Silberay, so they would see what she had promised on their behalf. She still needed to lift her chin and call on Marheh the Great for courage when she thought about the possible reaction to her initiative. At least she wasn't an apprentice to be grounded or put on probation, and she could cope with anything else.

After the fourth letter had arrived from Hemera she had told Fylan and asked her to keep the letters, just in case. She had even retrieved the first one from the rubbish. Fylan wanted her to go to the police, but she was reluctant. If they came to the Harbour to investigate they might even agree with Hemera about her.

Bixa arrived on a bitterly cold day on the Monday of the first week in February. Marheh was congratulating herself that she had finished delivering her leaflets before the weather turned. Walking in this sleet and wind would have been testing enough without needing to keep the leaflets dry. She certainly did not expect any visitors. There would need to be a very good reason for anyone to be outside. Then she looked up from her desk and saw a boat, battling the wind, crossing the basin to moor at the loading dock.

The figure that stepped off was so wrapped up against the weather that she could only assume that it was Bixa, since she recognised *Spring Song*, her boat. Jumping up, she grabbed her coat and raced out to help her moor. The quicker she could be finished and get inside the better.

"Oh good," Bixa shouted against the wind. "Can I put her straight into the dry dock?"

Marheh grinned and nodded and ran to pull up the little footbridge that crossed the entrance. The dock was still full of water from *Sunrise*'s departure, so it was not many minutes before *Spring Song* was floating under cover.

"Sometimes I think you have to be crazy," Bixa said cheerfully, when Marheh had joined her on the edge of the dock.

Marheh laughed.

"It's good to see you, but you didn't need to brave the elements to quite this extent."

"I don't mind. It's exhilarating really."

She stretched widely. Water was still dripping off her coat and her hat clung damply to her skull. She was a tall woman and well built. She pulled off her hat to reveal short, straight grey hair, rather spiky with being released from the cap. She glowed with good health and Marheh thought she looked much younger than the seventy years she must have reached if she was to become a mentor this Gathering.

She turned to Marheh and made a little bow.

"Thank you for your help Harbour Master."

"My pleasure."

"How is it going? Have you healed now? How many sacred cows have you overturned already?"

Marheh made a face then grinned and lifted her chin, mocking herself.

"Which question shall I answer first?"

"Have you healed?" Bixa said again, serious now.

"Yes, I'm fine."

"Good. Come on board and I'll make sperit and we can discuss everything else in the warm."

Bixa wound the centre line around the bollard at the edge of the dock and ran her hand lightly along *Spring Song*'s roof.

"It will be a big change, an apprentice. I'm not sure I'm ready for it, but you can't turn back the years and I suppose I'm lucky to have one."

"The apprentice will be lucky to have you," Marheh said. "Are you sure you want a visitor? I should be making sperit for you."

"I want a visitor, seeing it's you and I'll let you put the kettle on while I dry off."

Once they were sitting together in *Spring Song*'s saloon conversation turned to practicalities.

"I'll get the blacking out of the way first," Bixa said. "I imagine there will soon be a run on the dry dock."

Marheh nodded.

"If I remember rightly Whin will be coming in next week."

"I'll be out by then."

Marheh saw her look around the saloon where they sat. *Spring Song* was quite different to *Day Bringer*. Instead of her pale green topsides *Spring Song* had wood panelling, its golden glow enhanced by the yellow curtains at the windows. Where Marheh's work space was quite crowded with its drying racks, bins for clay and work bench, Bixa's just held a desk and a typewriter.

"It will be a big change, won't it?" she said sympathetically. "Have you thought where you'll put your typewriter?"

"There'll be room for a little desk in my cabin. It will have to live on that, but I'm not sure I'll be able to use it. I'll miss the silence and the thinking space. Still, the world won't come to an end if there isn't a new novel by Bethany Spencer next year."

Marheh turned quickly. Bixa was smiling at her, a hint of challenge in her eyes.

"Really? You? I didn't know."

"Not many people do. You'll keep it to yourself, won't you?"

"Of course. I'm honoured. Your books always make me think as well as taking me somewhere else."

Bixa grinned at her and nodded a little acknowledgement of the compliment.

"I wouldn't have minded not have an apprentice and this one is breaking with tradition, but the mentors did not want to refuse her. She's twenty-four, not the usual twenty."

"You couldn't not be a mentor, they need you," Marheh said warmly.

"Couldn't not!"

"Oh well, you know what I mean."

Bixa laughed.

"I do, but enough of me. How have you been coping?"

"Up and down." Marheh made a face. "I have been sticking my neck out rather."

"It wouldn't be you if you didn't. We've needed a bit of a shake up I think. So what have you done?"

It took some time for Marheh to explain, the finances, the neighbours, the trouble with the cult, the open day, all the problems and possible solutions she had juggled with over the last couple of months. When she finally ran down she apologised.

"You shouldn't have to be thinking about my problems, especially since most are of my own making, but I'm grateful."

Bixa studied her in silence for a moment.

"It seems to me that the series of accidents that put you in the position of Harbour Master will have greatly benefited the Silberay." She gave a short laugh. "Mind you I can think of one or two who might want to spank you for presumption, but I'm sure you can handle them."

"They'll be the ones who think it funny for me to be Harbour Master, even as a stand-in."

"Well you must admit it isn't quite what we expect of you – but given that, you are always surprising us." Bixa's smile was affectionate. "You've always managed everything we've thrown at you, so I don't know why we should be surprised at anything you do."

"I try," Marheh said lightly, turning the compliment, which pleased and embarrassed her. "Do you want to finish the docking today? I probably should get back to the office if you don't."

"Tomorrow will do. I've a bit of sorting out to do and I'll move my things into the annex. It will be easier to do that while she is still floating."

Marheh nodded.

"Let me know if you need a hand and come and eat with me this evening if you are prepared to take a chance on my cooking. I'm not using the flat, so you could move in there if you'd rather."

"Best not. The annex will be fine." She grinned. "And I'll enjoy taking a chance on your cooking."

Marheh ran back to the office through the rain, shook out her coat and sat down at her desk, smiling to herself. Bixa would be here now until the Gathering. She was such a capable person, and kind too. Imagine her being Bethany Spencer.

She could make a vegetable tart for their supper. She'd best contact the carpenter and let him know there would be work for him by the end of the week. Only a month until the Gathering. The afternoon post would have arrived by now. She'd best go and collect it. Would Hemera have written again? The possibility sobered her, but only for a moment. Bixa's support would make such a difference. It had already.

The cold wintry weather continued for most of the week, but Bixa was able to finish blacking *Spring Song*'s hull and move her into the wet dock for the carpenter. She spent time cleaning out her cabin and making it ready for her apprentice but that did not take long. Neither did discussions with the carpenter about her own new cabin. Marheh was able to make use of her skills and experience and did so gratefully.

I didn't realise, she wrote in her journal four days after Bixa's arrival, *how kind Bixa is. It's almost like having Nemle back. I'll need to be careful not to abuse her kindness. She has been singing with me and I have felt the song expand and the light spread from it in new ways. When she learned that I had been practising mind control with Fylan and Teg she offered herself. She said it would be a good challenge for her to practise with me and helpful for when she has her apprentice. She is very well defended and I have not yet managed to enter her mind undetected, but when it comes to attack her skills are like Kel's. Actually in many ways she is rather like Kel, kind and dependable. I use the same handicap with her that I use with him.*

Tomorrow she is coming with me into Sefton Middle. I've made an appointment for us to see the town clerk. It is obvious that we need to do something to correct the information they have about us and perhaps find a way in which we can be of service to the town in a more tangible way than our singing. Hopefully, with two of us, we might be believed, or at least listened to instead of laughed at or feared. She has suggested that we ask the police for advice about the letters from Hemera too. I know Fylan would agree with that and I would prefer it to having them come here where they might feel confronted by the Harbour.

Next morning she and Bixa set off to walk into town. It was still very cold and the sky was grey and threatening but the walk gave them time to discuss strategies. If it rained later, or if they felt too burdened by the shopping they were planning, they could always return by bus.

The town clerk kept them waiting for ten minutes or so although they were precisely to time and when they were finally ushered into his office it was clear to them both that the interview was unlikely to be productive.

He was a tall, slight man of early middle age, very pleased with himself, and even his greeting was patronising. Two women, two older women, what would you know of business or administration, he seemed to be saying.

They had agreed that Marheh would be the spokesperson and she began by explaining that the rates notice had been incorrectly addressed to Mr Silberay, who did not exist. That was not difficult to understand but he appeared to consider the information beneath his notice.

"The office can put that right. Presumably you've some idea, some proof of who does own the property."

"The property belongs to the Silberay," Marheh said. "It has done for about one hundred and fifty years."

"You've just told me there is no Mr Silberay." He gave her a condescending smile. "Are you quite sure you have your facts straight?"

Marheh drew herself up, lifted her chin and looked him in the eye.

"Quite sure," she said. "There is no Mr Silberay, there never has been a Mr Silberay and *The* Silberay have owned the property since it was left to them by Sylvia Durand in 1803."

She was quite proud of herself for remembering Sila's family name as well as the date of her death. She continued to look at him, Marheh the Great very much in evidence. He picked up a paper from his desk, looked at it and turned it over. Then he stood up.

"I'm very busy ladies. I don't have time to waste on this nonsense. Have your Managing Director get in touch with the office if you need further advice."

Marheh and Bixa remained seated. Marheh looked up at the man.

"Mr Woodard, I don't believe you have been listening to me, and I have not finished yet. I had hoped to discuss the possibility of coming to some arrangement whereby the town might benefit by the use of our land and we might benefit by a reduction in our rates."

Somewhere in the back of her mind she was marvelling at this grand speech and she could sense Bixa's amusement as well as her approval.

"Perhaps however, you are not the appropriate authority and we would do better to approach the Mayor directly."

The man slapped down the paper he still held and glared at Marheh who gave him her best smile and waited. She could see him debating his response. After a few moments he returned to his desk.

"Perhaps you could explain what kind of business you are involved in," he said, his reluctance very evident. "Then I might begin to understand how

I can help you."

"The Silberay are not a business," Marheh said carefully, not wanting to provoke him further now that he was listening to her. "We are a group of individuals with a common goal and a particular, little known skill, which we do not use for profit but for the good of the community."

"A charity then."

"Not really," Marheh said. "But I suppose if we need a pigeon hole you could put us there."

"As a charity you could well be eligible for a reduction in rates. Ask for an application form at the front desk on your way out."

"I doubt we will meet your criteria," Marheh said. "But thank you for your time."

She stood up and delved in her backpack.

"Perhaps you might consider attending our open day," she said, producing one of her remaining leaflets and offering it to him. "It might be easier to show you than to tell you who we are."

He made no move to take it so she laid it on his desk, smiled graciously and turned to go.

"Do come," Bixa said, getting up to follow Marheh. "You might enjoy it."

As the office door closed behind them they looked at each other.

"Perhaps you are not the appropriate authority," Bixa quoted and they both laughed.

"Patronising little man," Marheh said. "I suppose we might as well pick up one of his application forms."

Bixa nodded.

"No harm in looking at it at least."

They collected a form and Marheh tucked it away in her pack then they headed for the police station.

A large, kindly man in uniform greeted them from behind a counter.

"How can I help you ladies?"

Marheh put the letters she had received on the counter.

"I just need some advice," she said. "I've been sent these letters, threats really, and my friends have suggested I should report them to you in case the writer decides to act on them."

The policeman turned them over one by one.

"Nasty," he said, when he had read them all. "Do you know who this Hemera is?"

"I had a visit from someone who I think is the leader of a cult here in Sefton Middle. He threatened me in similar language."

The policeman sighed.

"It'll be the Holy Temple of Light. You're not the first woman they've targeted, but this is a bit excessive, even for them."

"It is disturbing," Bixa said. "I'm concerned for my friend. What do you think we should do?"

"There's not a lot you can do, except take reasonable care. I wish I could say different, but if it is any consolation I've never known them to act. All talk they are."

Marheh nodded.

"Thank you for listening." She gathered up the letters. "At least you know about it now."

On a sudden impulse she brought another of her leaflets.

"We are hoping to share ourselves with our neighbours, become a bit better known," she said. "Perhaps you might find it worthwhile to come."

The man took the leaflet and read it.

"Sounds as if you're on the right track. Good neighbours are important. What's this water dimension then?"

Marheh smiled.

"I hope you'll come and find out."

Night visitors

Chapter Ten

The two women were quite pleased with their foray into Sefton Middle. Although the town clerk had not been particularly helpful they had, at least, made a start at the town hall and the policeman had seemed interested and honest about his inability to help. They loaded themselves with provisions and took the bus back to the Harbour feeling positive despite the grey day and the rain that had accompanied them since they left the town hall.

Marheh went straight to the office, aware that she had been away for sometime, while Bixa made sandwiches for them both for lunch before heading for the wet dock to see how the carpenter was progressing.

Marheh ate at her desk, opening the morning's mail between bites. She would not send anything on now, since the Gathering was so close, but she put the little pile of personal letters to one side to distribute to pigeon holes at the end of the day, except the one for Bixa, which she would deliver personally.

The telephone was quite busy. Suddenly the scattered Silberay were realising the approach of the Gathering and wanting to arrange for work to be done on boats or to warn the Harbour Master of special deliveries they had organised. There were a few grumbles from callers who had not been answered that morning and a few managed to imply that Marheh was not reliable enough for the job she was doing. She managed to bite her tongue and apologise nicely to those she recognised as her elders, with her contemporaries she was not quite so restrained.

Fylan had invited her and Bixa to join her for a late supper after the old ones had retired for the night. She was interested to hear about their visit to Sefton Middle as well as the developing plans for the open day.

"My letter was from my apprentice," Bixa said as they sat around the table enjoying Fylan's steak and kidney pie. "She seems like a sensible young woman. She wondered whether she could visit the Harbour beforehand to see what sort of space she might have so as to know what she could bring."

"Don't prospective apprentices get a list of essentials any more?" Marheh asked.

"Not like we did," Bixa said. "I can remember thinking it was like going back to school. I was a boarder and the list was very prescriptive."

Marheh laughed.

"I remember how proud I was of my new clothes, especially my boots and my trousers. Of course I had never worn trousers before, very different to women these days."

Bixa smiled.

"I remember your first Gathering. I think everyone knew how proud you were and how young."

"Was I so transparent?"

"Tell me more," Fylan said. "I wasn't there, don't forget."

Bixa looked at Marheh thoughtfully and smiled again.

"It was the last Gathering before I graduated so I wasn't involved in apprentice classes and my mentor needed quite a bit of my time, but even so, at any time the Silberay were gathered in any number, there was this shining child, glowing with purpose, absorbing everything. Sometimes her eyes seemed three times normal size. She made me feel quite elderly. There were whispers about her already. She was the third generation of her family to be apprenticed to the Silberay, she was talented, she was young, only turning twenty in the last days of that Gathering. There were one or two who thought she should have had to wait until the next Gathering and a couple of grumpy old men were heard to say that she would be a handful."

Fylan laughed.

"I think one or two might say that she is still."

Marheh put her chin in the air and looked down her nose at her companions.

"You should both be more respectful of the Harbour Master," she said severely, then spoiled the effect by joining their laughter. "Poor Nemle, she was the one who had to put up with me."

"She loved you," Bixa said.

"Yes, she did," Marheh agreed, sober now. "And I was not very lovable, especially at first." She looked at Bixa. "That must be quite challenging, knowing you will be living at close quarters with a stranger, someone you are enjoined to care for, if not love."

Bixa nodded.

"We have, at least met briefly, unlike you and Nemle, but yes, I do feel a bit apprehensive."

"I was so pleased with myself I couldn't imagine that I might be difficult to live with," Marheh said. "At the end of our first week together Nemle punished me for something I didn't think was my fault. She apologised afterwards, but I was too immature to accept that and spent the next six weeks or so being as rude and uncooperative as I could. I knew I was trying her patience to the limit and I was pleased when I could see a reaction."

She paused, lost in memory.

"What happened?" Bixa asked when it seemed as if she would stop there. "How were things resolved?"

Marheh gave a little smile.

"After one particularly outrageous piece of rudeness Nemle tucked me under her arm and gave me a hiding."

"How on earth did that help?" Fylan asked.

"It brought things to a head, made me wake up to myself. Nemle had been so forbearing up until then, trying so hard to make up for losing her temper with me the first time." Her face softened. "She came down from the back deck into my cabin and apologised for punishing me when she was angry and asked if we could begin again."

"And you did," Bixa said softly.

Marheh nodded and brushed away a tear.

"I still miss her sometimes."

They were all quiet for a moment then Bixa spoke.

"I hope I can rise to the challenge as Nemle did."

"You will." Marheh grinned at her. "And I doubt you will need to resort to spanking, not if she has already met you. She'll have to be more mature than I was too. What's her name? Will you invite her to come and see *Spring Song* before the Gathering?"

"Her name is Beuda, and yes, of course. If she wants she can come and stay in the annex with me. That will give her a chance to back out if she decides she can't bear my company."

"Don't be silly."

Marheh gave a little chuckle.

"Bixa and Beuda, perhaps we should rename *Spring Song* the Beehive."

"Don't you dare." Bixa sighed and regarded her empty plate. "Fylan, that was delicious. Thank you so much."

"It's good to see you both." Fylan stood up and reached for their plates. "You'll have a piece of cake with your sperit?"

Cake was eagerly accepted and by the time they each had a large piece and a mug of sperit in front of them the talk had turned to the Gathering.

"This feels like the lull before the storm," Marheh said. "Whin arrives with *Cloudburst* next week and there were two more bookings for the dry dock this afternoon as well as requests for the welder and the carpenter. Just as well I managed to get Toby on side."

"How are we off for blacking paint?" Bixa asked.

Marheh looked startled.

"I've no idea. I suppose I'll need to put in an order, but how we'll pay for it I don't know."

"Most of us expect to pay for it ourselves," Bixa said. "It is essential maintenance after all."

"What else should I get in? There won't be a boot maker this year, he's retired."

"What about the new tunics for the apprentices?"

Marheh nodded.

"They're ordered, all except the ones for the first years and I don't know the sizes for them. The colour for the fourth years is not quite right and the tailor said he couldn't get anymore of the good wool fabric, but there will be tunics for the ceremony."

"Am I right in thinking there will be three people retiring?" Fylan asked.

"Yes," Marheh said. "Of course that will affect you. Are there things I need to get for you?"

Fylan shook her head.

"Not immediately anyway. They will bring their own bedding and I have rooms enough. After the Gathering I might need to find a helper for a while though. Mieka is very dependent now and it will be hard to give them all proper care."

"Of course you must have a helper," Marheh said. "But I very much hope that I will have been relieved of my position by then."

Bixa and Fylan smiled at her emphatic tone.

"Have you heard from Gilt?" Bixa asked.

"Not for ages," Marheh said. "At least a month. He said then that his father was failing fast, but he warned me not to expect him back for the Gathering."

"It might be a good idea to contact him and find out if he wants to continue in the position," Bixa said. "If not we will need to appoint someone else this Gathering."

She smiled at Marheh.

"I'd vote for you, but I know that is not what you want and I think your talents are better employed out and about."

It was quite late by the time Marheh and Bixa left Fylan and the warmth of her kitchen. The night was still and starry but very, very cold.

"I'm so grateful for you and Fylan," Marheh said quietly, her breath visible in the chilly air. "I would have been quite lost without you."

"I doubt it," Bixa said. "But I'm happy to be of use."

They were hurrying, Marheh to *Day Bringer* and Bixa to the annex. The cold bit despite their coats and hats. As their ways parted they paused to say goodnight.

"Sleep well," Bixa was saying when something caught Marheh's eye.

"What's that?"

"What?"

She turned to look out over the water as Marheh was doing.

"There is someone intersecting with the water dimension," Marheh said quietly. "Quickly, let's get onto the gantry where we can watch without being seen."

Bixa followed her the few necessary steps and they stood together watching a dark shape walking about in the waters of the Harbour. It was clear that the person was not in the water dimension. Not only was his movement unimpeded by any drag against the water, but they saw him walk right through a gantry. His steps seemed to have purpose though.

"What could he be doing?" Marheh said quietly.

Bixa shook her head.

"I've no idea, but look, there is another."

They stood watching, huddled together against the cold, glad of each other's company. Even though they both understood what they were seeing it was still eerie. The two figures, up to their armpits in the still, dark water, walking about as if performing some particular action, without causing even a ripple.

Marheh shivered suddenly.

"They're very intent on what ever it is, very determined. Ordinary people usually feel very uneasy when they intersect with the water dimension," she commented. "At least so Nemle said."

Bixa nodded.

"I've been told the same."

"Come and watch from *Day Bringer*. I don't think you should go back to the annex while they're still here. There's something... something furtive about them."

It was a relief to go down into *Day Bringer*'s cosy saloon out of the chilly air. Marheh bent to add coal to her fire but did not light the lamp. The soft, warm darkness was comfortable and meant they see out once Marheh had opened the curtains.

"I think he is holding something," Marheh said at one point. "I thought I saw some kind of container."

They were walking in some kind of pattern that brought one of them quite close to *Day Bringer*.

"I think that might be that father I told you about." Marheh could not help whispering although it was unlikely her voice could be heard beyond the water dimension. "He's from the cult."

Bixa nodded without taking her eyes off the men.

"I think they've finished whatever it was they were doing," she said as the two men met and began to walk towards the administration building.

As they left the area where the water dimension overlaid the land it became obvious that both men were holding a container, some kind of bottle, big enough to hold a couple of pints of liquid. There did not look to be any weight to them, but it was not until they saw one of the men tip his up and shake it that they recognised that they were empty. Marheh tried to take note of where he stood. Perhaps in the morning there might be a few drops still visible, or at least some sign.

The men were obviously relieved to have finished whatever it was they had been doing. They hurried away towards the street without a backward glance. Marheh and Bixa watched them out of sight.

"I don't like it," Marheh said. "What if that was fuel? What would happen if they tried to light a fire beneath the water dimension?"

Bixa shook her head.

"I doubt it would burn for long, if at all. It's only grass after all and probably still with snow lying."

"Of course! Mother and Father commented on the snow when they were here, though the rain on Monday probably got rid of most of it. Everything would be very wet still."

Bixa nodded.

"I believe the water dimension impedes drying too."

Marheh turned away from the window and moved restlessly around the saloon.

"They must have been doing something they thought would trouble us. How can I fix it if I don't know what it is?"

"I'm sure Toby, or William would tell us if there is anything to see."

"William?"

"The carpenter. He's doing a lovely job on my cabin and he knows the Silberay."

"Of course."

Bixa went to Marheh, took her arms and gave her a little shake.

"Stop pacing. There is absolutely nothing we can do tonight and nothing you have to do alone."

Marheh screwed up her face.

"I know really. It's just…"

"It's just bedtime," Bixa said firmly. "They've gone now. I'm going too. It's a puzzle for tomorrow, not now."

Marheh raised her eyebrows and grinned.

"Yes Ma'am, anything you say Ma'am!"

Bixa laughed.

"If I'm being bossy it's for your own good. Come and see me out."

Marheh stood on the back deck and watched as Bixa negotiated the gantry, stayed there until she saw her disappear against the dark shape of the annex, then went back inside and put herself to bed.

Next morning she was up and dressed early and out at first light to inspect the place where the intruder had shaken out his container. She could not be sure she had identified the exact spot, but an inspection of the general area revealed nothing unusual, only the short grass, the same as that she believed to be beneath the water road, the same as that covering the front garden between the houses and the street.

She went back inside to make herself a Saturday breakfast and puzzle over the actions of the intruders. Later, in the office, the mail and the telephone were enough to move her thoughts away to more immediate issues. In the mail was the bank statement for January, showing a dire picture of the state of the Silberay's finances. The bill from the tailor and accounts from the suppliers of gas and electricity arrived at the same time and caused her to tear her hair over the problem of how she would be able to pay them.

There was a phone call from Whin confirming his arrival, probably on Monday, possibly Tuesday depending on the weather and would he be able to go straight into the dry dock? Another caller wanted her to order him some dark blue marine paint and keep him a place in the wet dock so he could repaint the topsides during the Gathering when he might have some help. Someone else wanted to be sure of being able to replace worn lines and a third caller needed new fenders.

Marheh realised she had not given any thought to stocking the little store room they called the chandlery. Surely Gilt would have mentioned it if she needed to order the basics but she had better go and take a look. It was located in the annex at the end nearest the dry dock and so easy to overlook. If it became critical, she could probably get in a few necessities on credit, but there would be no free supplies for the Silberay, everything would have to be paid for.

She was still in the office at one o'clock when Bixa came looking for her with sandwiches she had made for their lunch.

"Silberay panicking are they?" she asked. "I thought we were lunching an hour ago."

"There are so many things I haven't thought of and every day more things to do."

"Well you're off duty now. I thought we were going to the pub this afternoon."

Marheh nodded.

"I want to take this poster I've made about the open day and see if they can put it up somewhere. Perhaps we might even meet a couple of our neighbours."

The telephone rang and she looked apologetically at Bixa before picking it up. A brisk word of introduction and the she sat listening for some time.

"I'm sorry Juni," Bixa heard her say at last. "I can't answer that without talking to Fylan. Can you ring back on Monday when I've had a chance to speak with her?"

A few more minutes of polite listening then a firm goodbye before she put the phone down.

"Come away now," Bixa said. "You can tell me over lunch if you want but if you can't hear the telephone you can't answer it. I'm taking the sandwiches back. We are lunching in the annex."

Marheh nodded.

"I'm sorry, it's just... can I just check the chandlery before we eat?"

Bixa raised an eyebrow quizzically.

"After we eat," she said firmly.

As they walked together towards the annex Marheh spoke of her latest telephone call.

"Juni wants to stay on Summer Breeze, not move into the house. She says she realises that boating alone is too much for her now but otherwise she can still manage for herself. I can sympathise with that. Since she doesn't have an apprentice there is no one to take over the boat, but it might not be wise to set a precedent and I'm concerned that it will mean more work for Fylan if her charges are not all under the one roof."

As they reached the door to the annex Bixa stopped and looked at Marheh then continued on toward the chandlery.

"Come on. I can see you are not going to relax until you've looked. Did you bring the key?"

For answer Marheh pulled it out of her pocket.

Inside the store was dim and dusty. Bixa found the light switch and flicked it on.

"It doesn't look as though anyone has been in here since the last Gathering," Marheh said after a lengthy silence.

"It does look a bit... neglected."

Bixa chose her words carefully, not wanting to seem too critical of Gilt, but rather appalled at what she saw. She went to Marheh, put both hands on her shoulders, turned her around and propelled her outside.

"You've seen it now. It probably isn't as bad as it looks and everything will look better after lunch."

They walked in silence to the annex. As well as the attic dormitory with its curtained cubicles, the three bathrooms and the laundry, there was a little sitting room with a fireplace, several comfortable chairs, a small sink and an electric kettle. Bixa put the sandwiches down on the little table between two of the chairs.

"If you take the guard away from the fire I'll put the kettle on," she said.

Marheh did as she was asked then sank into an armchair.

"Everything keeps piling up," she said. "I'll need to spend a couple of days making an inventory in there just to work out what to order."

Bixa came across to her carrying two mugs of sperit. She put them down beside the sandwiches and looked at Marheh sprawled in the chair as if she did not have the energy to sit up straight.

"On Monday we will do it together. It will not take so long with two of us. This afternoon and tomorrow are for going to the pub, sleeping in, maybe taking a walk and enjoying ourselves without thinking about the Gathering or the needs of the Silberay."

Marheh opened her eyes and gave a wry smile.

"I can certainly use your help, even if I don't want to take it."

Bixa passed her the plate of sandwiches.

"Here, curried egg and cheese and pickle."

Marheh reached for the nearest which turned out to be cheese and pickle. Bixa waited to see her take a bite before selecting one for herself.

"I think you should ask Teg if he could help as well," she said. "He could sit and scribe while we run about sorting and counting. I think he'd be pleased to be able to contribute."

Marheh demolished her sandwich, sat up straight and reached for another.

"Yes, I think he would."

They finished their lunch in amicable accord, not needing to talk much, feeling comfortable with each other. Bixa commented on the cleanliness of the annex and was interested to hear how Tippa had offered her services in lieu of payment for the work on *Sunrise*. Marheh spoke of her reluctant approval of Marheh's ideas and of their emerging friendship.

When the food was eaten Bixa suggested that they sing. It was a conscious relinquishing of self. Marheh thought afterwards that she had felt her spirit expand unhindered by her mind's preoccupations with needs and problems and uncongenial tasks.

The afternoon was well on by the time they reached the pub. The clientele seemed much the same as on Marheh's previous visit. Once they were sitting comfortably with their drinks she looked around to see if she could spot the woman who had spoken with her then. The warmth of the open fire, the cheerful barracking of the darts players and the talk and laughter from the other tables created a convivial atmosphere that no longer made her feel excluded now that she too had company. She saw the woman she had met, caught her eye and smiled, raising her glass in acknowledgement. A moment later she saw her speak briefly to her companions before making her way across to them.

"May I?" she asked, indicating the empty chair at their table.

"Please," Marheh said. "I was hoping we might meet again. I'm Mary and this is my friend Bethany."

"Ellen," the woman said.

There was an awkward pause then Bixa spoke.

"This is a pleasant pub. Are the patrons mostly local? You all seem to know each other."

Ellen agreed that yes, the people were mostly local, and for a while they made polite conversation about nothing much. It became clear to Marheh and Bixa though that Ellen had a particular purpose in joining them.

"A lot of us got a leaflet about an open day at that place where you work," she said at last. "There's quite a bit of feeling about it, not all of it positive." She looked at Marheh. "What's it about then? It's never happened before."

"We've started to realise," Marheh began. "We've come to understand that our neighbours don't know anything about us, and that doesn't seem right."

"What's there to understand? I thought you said old people live there."

"Yes, they do, but..." she hesitated, looked at Bixa then back at Ellen. "Have you ever heard of the Silberay?"

Ellen shook her head.

"What is it, some kind of club?"

"In a kind of a way I suppose." Marheh was choosing her words carefully. "It is difficult to explain, that's part of the reason for the open day. It will be easier to show then to explain."

Ellen stood up.

"I don't know. It doesn't make much sense to me."

"Perhaps if you come," Marheh said as she turned to go. "I hope you will."

Ellen left without replying. Marheh sighed.

"Perhaps no one will come," she said to Bixa.

"I think curiosity will bring them," Bixa said. "You could see she was asking on behalf of all the others."

"Do you think so?" She brightened. "It's a start anyway."

They finished their drinks and departed without any further overtures from the locals but the landlord was happy for Marheh to put her poster on his community notice board so they left feeling satisfied with their afternoon's outing.

Sunday passed quietly. Marheh spent time with her clay as well as with the soul song and practised the discipline of the mind with Bixa and Kel, challenging herself by encouraging both of them to come at her at once. Even then she handicapped herself, keeping part of her mind occupied by singing all the songs she knew from the Silberay songbook. The two of them together defeated her in the end, but not before she had pushed them to the limit of their skills.

"What happens now?" she understood Bixa to be wanting to know as she wriggled under their control and continued to sing. She felt Kel's laugh, felt the light smack on her rear that was the usual way he celebrated his rare victories then felt his hug, warm and reassuring. There was warmth from Bixa too and gratitude as she withdrew. Marheh understood that she was giving her space to be with Kel and stopped her singing to share herself with him, letting him know something of her activities as well as her love for him.

In the evening Bixa came to *Day Bringer* bringing supper to share.

"You are being very kind to me," Marheh said, breathing in the smell of the casserole.

"I could say the same of you," Bixa said. "I learnt so much this afternoon during our practice. I haven't worked so hard at the discipline of the mind for years, if ever."

Marheh grinned.

"I'm glad I made you work. Do you feel the need to celebrate your victory too?"

Bixa laughed.

"I'll save it for when you need admonishing. Let's eat."

Next day Whin arrived quite early. The dry dock was ready to receive him and Marheh enjoyed a short break from the chandlery helping to operate it. The work there was going better than she had expected and it was obvious to her and to Bixa that Teg was enjoying being useful. She did not know Whin very well and found him quite demanding to deal with as well as being rather patronising in a kindly, avuncular way that had her biting her tongue to keep back the retorts she wanted to make.

"I feel as if I'm being patted on the head and told to run away and play," she told Bixa and Teg. "Until he wants something, and then I'm slow and inefficient. I would feel sorry for his apprentice only I suppose, since the apprentice will be male, he won't treat him like a child."

Bixa nodded sympathetically. She too had been patronised in the nicest possible way when she was Harbour Master and she had been more than a decade older than Marheh.

"Some of these older men can't help themselves," she said. "I don't think they understand what they are doing."

"Six half inch D-shackles and four one inch," Marheh said. Teg wrote it down as she spoke. "Teg doesn't do it and he's older than any of them. Jik doesn't either."

Teg smiled at her.

"I can't speak for myself, but Jik has obviously been brought up properly by his niece."

"2 inch brass cleats, twelve," Bixa said. "Are you going to tell him about the open day?"

"Three 5 inch brass T-studs and one 6 inch. He won't like it. I'll be in trouble if I tell him and if I don't."

"He's just a young whippersnapper," Teg said. "You send him to me if he gives you trouble."

Marheh giggled. She was busy measuring what was left on a reel of rope. "What am I then, a babe in arms?"

"You're the Harbour Master," Teg said. "And not to be trifled with."

"There are only thirty five yards of this rope so I hope Fid's the only one who wants new lines."

They finished the inventory late in the afternoon. As they were walking back towards the administration building Whin came out and approached them. He did not look happy. He had something in his hands and as he came closer Marheh realised that it was one of her leaflets advertising the open day. He could only have got it from her office and she was not sure how she felt about that.

"What's this then?" he demanded when he reached them. "Enter the water dimension! Boat rides!" he quoted.

"It's a new idea for the Gathering," Marheh said demurely. "For the neighbours to get to know us."

"Boat rides! It makes us sound like a fun fair. Who, may I ask, is going to provide these boat rides?"

"We are," Marheh said. "The Silberay."

"You must have taken leave of your senses," he said.

"I don't think so," Teg said quietly. "I think she is helping to bring us to our senses."

Whin looked at Teg as if he had never seen him before.

"You surprise me," he said, obviously having difficulty restraining himself from saying something more forthright.

Marheh did not dare look at Bixa for fear she might laugh, remembering Teg's opinion that Whin was just a young whippersnapper.

"Think about it," Teg said. "How many apprentices began when you did?"

Whin shook his head as if the question was irrelevant.

"There were seven of us," Bixa said. "But Tope decided the life was not for him after a few years."

"And how many of you are able to take an apprentice this Gathering?"

"Just the two of us I think," Bixa said, looking at Marheh for confirmation.

"Doesn't that make you wonder?" Teg asked.

Whin did not look convinced.

"I doubt I'll have time to be involved," he said. "After all, my apprentice will have to come first."

"Of course," Marheh said sweetly. "But it might be something that could involve your apprentice, good training in neighbourliness." She smiled and held out her hand. "Could I have my leaflet back please? I don't have many left."

He gave it to her rather reluctantly and they went on their way, Whin heading for the annex, while Marheh and Bixa went with Teg to the house. Marheh thanked him as they said goodbye and he gave her a grin that revealed the boy that was still somewhere inside despite his ninety four years.

"Haven't had so much fun since I retired," he said. "You stick to your guns young woman."

The next few days were busy but uneventful. Whin was occupied in the dry dock with Toby and Bixa was busy touching up *Spring Song*'s paintwork. Phone calls, orders, deliveries and invoices kept Marheh occupied without much time for anything else although Whin's response to her plans had started her thinking about her welcome speech. It would be her best chance of persuading the Silberay to support the open day but when she pictured herself delivering it all she could see were the pitfalls that would bring scorn and opprobrium upon her.

She had all but forgotten the actions of the intruders she and Bixa had witnessed the previous week. Then, on Friday, she and Bixa went into town for provisions. Bixa had insisted she needed a break from the office and since the day was fine and sunny she did not put up much resistance. On the way in they were hurrying to catch the bus, but returning along the drive, laden with bags and back packs, there was time to look around.

"There's something wrong with the grass," Marheh said, stopping for a moment.

Bixa stopped beside her and looked across at the lawn that lay between the buildings and the road.

"There are some very brown looking bits," she agreed. "I wonder why."

Marheh put down the bag she was carrying and walked across to the nearest place.

"It looks as if it is dying," she said, bending to touch.

Bixa put her bags down too, but instead of going closer she stepped back.

"I don't think it's natural," she said, scanning the area. "In fact," she hesitated for a moment, squinting a little. "I think I can make out letters. That bit where you're standing looks a bit like a B to me."

"What!"

Marheh stepped back to join her.

"Do you see? And further along there's a T and an H."

Marheh stood staring at the areas of dying grass.

"It was them," she said suddenly. "The men we saw the other night. That's what they were doing, writing BURN WITCH in the grass. That's what they were shouting at me when they came. They will have written it under the water dimension too. No doubt it will show up very clearly by the time the neighbours arrive for the open day, if they do."

"There must have been some kind of weed killer in the bottles," Bixa said. "But why do you think it will say burn witch?" She squinted again, trying to fit the brown patches into the words. "Mind you, you could well be right."

"I am," Marheh said gloomily going to pick up her bags. "You weren't here when a group of them came and shouted at me."

She set off again towards the administration building. Bixa picked up her bags and hurried after her.

Not until they were in the kitchen beginning to empty their bags did Marheh speak again.

"What on earth am I going to do to fix it?" she said, thumping the tins of tomatoes she had been carrying onto shelves in the pantry.

Bixa said nothing, just unloaded her tins of beans onto the next shelf. Now that Whin had arrived and with Beuda coming in a couple of days it made sense to pool their resources and eat together. Back and forth they went, two or three times, until everything was put away appropriately.

"We will need to use the mince meat today," Bixa said. "I'll cook."

Marheh swung around, angry and upset. She scanned the kitchen as if she had never seen it before then grabbed a cup that dangled from a hook on the dresser, lifted it with both hands and smashed it as hard as she could on the floor. It shattered into little pieces.

"Better now?" Bixa asked after the initial shock had passed.

Marheh turned on her.

"Don't be nice to me," she shouted.

Bixa gave a wry smile.

"I'll smack your bottom and stand you in the corner if you prefer."

Marheh covered her face with her hands.

"I'm sorry." The words were muffled. "I can't do this any more. It's too hard."

"It is hard," Bixa said slowly. "But you've done hard things before, harder things I would have said."

Marheh looked at her.

"Yes, but they were my hard things, things that used my skills and talents. This isn't... this doesn't fit me."

Tantrum

Chapter Eleven

That night in her journal she drew a little picture of a screaming baby Marheh.

I behaved so badly, she wrote. *Like a child. Bixa was so patient and sensible but it isn't good enough for me to get over it and apologise, I shouldn't have behaved that way.*

She scribbled another little drawing, Bixa putting the bad child in the corner.

There are times when I don't think I'll ever be a proper grown up person and I'll be fifty-two next month. I hate this job. I'm afraid of that cult and what they might stir up and I'm afraid of what the rest of the Silberay will think about what I've put in motion. That's honest at any rate. I'm trained to act against the Yareblis, but there isn't a Yareblis in sight here, nor likely to be. They've not been known to come to the Harbour. So what am I doing upsetting things?

It's just as well it was only Bixa who witnessed my outburst. Whin would have felt totally justified in his criticism. Why couldn't I have just sat at my desk and gone through the motions?

This time the drawing was of a very bored and indolent Marheh lounging at a desk.

I couldn't of course. That would have let Nemle down as well as myself.

She closed the journal and sat for a bit longer. Nemle had believed in her, but it wasn't just Nemle. Kel did and Jik and Dom, Bixa did and Teg too. Tomorrow was another day and she had things to do.

"Do you think a gardener would be able to help?" she asked Bixa next morning.

She had got up early and made her a little drawing, a series of little drawings really, like a cartoon strip. The tantrum and the child in the corner with, between them, the spanking and to finish the tearful, sorry face. Bixa had laughed as she studied it.

"I keep forgetting that you are an artist, along with all your other skills," she had said.

"Well I am truly sorry I subjected you to my lack of self discipline," Marheh had said before turning the subject to the words in the grass. Bixa, it seemed, had been considering the problem.

"I think the best thing to do would be to find someone with a digging thing, or perhaps a plough," she said. "There are nearly two and a half weeks till the Gathering and four before the open day. If the soil was turned over and left for a week there would still be time to throw a bit of seed over it. It won't be perfect but at least it won't be readable."

Marheh nodded.

"If I had half a brain I could have thought of that. Thanks, I'd better go to the office and look up the telephone book."

Bixa shook her head.

"Be a bit kinder to yourself. You have a lot on your plate just now."

Marheh grimaced.

"That's no excuse. See you later. Shall we brave the pub again this afternoon?"

"Let's. You never know, we might find a friend, or even someone who knows someone who digs."

The office seemed particularly unappealing this morning. The telephone was insistent to the point where she almost gave up on any other work. The Silberay were suddenly realising that the Gathering was not far off and bookings for the docks not made, goods and provisions not ordered. In between calls she shuffled papers, trying to sort them a bit so that she could deal with them efficiently. The invoices were the most worrying. Which should she pay with the little bit of money that was left? If she did find someone to dig over the dead grass how would she pay for the work? Was there any point in trying to persuade the cult leader that the Silberay were not dabbling in black magic?

She went to the front door to collect the mail in a moment of quiet but came back to find the telephone yelling at her and an irate creditor wanting payment for something she had no knowledge of.

She was still struggling with paperwork and answering the telephone when Bixa came to visit, intent on rescuing her from the office.

"You are not obliged to be here after eleven on a Saturday and it is now midday," she scolded. "It is no wonder you get a bit overwrought. Give yourself some space."

Marheh looked up from the invoice she was studying.

"What a nice way of putting it," she said with a little grin.

She might have said more but the telephone rang again.

"Silberay Harbour," she said.

"This is Beuda," the voice at the other end said.

Bixa saw Marheh's face change.

"Beuda," she said warmly. "You're one of our new apprentices. How nice to hear from you, and what good timing. Bixa is here in the office. I'll put her on."

She handed over the receiver and sat back in her chair to listen to Bixa's half of the conversation.

"No, no, you are very welcome."

"Marheh is acting Harbour Master, I think you will have dealt with Gilt before."

"Come and stay if you wish, or just visit, whatever suits you best."

"We'll look forward to seeing you."

Bixa hung up the receiver then carefully removed it again.

"She's coming tomorrow, just overnight, then she's going home to pack – and I'm not putting the phone back until you've left the office. Whin is in the kitchen with the soup and sandwiches and if you don't come now he will have scoffed the lot."

Marheh laughed.

"Alright, I'm coming."

She took a moment to straighten the papers she had yet to attend to and pick up the envelopes she had ready for the post while Bixa watched her, eyebrows lifted.

"We can post these on the way to the pub," she said. "Then they, at least, will be out of the way."

Bixa did not reply, just looked meaningfully at the door. Marheh scurried past her and into the corridor then waited to see her replace the receiver before joining her, closing the office door firmly as she did so.

There was time, after lunch, to go back to *Day Bringer* for a while and sing before meeting Bixa again to walk to the pub. Whin had declined their invitation to join them. He had found a copy of *Mentoring the Young Apprentice* in the library and wanted to spend the afternoon perusing it.

"I didn't tell him I found a dozen or so copies in a cupboard in the office," Marheh said as they strolled down the drive. "It was already old fashioned when I was an apprentice. Nemle put her copy in the fire, she told me, after about six weeks of trying to follow its precepts." She gave a little chuckle. "She used to tease me though, by pretending to quote bits at me, bits she made up to suit my offence."

"You always speak as if you were a terrible trial to Nemle, but I don't really believe that."

Marheh laughed.

"No, after the first uncomfortable weeks it was more of a game between us."

"So you don't recommend that I read this gem?"

"Far be it from me to advise my elders and betters,"

She skipped away from Bixa's swipe at her rear.

"I suppose I shall have to offer Whin a copy if he is really taken with it, but I would be concerned for his apprentice."

"Perhaps I had better have a copy to tell me what not to do."

The day was almost spring-like and the short walk to the pub gave time to enjoy the sun and the blue sky. Some of the little front gardens in the houses opposite were showing signs of growth, new leaves and buds and a few snowdrops.

"I wonder if the bluebells under the trees along our fence will be out for the Gathering," Marheh commented. "It's been so cold the last couple of months."

"Even if they are not out at the beginning they should be out for the open day."

"It's good to see the days getting a bit longer."

"And to feel a touch of warmth in the sun."

The pub, when they reached it, was comfortably full with the same Saturday crowd as before, talk and laughter, barracking for the darts players and even a few nods of greeting. Marheh went to the bar while Bixa looked for a table. As she made her way across the room she saw Ellen smile and beckon.

"Come and join us," she invited. "We're all curious about you and that place where you work."

Bixa smiled her thanks and looked at Ellen and her companions, two men and another woman. One of the men stood up and grabbed an empty chair.

"Here, have a seat. I'm Dave."

"Bethany," Bixa said. "Is there room for two? My friend is at the bar."

"Of course," Ellen said. "We saw you come in together."

Dave was already swinging another chair into place. Bixa looked to make sure Marheh had seen her then made herself comfortable beside him.

Looking around the table she decided she was probably the oldest of the group. The others looked to be closer to Marheh's age. Two couples, she wondered. Marheh arrived then with their drinks, lager for Bixa, cider for herself. She slid into the empty chair beside Ellen and smiled around the table.

"I'm Mary," she said.

The man on her other side offered his hand.

"Ben," he said. "I think you've met Ellen, next to her is her husband Dave and next to me is my wife Jill."

Marheh lifted her glass to salute them all.

"It's nice to meet you."

There was a little silence then, but Bixa spoke before it had time to become awkward.

"You obviously know each other well. Are you neighbours as well as friends?"

"That's right," Dave said. "We bought when the new subdivision opened, it would be five years ago now. I'd say the same of most people here. You two would be the first we've met from the Harbour, keep yourselves to yourselves mostly don't you?"

"Most of the people who live there all the time are quite old," Bixa said. "Over ninety, they can't get out much."

"Is it an old people's home then?" Ellen asked. "The Harbour is quite a good name for an old people's home, you know, like coming in to harbour after an active life."

"Except that leaflet you put out said boat rides," Ben said. "What's that about?"

Marheh and Bixa looked at each other. Bixa gave a little nod that meant this is your story, you tell it.

"Old people do live there," Marheh began. "But it isn't really an old people's home, just a place where Silberay retire to be cared for."

Ellen, Dave and Ben looked blank, but Jill's eyes widened. Marheh looked at her.

"That's a word I haven't heard since I was a child," she said. "The way my mother told it the Silberay were like good fairies, just a nice story to tell at bedtime."

"What was the story?" Marheh asked. "Do you remember?"

"Not much. It must be forty years or more since I needed a bedtime story to sleep." She frowned. "These Silberay appeared when there was trouble," she said slowly. "You never saw where they came from, but when they came they made everything all right."

"I wish we could," Marheh said. "Sometimes we can help, that's all."

The four neighbours stared at her.

"You're not joking are you?" Dave said. "You really think you are one of these good fairies."

"But we're not," Marheh protested. "We are just ordinary people. We do try to be helpful and we're trained in some special skills, but we are certainly not fairies, or witches. I don't believe either exist."

Dave turned to Bixa.

"Are you her keeper? She seems quite normal otherwise."

Bixa smiled.

"I'm her friend. I'm Silberay too."

"This has to be some kind of elaborate con job," Dave said. "But I can't see what you hope to gain by it."

Marheh looked around at them all, Dave seemed on the edge of anger, Ellen troubled, Ben curious and Jill thoughtful.

"We hoped… we wanted our neighbours to understand who we are. The Harbour has been our base for about two hundred years but it is only in the last five or six that we have had close neighbours. It has changed things." She turned to Ellen. "You told me about the rumours and about your friend who has seen people appear and disappear. We don't want our neighbours to resent us or be afraid. We've kept ourselves to ourselves for too long already."

"You're asking us to believe the impossible," Ben said slowly. "But suppose we manage to keep an open mind about the truth of what you say, tell us more about what goes on at this Harbour of yours."

Marheh flashed him a smile.

"It's our centre, the place where we return and where we retire once our active lives are over."

She went on to explain about the old ones, about the water road, about her present job as Harbour Master and about the approaching Gathering, Bixa occasionally adding a few words of clarification.

"I'm sorry, I've been talking too much," she finished. "I really hope you'll come to the open day and get to know us a bit better, but I'll understand if you'd rather not."

She drained her glass and put it on the table.

"Thank you for inviting us to join you," she said. "You might wish you hadn't now, so we'll leave you in peace."

She stood up.

"Perhaps we'll see you next Saturday," Ben said thoughtfully. "You're very convincing."

Bixa stood up too and smiled a farewell.

"We'll look forward to it," she said.

They made their way across to the door very conscious that their four recent companions were following them with their eyes and bursting to discuss them and their story.

"You know," Bixa said as they walked towards the Harbour. "I think it would be good to have some copies of Hafa's history available at the open day. Bethany Spencer could organise that if you like the idea."

"It's a great idea, but won't it be rather expensive?"

"I think I can afford one hundred copies or so. Perhaps people could be asked to pay sixpence if they want one, that way it won't just be thrown away."

As they turned into the drive at the Harbour Marheh stopped suddenly.

"I forgot to ask if anyone knew someone to dig," she said in dismay.

"We can go back if you like."

They both gazed at the grass. Another day of sunshine had made the damage even more evident.

"No I'll get on the telephone on Monday. That will be more businesslike."

They spent the evening together with Whin who was keen to discuss his afternoon's reading with Bixa. Marheh thought he only just tolerated her presence, but since she was Harbour Master and since she had shared the evening meal with them he could hardly send her away. He looked rather disapproving when he learned that Bixa's apprentice was coming to the Harbour before the Gathering and that she was twenty four instead of the usual twenty. Marheh admired the way Bixa dealt with him. She knew she would have lost patience and said something sharp if he had been speaking to her.

There were not many buses on Sunday so Marheh and Bixa arranged to meet each one in order to be there to welcome Beuda. Next morning at ten past ten they were both at the stop when a tall, sturdy looking young woman with a backpack stepped off and turned to smile at them.

"You must have been up bright and early," Bixa said, going forward to greet her.

"I didn't want to waste the day," Beuda replied.

Marheh looked on, curious about this young woman who was planning to change her life in a radical way and join the Silberay.

"This is Marheh," Bixa said. "The Harbour Master."

"We spoke on the telephone I think," Beuda said, offering Marheh her hand.

"That's right," Marheh said. "Did you have a good journey?"

"It was very straightforward," Beuda said. "A train to Cuddes and then the bus, but because it is Sunday I didn't have much choice of times."

"I'm surprised there was a train at all," Marheh said.

"I'll have more flexibility tomorrow."

"Well, you're very welcome. Come along and get settled."

Marheh turned and led the way down the drive to the administration building, then around the side to where there was a view of the Harbour.

"This is it," she said, pausing for a moment. "The heart of the water road." After a few moments of silence she turned to Bixa. "Why don't you take Beuda to the annex to settle in then, when you're ready, the two of you come for sperit on *Day Bringer*?"

"That would be lovely," Bixa said. "Come along and I'll show you where you'll be sleeping."

Marheh watched them go then turned and made her way along the gantry to *Day Bringer*. Beuda seemed pleasant enough but she couldn't help feeling for Bixa. The thought of sharing her life with this stranger must be quite confronting. It was not just the changes to her boat, but the constant need to consider someone else.

As she stood in the galley, moving the kettle onto the fire, looking out a couple of extra mugs, she thought about how *Day Bringer* had looked when she and Nemle were together. Nemle's cabin had been where her work space was now. The doors into the well deck that she kept open all summer had not given the saloon light and fresh air as they did now. Taking an apprentice meant a relinquishing of self that she was only just beginning to appreciate. Would there be an apprentice for her when the time came? Would she want one?

She went into her work space. There would probably not be enough time to get out her clay but she could check on the few pieces she had completed over the last weeks and make sure they were not drying out too much to be safely transported. As she pottered she kept thinking about Bixa and Beuda and the challenge of an apprentice. They were taking their time coming. That was probably a good thing since they would be getting to know each other.

A whole hour had gone by before she saw them approaching along the gantry. Beuda was smiling and striding out but Marheh thought Bixa looked subdued, or perhaps she was just thoughtful. Maybe she was putting too many of her own feelings into her interpretation of Bixa's. She went up to the back deck to welcome them.

They stayed about an hour with her, sharing sperit and talking. Marheh showed Beuda over *Day Bringer* and listened while she compared her with *Spring Song*. She had heard of Marheh Carron of Carron Pottery and was, Marheh thought, a bit too ready to admire once she had made the connection. Bixa said very little although Marheh tried to leave room in the conversation. When they left Marheh looked after them with troubled eyes. She had come to care for Bixa very much and value her kindness and quiet wisdom. This confident young woman seemed almost to be taking over, as if Bixa was already an old woman to be side-lined instead of a mentor to be valued for her teaching, her knowledge and her experience.

She thought back to the early years of her own apprenticeship. Had she treated Nemle that way? She thought not. Her own bad behaviour had been sulky and childish but Beuda was neither, just very confident and a bit dismissive of other people. The Silberay placed a value on humility. It was something she still struggled with, but Nemle's example and teaching had helped her to understand the difference between true humility and the kind of false modesty that made a show of putting oneself last.

Everyone had learning to do. It didn't matter how old you were. The important thing was to recognise that and be open to listen, evaluate and change if it seemed wise and good. She laughed a little. Here she was pontificating as if she had life under control when most of the time she was running to keep up or tightrope walking over half understood problems, even dangers.

They all met again in the kitchen for the evening meal. Whin was there too and Marheh was grateful for his presence. He could not be said to be an example of humility, but he did try to be kind and during their meal his kindness took the form of sharing with them all, but especially Bixa and Beuda, some of the precepts acquired from his study of *"Guide to Mentoring the Young Apprentice"*.

Marheh tried to reproach herself for the wicked delight she took in Beuda's reaction to some of these. *"Your goal in the early years is to guide the apprentice towards the necessary humility, patience and thoughtfulness for the later progress towards wisdom,"* were words that offered the possibility of a useful discussion, but Beuda thought that humility was an outdated concept and did not seem prepared to consider any other point of view.

Then there was *"Maintain firm discipline. Instruct the apprentice in obedience and service and expect both at all times"*. Obedience was apparently outdated also. Marheh tried to suggest, as Nemle had to her, that the obedience required of the apprentice was a practice for the obedience to an ideal, an idea of service that was embedded in the Silberay promise. *"Discipline"*, *"Obedience"*, *"Humility"*, these were at the heart of the life the Silberay chose. Marheh had never questioned that. Although she was aware of her many failures she continued to strive for a more disciplined approach and a greater understanding of the disciplines of mind and soul, for a more perfect obedience to the ideal to which she had committed herself and for the humility to listen, learn and serve.

Bixa, she thought, was much closer to the ideal than she would ever be. Surely Beuda would see that, perhaps not immediately, but, before she made her promise. There would be three weeks of classes and discussions about the Silberay, as well as practical work, before the promise must be made.

"What brought you to the Silberay?" she asked towards the end of the evening. "You are choosing to make a big change from the life you had."

It was a question all new apprentices were asked, but, at twenty, lives were not established as firmly as they were at twenty-four. Beuda had been to university and set out on a career in the Public Service she had told them.

"I was on holiday visiting a friend in Highington and I met Myl at the market. He was selling some beautiful leather. We got on really well. He told me about the Silberay and invited me to visit his boat. When I discovered I could see the water it seemed as if I was meant to join." She paused and looked earnestly at the three Silberay. "I was wasted in the

Public Service, too many time serving staff between me and any position of influence."

Marheh tried to place Myl, but it was not until Bixa asked after Yog, his mentor, that she remembered the good looking young man, his mentor, who had a heart condition, and Mistral, their boat.

"I didn't meet Yog," Beuda said. "Myl said he sleeps a lot, but I met Myl quite a few times. He really encouraged me to apply to the Harbour so I could use my gift."

"He did tell you, didn't he?" Marheh asked carefully. "That there is a long apprenticeship. You know that Myl is still an apprentice and will be for quite a few years yet."

"Yes, of course, he told me that, but he doesn't do classes any more, just keeps an eye on Yog."

"I think," Bixa said with quiet emphasis. "I think that Myl would say that he cares for Yog, as I know he does, and understands that the service he gives is part of his learning."

Marheh smiled at Bixa, thankful that she had joined the conversation after saying very little for most of the evening.

"Yes, of course," Bixa said hastily, but Marheh was not sure that she really understood Bixa's point.

They separated then, heading for bed. Marheh still felt troubled and settled herself to sing before she slept holding both Bixa and Beuda in her mind as she entered her portal. There was no soaring joy, no golden light, but the music held warmth and eased her concern somewhat. Bixa was wise. She would know how to proceed with Beuda.

Welcome breakfast

Chapter Twelve

Next morning Marheh was in the office early. The official opening of the Gathering was just two weeks away and she could expect Silberay to start arriving any day. She needed to find someone to dig over the grass. That was the most urgent job since the words were now so legible that both Whin and Beuda had commented. She needed to order more bituminous paint since most of the dry dock bookings were for hull blacking, she needed to timetable rooms for apprentice classes, and she needed to find time to work on her welcome speech. Just the thought of it made her stomach turn over. It would be bad enough if all she had to do was say a few words of greeting, but she had set herself to persuade them to support the open day and she feared their response.

Around midday Beuda came in with Bixa to say goodbye. She was about to go for the bus back to Cuddes and her train. She was perfectly pleasant but Marheh couldn't warm to her, though she took herself to task for thinking that way.

About half an hour later Bixa came back alone. She did not speak and Marheh thought she looked weary and weighed down. She stood up and went around her desk to give her a hug.

"Well," Bixa said when the hug ended. "We've obviously both got some learning to do."

There was a little catch in her voice and Marheh knew she was referring to her prospective apprentice. She took her arm.

"Let's go and make sperit. I've got bread and cheese on *Day Bringer*. Will that do for lunch?"

It was not until Bixa was comfortably settled in the armchair and Marheh was preparing sperit and cutting bread and cheese that she spoke again.

"She has a fairly good opinion of herself," Bixa said.

Marheh was relieved to hear the resolve in her voice.

"Obviously she thinks that once she's had a few steering lessons I'll be surplus to requirements, but she has another think coming."

Marheh grinned.

"Take a leaf from Nemle's book. After she spanked me she told me she wouldn't teach me to steer until I'd learnt some humility."

Bixa laughed.

"I doubt I'll spell it out quite so explicitly but the intent will be there. I can't say that I'm looking forward to the next couple of months, but no doubt we'll learn together. How long did you say it took you and Nemle?"

"Six, maybe eight weeks, before I realised that I was not the special person I thought I was and that Nemle was someone to respect."

Bixa looked affectionately at Marheh as she accepted the mug of sperit she handed her.

"The difference is that you were much younger and you knew more about the Silberay and what you were choosing. Myl would have tried to tell her I think, but I have a feeling she paid more attention to his good looks than to his words."

They were still sitting together over their bread and cheese when they felt *Day Bringer* rock and looked up to see *Autumn Wind* manoeuvring into position to moor behind *Day Bringer*. Without needing to consult they both stood up and made their way out onto the gantry. Marheh thought Bixa seemed almost as pleased to see Jik as she was. She had never thought of Jik as having a soul friend, not everyone did and Jik had always, she realised rather ashamed, been defined by his relationship with her, but Bixa would be perfect.

Marheh was aware that she had been out of the office rather longer than she should have, but there was time for a hug and a greeting before she hurried back to her duties. They would all gather for the evening meal, she felt sure, and Jik would probably visit the office once *Autumn Wind* had been attended to.

As usual the telephone was shrilling madly as she entered, but stopped abruptly just as she reached it. She could only shrug and assume the caller would ring again if it was important. She was expecting some deliveries this week, a few items for the chandlery, a couple of parcels individual Silberay had told her to expect as well as the new tunics for the apprentices. She needed to be in the office, sometimes she needed to sign for things. The blacking paint she had ordered that morning was promised for the end of the week too, but she still had to find someone to dig over the grass. That had to be a priority. Already those neighbours with a view over their front lawn would be able to read what was written and wonder about it. She grabbed the telephone book and made a start, wondering whether she should look under digging or gardeners, or perhaps excavating.

She was still dithering when Jik put his head around the door.

"How goes it niece?"

"Don't ask! I wish I had opted for a nice quiet convalescence at home in Deerford."

"It is a busy time leading up to the Gathering."

He had not finished speaking when the telephone rang and there was a loud ring from the front door.

"Very busy! I'll get the door."

By the time Marheh had dealt with her caller he was back with a couple of parcels and the afternoon post.

"How can I help?" he asked, wondering where to put the parcels.

She looked up at him. He was studying her over the parcels, his expression kind and sympathetic. He had done this job. He knew what she was experiencing. She let out her breath in a long sigh.

"Find me someone to dig," she said.

It was a request that needed explanation and then he had to go out and look at the problem, but then he took over the telephone and began calling.

The advantage was twofold, not only had he undertaken one of her tasks, but while he was doing it the telephone was engaged. She tackled the post with new heart.

The next two weeks flew past. Each day seemed to contain more problems, more jobs to be done, more things to resolve. Silberay began to arrive, one or two, then four or five, until, a week before the official opening of the Gathering, there were already a dozen or more boats in the Harbour and a dozen or more Silberay expressing surprise at Marheh's position and making demands she could not always meet. Without Jik and Bixa she would have given up in despair, she thought, wondering how they had managed alone. It was not just that they had taken over some of the tasks that still needed to be done, but they were caring for her too. Always they collected her from the office at dinner time and made sure she was fed then they would insist she sing with them. It stabilised her, she knew, more grateful than she could easily express.

Bixa had carried out her promise to have copies of *The Short History of the Silberay* printed and also had the printer do another hundred copies of Marheh's leaflet. The ones she had kept for the Silberay had unaccountably disappeared from her desk. Jik, being a mentor, knew what was wanted in the way of apprentice classes and took over timetabling the rooms and the mentors who would teach the various subjects.

Even with their help, Marheh sometimes felt she needed to be in three or four places at once. The chandlery, the wet dock, the dry dock, all needed to be checked. Arbitration was occasionally needed when requirements clashed or overlapped. She still had the telephone and the mail to deal with. The letters from Hemera continued but the worry of these was now overshadowed by the worry of the increasing pile of unpaid invoices. All was in hand for the welcome breakfast although the caterers had been rather disapproving of the kitchen facilities. At least, thanks to Tippa's ministrations, it was clean. The old ones valued her visits, or so she thought, and she did not want to neglect them even if she only spent fifteen minutes over a cup of sperit.

The thought of her welcome speech continued to press. She had managed to jot down one or two ideas, but never found the extended period of uninterrupted time she needed to make a coherent whole. Very late on the Friday night before the breakfast signalled the official beginning of the Gathering she was still despairing over it when Kel came to her.

"Go away. I have to write my speech."

He continued towards her, took the pen from her hand and pulled her into a hug.

"You're too tired to do it now. You'd be better to get some sleep. You know what you need to say."

She let him hold her for a few moments, luxuriating in the comfort of his embrace.

"You've been running all day."

"I need to get it right. They have to understand."

"Suppose you tell me then. I'll write it down."

She looked at him, pulling back a little so she could see his face. Unlike Jik and Bixa he had not been here to listen to her arguments or discuss her ideas. A new listener might be just what she needed.

She let him lead her to the armchair and watched as he took up the pen and paper she had abandoned and sat on the footstool at her knee.

"Welcome to breakfast," she began. "And to the ninety first Gathering of the Silberay…"

Next morning she began the same way.

"Welcome to breakfast and the ninety first Gathering of the Silberay. I want to thank Jik and my father, Sef Carron, for providing this generous welcome meal for us, and, since it would be a shame to let the food spoil, I'm inviting you to eat first. That way, those of you who know why I am here instead of Gilt can share your knowledge and hopefully you will all be comfortably replete when I need you to listen to me again."

There was a moment of surprised silence, a chuckle or two and a burst of applause, led by Tippa. Marheh blushed and waved in the direction of the laden tables.

"Help yourselves."

She looked at Kel, sitting where she could see him, with an empty seat beside him. He smiled and nodded. She hesitated for a moment then, as the Silberay began to move towards the food, she went to join him.

"What would you like?" he asked. "I'll get it for you."

"I couldn't eat anything."

He stood up.

"I'll choose then and perhaps you'll change your mind."

A few minutes later he was back. The plate he placed in front of her held a perfectly poached egg on a round of toast, a portion of fried mushrooms and two rashers of bacon. His own plate held sausages and grilled tomatoes as well.

"Go on," he said. "It would be a shame to waste it."

He'd chosen well, she thought, studying her plate. She wasn't hungry, but she did enjoy bacon and the mushrooms looked to be just as she liked them.

There was no particular protocol regarding who should sit where on an occasion like this, so she was surrounded by friends, not just Kel, but Jik and Dom, Tippa and Pon, the other person who had been apprenticed when she was. It would have been nice to have had Bixa there too, but she was with Beuda who had made a beeline for Myl. Whin was there too with his new apprentice Glik and Myl's mentor Yog.

Marheh made a note to herself to welcome the two new apprentices formally. They were to visit her in her office later in the day too, for the traditional interview with the Harbour Master. In her day the interview had been with the Apprentice Master, very solemn and full of rather heavy handed advice about the way a Silberay apprentice should behave. She had no intention of doing that, she would feel a hypocrite.

She looked at her plate and realised it was empty. There were conversations buzzing all over the room as well as at her table, but her companions had recognised her abstraction and left her to her thoughts. Any minute now she would have to get up and address the Gathering. A fist seemed to clench in her stomach and she wondered whether she should have eaten. When she stood up and went to the dais would they listen to her? How would they react to what she had to tell them? She swallowed and sat up straighter. Where was Marheh the Great when she needed her? She took a deep breath and stood up. Across the table Jik smiled at her.

"You can do it," he mouthed.

She lifted her chin, grabbed her notes and marched up and onto the dais.

It took a few moments for all the chatter to die down but she waited, gazing out over the big room at the tables and the Silberay sitting around them. Then she saw chairs being turned towards her and faces lifted. She swallowed a moment of panic, took a deep breath and began.

"I think I should say at the outset that I know I am too young and nowhere near responsible enough for the job of Harbour Master, but here I am!"

Smiles and a few chuckles greeted this opening and she relaxed a little.

"Gilt rang a day or so ago and sends you his greetings and advised me that he does not wish to continue in the position, so all you mentors will have some thinking to do to appoint someone else."

She had decided not to announce the death of Gilt's father, nor that Gilt was considering leaving the Silberay. This news could be left for another, less formal, occasion.

"It is my special pleasure to welcome our two new apprentices and to congratulate our two new mentors. You all know Whin who will have Glik as his apprentice."

There was some applause and Marheh gestured for the two to stand as the clapping continued.

"Bixa, our wise and talented former Harbour Master, will be mentoring Beuda."

More applause as Bixa and Beuda stood with the other two.

"I owe a special debt of gratitude to Bixa who has been mentoring me over the past month as I struggled to work out what needed to be done in preparation for the Gathering. If things run smoothly you can thank her, but please blame me for the mistakes."

She went on to outline what she referred to as housekeeping details; timetables for classes, where and when meetings were scheduled, where details of dry dock and wet dock bookings were posted. Then she paused and looked out over the gathered Silberay. This was it! Now she had to announce the open day and persuade them to support it.

"I had never spent much time at the Harbour," she began, when she saw she had their attention. "I had not realised that Sefton Middle had expanded and come so close to us and I had certainly not given any thought to what the neighbours saw when they looked at the Harbour. Living here, walking into town, visiting the pub, talking to people, opened my eyes to problems and possibilities. No one knows us any more and so things about the Harbour are frightening.

Imagine how it would feel to look out of your bedroom window and see someone appear from the water dimension and then disappear back into it again. What do people think when they see the field beneath the water dimension with no crop or grazing animal?"

She went on to tell the story or how she and Sef had talked to Toby and how she had taken his family for an outing on *Day Bringer*.

"And so," she finished. "It seems to me that we have a responsibility to make ourselves known to our community, and ... this is where some of you may think I have exceeded my authority ... I have committed us to host an open day, two weeks from today."

Tippa and Dom stood up and moved to distribute leaflets to the tables.

"I will give you a minute to look at what is planned and then I will try to answer any questions."

As soon as she stopped speaking there was a buzz of conversation. People grabbed for the leaflets and exclaimed over the offerings. Marheh could not tell whether the general mood was positive or negative, but Jik, Kel and Bixa were smiling at her which gave her courage for the questions which would come. The noise level in the room was rising and it was obvious that there was some heated discussion at a couple of tables and some head shaking at others. There would be even more head shaking when she explained the state of the finances, but that was something for a mentors' meeting, not for now.

She looked over the room. Roughly seventy people all of whom she knew, some were friends, others just acquaintances. There were those like Bixa and Jik and Kel who loved and supported her and others who disapproved. She could never quite forget that anyone older than she had been present in this room when she had been accused and found guilty of misusing the discipline of the mind, and, a few days later, had watched while she had been beaten. No matter that she had been exonerated later, the humiliation of the beating still returned to plague her at odd moments.

At one of the tables there was a group of mentors and it was from one of these, an older woman called Nisfa, that the first challenge came. She stood, not without some difficulty, then took her walking stick and banged it on the floor for attention. Marheh met her gaze trying not to feel defiant. She was not a naughty child whatever Nisfa might think. She lifted her chin a little.

"Well Marheh," Nisfa said. She had a nice voice, warm and strong despite her age. "You've always been a rebel, haven't you?"

"Is that a question?" a voice quipped from another table.

Nisfa responded with a small frown towards the interruption.

"Why did you make such a significant change to our normal program without consulting the mentors?"

Marheh took a deep breath before she answered, knowing she must not sound defensive.

"I did think about waiting," she said. "But the more I learned, the more I felt it important not to delay. By the time of the next Gathering perceptions and prejudices would be even harder to change. Even now it might be too late."

Nisfa nodded thoughtfully. She seemed to have appointed herself spokesperson for the mentors. Marheh saw her look at the group around her then draw herself up to speak again.

"You've obviously given some thought to the problem. What does concern us is the opportunity this might give the Yareblis. By issuing a general invitation like this you've opened the door for them to invade our home. That would be a defilement of our centre, our haven, our place of safety."

She stopped abruptly, obviously troubled.

Again Marheh took a deep breath looking for time to form a response.

"I admit," she said slowly. "That is not something I had considered, but I believe the risk is small. We know that the song of the old ones is strong here. Yareblis would be uncomfortable living close by. They are not our neighbours and it is our neighbours who have been invited. I distributed leaflets like the ones you have to the houses close to us, I put a poster in the pub and I gave one to the town clerk and one to a policeman in Sefton Middle. Nothing has been distributed further afield than that."

Nisfa nodded and looked around the room.

"What about the rest of you? I'm surely not the only one with an opinion."

There was a short silence then Bixa stood up. Marheh looked towards her and noticed Beuda beside her. She seemed uncomfortable and for a moment Marheh wondered why, but then Bixa began to speak.

"As most of you know, I held the position of Harbour Master before Gilt." She stopped to smile at Marheh. "I know some of you think that Marheh has been too quick to act without consultation, so I want you to know that she has consulted with three former Harbour Masters, Teg, Jik and me, because she wants to do the best she can in a position that has been thrust upon her. I think she is to be thanked and congratulated for putting the good of the Silberay before her own good and giving herself wholeheartedly to work that is not particularly congenial to her."

"Hear, hear," Tippa said loudly.

Someone else began to applaud and the whole room took it up. Marheh stood, scarlet faced and suddenly tearful at this evidence of appreciation. Bixa went to her, gave her a hug and then a little shake.

"Just explain what you want them to do and tell them where they should be next," she said quietly before going back to her seat.

The clapping still continued. Marheh looked across the room. At that moment she loved them all. She had been so sure there would have been disapproval but Nisfa's questions had been for information, not challenge, and now she too was applauding.

A few moments more she stood speechless then held up her hands for silence.

"Thank you, thank you so much. I'm very grateful for your support and especially grateful to have had Bixa, Jik and Teg as mentors and advisers.

I've put up three sign up sheets on the notice board outside my office. One is for those of you who might be prepared to offer boat rides, one is for offerings of afternoon tea and one is for people to lead tours of the property. Please think about adding your name to one, if not all, of them."

She paused to smile and look around again.

"Now I think it is probably time to move on. The program for today is posted on the notice board in here, but, to begin with, at ten o'clock the third year apprentices are scheduled to meet with Peli in room three. That will be a practical session on splicing and other rope related tasks. Beuda and Glik, you get to meet with me in the Harbour Master's office, fourth and fifth years there is a boat in the dry dock that needs your help with blacking and sixth years, you lucky people will be meeting Jik and Yog over at the hard standing for tips on engines and engine maintenance."

She finished by asking for a few volunteers to help with the breakfast dishes then went back to her seat beside Kel. She sat down with a huge sigh of relief and glanced at the clock.

"Half an hour."

Kel smiled at her.

"Time for some sperit, and would you like something else to eat?"

He got up to get it for her while the others were congratulating her on her speech and its outcome.

"You all helped," she said in response. "You listened and worked and supported me in so many ways. I'm very grateful."

Tippa gave her a grin and stood up.

"Pon and I are going to organise the kitchen detail. You are not wanted, understand?"

Marheh smiled her thanks as Kel returned with sperit and a toasted muffin liberally spread with butter and apricot jam.

"I'm proud of you niece," Jik said when Tippa and Pon had gone. "You did that very well."

"When Nisfa stood up I thought I was in for trouble, I've always felt she disapproved of me, but she was really quite mild."

"She calls a spade a spade," Jik said. "But you know where you are with her."

"I'm not looking forward to the mentor's meeting this afternoon. My report won't be good news."

"No," Jik said. "But that is not your fault. Bixa and I will be there to defend you if they try to shoot the messenger. Just present the facts and figures, be as matter of fact as you can."

Ready for the Meeting

Chapter Thirteen

Marheh was in her office sorting the morning's mail and feeling thankful there was only one delivery on a Saturday when Bixa and Whin arrived with the two apprentices. She stood up to greet them and suggest that they all go with her to the Harbour Master's flat where they could be less formal and have space to sit in comfort. She chatted to Glik as they went upstairs, recognising that he was diffident and unsure of himself in this new environment.

She had thought hard about this interview, wanting it to be welcoming, but wanting also to emphasise the serious purpose of the Silberay and the discipline their life involved. Of course Bixa and Whin would be both guide and example, but for now she represented all the Silberay. It felt like a big responsibility.

"I'm sure Gilt would have asked you this at your first interview," she began, when they were all seated in the living room of the flat. "But I would like to ask again, what was it that drew you to the Silberay? What do you hope to gain from us and what to give?"

She looked from one to the other. Glik leaned forward, eyes shining, mouth ready to speak, but Beuda got in first.

"I liked what Myl told me," she said. "And when he said that I might be eligible to become an apprentice because I can see the water I decided it was worth a try. It seems like a nice life, travelling, seeing new places, helping people. I'm good at administration and I'm pretty practical. Gilt said I might make a good Harbour Master one day."

"And so you might," Marheh said, smiling at her and wondering how much she really knew about what she was committing herself to.

She turned to Glik.

"My grandfather used to tell me stories," he said. "His uncle was Silberay. When Grandad realised I could see the water he told me how the Silberay changed things, how they made things better whenever they appeared. It seemed like a special thing that I could be part of. I hope one day I might be able to make things better too."

"I'm sure you will," Marheh said. "The hope of making things better for people and the landscape is something that underlies all our practice. We travel because it keeps us in touch with more people and places but the important learning is not boat management, but the disciplines of mind and soul." She leaned forward, eager to have them understand. "Those are what we bring to the landscape and it is those that require the lengthy apprenticeship that you will serve."

"Myl said it is twenty years."

Beuda sounded as if she didn't believe that. Marheh nodded.

"That's right. For the first ten years you will be involved in classes at the Gathering, and every Gathering, if you learn well, you will move up to a new level. You probably heard me speak of the third years and the fourth years, but in fact it is not the years, but the Gatherings that are numbered, so to be a third year means that this is your third Gathering but the beginning of the fifth year of your apprenticeship. Then, when formal classes are over you will learn the work of caring in a practical way as your mentor ages and needs more of your help. Don't be fooled though, your mentor will still have a great deal to give you of wisdom and knowledge of the disciplines."

"Isn't discipline a bit old fashioned these days?" Beuda said.

"In what way?" Marheh asked. "How do you think of discipline?"

"Oh, you know, being disciplined, punished, if you don't do what you're told. Having someone boss you. Something people used to do to naughty children."

Marheh laughed.

"Well, there will probably be times when you are expected to do as you are told, but discipline is much bigger than that. It's putting values, an ideal, ahead of your own desires and working at them, even when it is difficult or costly. It's practising the soul song, the discipline of the soul, when the joy and the music are absent and all around you is dark. Obedience to your mentor will be part of learning self discipline. If you are anything like me you will probably fail and fail again even after you have graduated but you will at least know enough to recognise your failure and begin again."

Beuda did not look convinced and Marheh again felt a stab of anxiety for Bixa.

"I really don't see why it should take twenty years to graduate either," Beuda said. "I'm sure I can learn to operate a boat more quickly than that, and I know how to help people already. Usually it's just a matter of telling them what to do, or how to do something better."

"Are you sure you want to be Silberay?" Marheh said sharply. "I don't think you've listened to a word I've said."

"What do you mean? Of course I've listened, of course I want to. I just think twenty years is ridiculous and I bet I'll prove it to you too."

"I see," Marheh said and turned to Glik. "Is this how you think?" she asked.

He shook his head.

"I think," he hesitated then continued in a rush. "I think being part of something special like the Silberay is never going to be easy and learning to be disciplined in everything is part of the job."

Marheh smiled her agreement then looked at them both.

"I think there is almost nothing more important than being open to learn all your life. That involves discipline, struggle, even pain sometimes. That's why you have a mentor for so long. They encourage and prod, and set an example. The Silberay are glad to welcome you both and will support you in every way they can. Being able to see the water is a privilege and a responsibility. Your mentors are skilled and wise and deserve your love and service."

She stood up.

"I'll let you go now, but please don't hesitate to come to me if you have any questions you think I can answer." She turned to smile at Bixa and Whin. "Only I can't imagine any question that your mentors could not answer better."

Beuda was first out the door followed by Glik and Whin. Bixa lingered a moment to smile at Marheh and mouth a word of thanks.

When the door closed behind them Marheh sank into an armchair and let her breath out in a long sigh. She would have to go back to the office in a few minutes, but she had put a lot of herself into the meeting with the apprentices and she needed some space to gather herself for the next challenge. Glik was a nice lad, she thought. Whin would be a conscientious mentor and if he was a bit conservative now, contact with the young would change that if necessary. Beuda posed more of a question. She had seemed to discount a lot of what Marheh had said, but perhaps she would think about it as the days went by. She hoped so for Bixa's sake.

She closed her eyes and reached for her portal to the soul song. She would spend a few moments singing for all the gathered Silberay, but especially for the two apprentices and their mentors. It was love she was singing, love she didn't know she could feel for all of them, not just the ones who cared for her, but her critics too.

The telephone ringing brought her back with a start. For a moment she was confused until she remembered that Jik had told her it rang in the flat as well as the office. It had stopped ringing by the time she had found it, but it had been useful in returning her to the tasks of the Gathering.

She made her way back to the office to prepare for her next challenge. After lunch she would address the mentor's meeting and give them the bad news about the finances. She was not looking forward to it. They would be upset, perhaps even angry. They would have questions and she had to be able to answer them without allowing herself to lay blame or become defensive. Thank goodness Jik would be there and Bixa.

There were fifteen mentors counting Zinda, who was about to retire, and Whin and Bixa, who were just joining the group. There was no formal leadership, but Nisfa was often spokesperson. In her mid eighties, she was very experienced, fit for her age, and respected for her commonsense. Marheh did not know her well and had been inclined to think she disapproved of her, although the morning's interaction had begun to change that feeling. Her apprentice, Sampi, was a musician, and often played her violin for the sing alongs that were a traditional entertainment at the Gatherings.

As she prepared for the meeting Marheh tried to think of all she knew of the individuals that made up the group of mentors.

Since Beuda had spoken so often of Myl, Marheh had looked out for Yog, his mentor, and made a point of speaking with him when Mistral arrived at the Harbour a couple of days before the Gathering. He was a quiet man and not in very good health, but she had discovered a dry sense of humour and a strong sense of duty. Peli, who had taken the third years that morning, was one of the younger mentors. Her apprentice Rima was a third year. There were no second years of course, since there had been no new apprentices last Gathering. The other third year was Onn, his mentor was Luff. There was one fourth year, Dom was the only fifth year, and there were three sixth years, who would move past formal classes this Gathering. She realised she knew the apprentices better than the mentors, probably because the mentors tended to do things together.

Five minutes only now, before the meeting. She picked up her summary of figures and the two most recent account books, glanced over the summary once more and set off for room two.

Jik and Peli were there when she arrived, moving the tables into a square. She put down her things and moved to help them, but they were nearly done. Jik smiled at her and showed her where to sit, then turned to greet Bixa and Whin. Nisfa was just behind them and in a few minutes all were gathered.

There were words of welcome for the two new mentors and for Marheh then Nisfa led them into the soul song. They did not spend long there, but the singing centred and united them so they were reminded to listen with hearts and minds open to hear the thoughts of their colleagues without acrimony, valuing each without judging, although there would perhaps be disagreement and discussion.

Marheh felt reassured by the experience. They would be shocked by what she had to tell them, but they would not blame her.

"Harbour Master," Nisfa said formally when the soul song was ended. "You have a report for us?"

"Yes, I do." Marheh glanced at her summary. "I do have a report and I'm afraid it is not good news."

The faces around her took on various expression of concern, but no one spoke.

"I've gone over and over the figures and asked Jik and my father to confirm my arithmetic. There have been times over the last five or six years when payments have been made drawing on capital. Interest rates are low at the moment and with reduced capital our income is significantly reduced.

Our land has been re-zoned from agricultural to residential and that has more than doubled our rates. I have bills amounting to around £350 that I cannot pay until some of the Silberay have paid their dues. We could not have had a welcome breakfast without the generosity of Jik and my father and the farewell dinner will have to rely on contributions of food from us all because I made the decision not to go into more debt. I have figures that I can show you if you want, but I believe that we have to make a radical change to the way we operate or we will be bankrupt within the next ten years."

A stunned silence greeted these last words then several people began to speak at once. After a moment Nisfa called the meeting to order then turned to Marheh.

"That is a very challenging statement. You've only been acting as Harbour Master for three months, are you quite sure you are not..." She hesitated. "Not dramatising what is really only a small problem? You do have a bit of a reputation."

Marheh took a deep breath. She was only a messenger, but for the mentors to realise that she knew she had to be unemotional, to speak calmly and above all, not to be defensive.

"Yes, Nisfa," she said at last. "I understand your concern, but I am quite certain of the figures. I have given a lot of thought to the problem and discussed it with Jik. I have some suggestions to offer, but I know the figures are correct."

Nisfa looked around at the group of mentors.

"Jik, Bixa, you have both been in the position of Harbour Master, can you comment?"

Bixa shook her head, but Jik answered.

"I went over the figures with Marheh's father. There have been some bad decisions in the past few years, made probably through lack of understanding. What she has reported is correct."

"Why take on the expense and inconvenience of the open day then?"

The comment came from Luff. Someone else muttered "Good question" and Marheh felt herself redden, but waited until Nisfa looked to her again.

"There has been no expense to the Silberay," she explained then. "Bixa has paid for the printing of Hafa's history and I paid for the leaflets. Another reason for having the open day is to show the neighbours what is here and perhaps allow them to hire rooms, or use the front garden when we are not here."

Nisfa smiled at her then.

"We will hear your ideas in a minute and any others people might have, but I want to say thank you on behalf of the mentors. Some of us might have disapproved of you from time to time, but I think we all know that you are totally committed to the values of the Silberay. It must have been difficult, taking on the job of Harbour Master, and I'm guessing that it would have been easy just to go through the motions rather than confront the problems as you have."

Marheh didn't know what to say. Her face felt hot and she knew she was blushing. She had not expected thanks or praise. Across the room Jik was smiling at her and Bixa, sitting beside her, put a hand on hers.

"What I suggest now," Nisfa continued. "Is that we listen to Marheh's ideas, then respond with ideas of our own before we adjourn to think things over."

She nodded to Marheh.

"Over to you."

Marheh took a deep breath and began to explain the ideas she had come up with, acknowledging the helpful discussion she had had with Jik and Bixa and how she and Bixa had gone to the town hall to speak with the town clerk. She mentioned the possibility of applying to be registered as a charity and emphasised how unknown was their purpose and their very existence.

"I know we haven't wanted to advertise ourselves," she finished. "But here where we have our centre, our heart, if we are not acknowledged for who we are we will be squeezed out of existence."

She stopped talking quite abruptly and for a minute or two there was a heavy silence. The radical changes she was suggesting were challenging and would demand work and thought. The Silberay were accustomed to a life of work and thought, but these changes would require a new way of thinking and work of a different kind.

"Thank you Marheh," Nisfa said at last. "Does anyone have questions or ideas?"

Another short silence was broken by Jik.

"I believe this matter should be discussed by all the Silberay, not kept to the mentors," he said. "We need the different understanding and energies of the young and the middle-aged, after all it is their future at stake."

Looking around the table Marheh thought that suggestion too was confronting to a few of the mentors who were used to being the decision makers for the Silberay as a whole, but Nisfa was nodding her agreement. She offered the opportunity for dissension, but although there were a couple of frowns and a bit of muttering from one corner no one spoke out against the idea.

"Harbour Master." Nemle turned to Marheh and spoke formally. "Can you schedule a general meeting for tomorrow afternoon?"

Marheh nodded.

"Will two o'clock suit?"

"Certainly," Nemle said, having looked around for agreement. "I suggest we adjourn until then."

She stood up and made her way around to Marheh who almost found herself bobbing a curtsy.

"Well done my dear," she said majestically and moved slowly onward and out the door.

That evening when she was finally alone on *Day Bringer*, Marheh took up her journal. The sing song had been fun, though they probably needed to include a few new songs with a more modern rhythm if they ever got around to publishing a new edition of "Songs of the Silberay". She was very tired now though. She picked up her pen, but was still staring at the blank page when she felt *Day Bringer* move as someone boarded.

Please don't let it be another problem for the Harbour Master, she thought, putting down her pen and getting to her feet.

Her visitor was either very bold or knew her very well. She heard the footsteps coming through without having waited to be admitted and looked towards them, expectant now, thinking perhaps she knew who it was.

When Kel appeared her face lit up and a moment later she was swept into a hug. She was so tired and the closeness was so comforting that tears came into her eyes as she leaned into his embrace. Then, without quite know how it happened, she found herself back in the armchair, on his lap, still held close. She let herself rest against him and closed her eyes.

He must have put her to bed, she thought, when she woke there next morning, She had been so tired, but too busy with thinking to sleep until he came. He knew her so well, the woman and the child that was still part of her nature despite her years. She pushed back the covers. The light and the silence told her that it was still very early but she felt refreshed and ready to tackle the day.

Would Kel be awake too, she wondered, dressing quickly and going through to make up the fire. She reached out with her mind, wanting to thank him for his care, and received a drowsy acknowledgement and an invitation to breakfast.

Half an hour later she was sitting opposite him at the little table in *Storm Cloud*'s saloon. He had made them scrambled eggs with bacon, then toast to have with their sperit.

"Thank you for looking after me," she said, spreading apricot jam lavishly on her toast.

He smiled at her.

"It's what I'm here for."

"I'm needing looking after in this job. I keep having to do grown up things and there's a little girl inside that keeps saying I can't, I can't."

"You're doing brilliantly."

But there has been a cost, he thought, looking at her. She was much paler than usual, less outdoors and too much office probably. She was too thin too, and, he searched for understanding, her light was dimmed somehow. He wanted to hold her, care for her until she shone again.

"Shall we sing?" he asked, as she swallowed the last mouthful of toast. "Or would you like some more toast first?"

She sighed and smiled.

"I'm full. It was a lovely breakfast thank you. Singing would be good."

There was a special closeness in the song that sustained her if they were physically near each other. He gave her so much she sometimes wondered what she gave to him in return. She loved him, she thought he knew that, but she sometimes felt that all she did was take from his strength and loving concern.

Her portal was quite elusive this morning, but she managed to enter at last. Once there though she seemed to have nothing to contribute to the music that surrounded and held her. She was singing however and gradually the other singers seemed to nurse her, nudge her soft, extended, sighing notes until she floated on a pad of harmonious sound. She could abandon herself completely then and let the music build until there was nothing else.

When the song ended she found she was still sitting at the table, her hands in Kel's, his familiar face opposite her, watching her with loving concern. There was no need for words. Stillness held them for a while as the memory of the song gently receded.

At last she let out a long sigh and stood up.

"Thank you."

He stood too and put his arms around her.

"You'll be back on the water road soon," he said.

"I'll come alive again then." She eased out of his embrace. "I have to hold onto that."

She moved through Kel's workspace and out into the well deck, Kel following. The sun was up now, the sky a clear, soft cobalt. Brass fittings on the boats shone in the light and the water sparkled. There was still an early morning chill in the air and little puffs of smoke drifted up from many of the moored boats. She looked back over her shoulder at Kel.

"Thanks again. On with the day."

She scrambled up and over the gunnel onto the gantry. Kel stood watching as she walked quickly towards the office. He had known she had courage for battling with the Yareblis, but it was courage of a different kind to give so much of herself to this uncongenial work. It was no wonder she was strained and tired. Surely they wouldn't expect her to continue in the job. She had told him that Gilt was not returning, but asked him not to speak of it since she had only just told the mentors. He would protest if they even thought of asking her.

Marheh was hoping she was early enough in the office to have an uninterrupted hour to think about the afternoon's meeting. Thankfully Nisfa had offered to chair, but she would need to be well prepared to answer questions as well as to explain her discoveries and ideas. At least there would not be mail to deal with and no formal classes for the apprentices. With any luck most of the Silberay would be having a lazy start to the day after last night's festivities.

She had been working for about an hour and a half and was beginning to think she had done enough when Bixa and Beuda came to the door. She had left it open on purpose, wanting to be accessible and Bixa was someone she was always glad to see.

She smiled a greeting. Bixa smiled back, but Beuda looked away.

"What can I do for you?"

"Beuda has something she wants to tell you."

"Oh?"

Marheh looked from one to the other and realised there was a degree of tension between them.

"Come in and sit down."

There was an awkward silence. Marheh waited, trying to look sympathetic.

"Bixa said I should tell you," Beuda said at last, sounding defiant. "When I was here before I took some of the leaflets from your desk and gave them out where I worked. She said you needed to know because of what you said about only distributing them locally."

"I'm glad you told me," Marheh said slowly. "It would have been sensible to ask first, but I dare say there is no harm done."

"I was just trying to be helpful. I would have thought you'd want people to know."

"It just makes things a bit difficult if our enemies feel themselves to be invited. Without an invitation they would struggle to enter but with one they could come in and we may not even know until too late."

Beuda's face suggested to Marheh that she didn't believe what she had been told, but she apologised with reasonable sincerity and headed off without waiting for Bixa, who sat down again and smiled ruefully at Marheh.

"She will have gone to look for Myl."

"Oh dear!"

"I feel sorry for him. She's very persistent and he is too nice to show her she is unwelcome."

"It will be better once you are out and about."

"I suppose so. I'm sorry about the leaflets. How many would she have taken?"

"About thirty I think. Probably not enough to cause a problem if she only distributed them to her work mates. I'd better confess to Nisfa that I misled her though."

"You've enough on your plate. I'll tell her."

She stood up to go. Marheh stood up too and gave Bixa a hug.

"Her heart is in the right place I think and you'll show her our values."

Half an hour more in the office and Marheh knew she had done all she could to prepare. As she made her way back to *Day Bringer* she stopped to look at the notice board where she had put the sign up sheets. Her own name headed the list for boat rides and tours but she did not feel confident enough of her cooking skills to offer to contribute to afternoon tea. She was not alone on either list, she was glad to see. Dom and Tippa had both offered to contribute afternoon tea, Jik and Kel were available for boat rides and Bixa and Whin were both listed for tours. Even Whin, she thought, with an inward smile and not just Whin but three or four others on each list. Nisfa's apprentice Sampi had her name on the boat rides list which must mean Nisfa approved. It was early days yet but it was clear that the Silberay were actively prepared to support the open day.

There would need to be a timetable for the tours and the boat rides, she realised as she walked outside. You couldn't have more than three or perhaps four boats moving around the harbour at once. There would have to be an agreed route too.

There were other Silberay out and about enjoying the sunny morning.

Most greeted her cheerfully, only one woman demanded she open the chandlery and scowled when she was told that it would not open until tomorrow. It had been a considered decision. After the meeting this afternoon the Silberay would understand why they would have to pay for whatever they wanted from the chandlery. She didn't want to have to argue the point beforehand.

She had not been back on *Day Bringer* for long when there was a visit from Sampi with an invitation to lunch with her and Nisfa on *Cloud Drift*.

"You've really made an impression on Nisfa," she said. "She wants to discuss your ideas before the meeting so she can support you better."

It was a bit like being summoned to dine with royalty, Marheh thought, when Sampi had left again. Jik, five minutes too late with his invitation, laughed when she said as much to him.

"You forget," he said. "You're the Harbour Master. You're royalty yourself."

She made a face.

"Not for much longer I hope. I'm abdicating the first minute I can."

Cloud Drift was a pretty boat, she thought as she walked along the gantry towards her mooring. Not, of course, as beautiful as *Day Bringer*, but different. Above the black hull her gunnel was picked out in blue and white, painted to look like a twisted rope and her topsides bore the soft clouds of a summer's day on a sky blue background. Marheh tried to think whether the artist was Nisfa or Sampi, but she couldn't remember.

Inside was also decorated with soft clouds and a bird or two, bringing the outside in.

"Sampi does it now," Nisfa explained, when Marheh had expressed her delight in it. "It is a bit beyond me, but we've worked together in the past."

Lunch was a thick vegetable soup with a toasted cheese sandwich. Sampi served them and sat on a folding stool at the end of the small table in the saloon. Marheh could not help thinking back to her own apprenticeship. The two fixed seats had been enough when she and Nemle had been alone, but the folding stool had always been her place if they had a guest.

During the meal conversation was kept away from the problems of the Silberay. Marheh was happy to listen while Nisfa and Sampi told her something of themselves. Nisfa, like Marheh's beloved Nemle, had been born last century and seen many changes. Unlike Nemle though, she had never needed to earn her living. Marheh thought it had perhaps given her a sense of entitlement and a confidence that enabled her to take charge of the mentors as if of right. Nemle, for all her wisdom, had never put herself forward unless she had needed to defend Marheh. That had happened more than once and Marheh suddenly realised how difficult it must have been for her.

Nisfa had, of course, known Nemle. She had joined the mentors before

Nemle retired and remembered her quiet, considered contributions to their discussions.

"She was very proud of you, and would have been proud of how you have tackled the job of Harbour Master."

Marheh smiled.

"I think she saw me through the eyes of love, but I try to do justice to her teaching."

Nisfa nodded with gracious approval and moved the conversation towards the forthcoming meeting.

Nisfa's support was more than she had hoped for, Marheh thought, walking back towards the office after lunch. There was half an hour before the meeting, time to go over her notes once more and jot down a couple of points that had come from the lunchtime discussion. She had told Nisfa that Gilt was resigning as Harbour Master and hoped she had made it clear that she did not want to continue in the position. Traditionally the Harbour Master was chosen from candidates in their sixties, a decade older than she. Surely there were suitable people amongst those.

All too soon she was on her way to the meeting hall. Sampi and a couple of the other older apprentices were just finishing arranging chairs in rows in front of the dais. Nisfa was standing at the lectern and beckoned Marheh to one of the two chairs behind her. Already Silberay were drifting in and taking their places. Marheh thought she could pick the ones who chose the front seats. For some it as a need to hear better, but for others it indicated a propensity for questioning and expressing an opinion.

Kel came in with Jik. They both gave her an encouraging grin and sat themselves in the fourth row, near enough for support, not near enough for distraction. She saw Dom come in with another couple of apprentices and Tippa with Pon.

The sound of conversation increased as the Silberay began to fill the room. All of them except the very youngest knew this meeting was a break with tradition. There would be those who came reluctantly, not wanting to waste the time they had in the dry dock or the wet dock. They would come though, curiosity would bring them, if nothing else.

Having explained it all to the mentors yesterday, Marheh did not feel nearly as anxious now as she had then and she was able to respond politely to Nisfa's words of advice and encouragement.

At precisely two o'clock, just as the last few Silberay were scrambling for a seat, Nisfa stood up and opened the meeting.

Ouch!

Chapter Fourteen

Marheh's news had been a nasty shock to the Silberay as a whole and some of them had wanted to shoot the messenger, but Nisfa had parried any accusing questions and made it clear that Marheh was not to blame for the predicament they were in. She went further and stated that it was the Silberay as a whole who had failed their Harbour Masters.

The meeting had gone on and on without any useful conclusions until Nisfa had finally sent everyone away with instructions to consider the ideas Marheh had presented and come up with some more helpful suggestions. They were to put these in writing and leave them in the Harbour Master's office. Another meeting would be held next weekend.

Marheh was in danger of being mobbed when she finally left the dais, but Jik and Kel fended off the questioners and whisked her away to *Storm Cloud* to be sustained with sperit and scones.

"Thank goodness that's over."

"They took it fairly well on the whole," Jik said. "Nisfa did a good job. I liked the way she refused to allow anyone to lay blame."

Kel nodded.

"No point in blame, though I do think that Gilt could perhaps have been a bit more diligent."

"He was probably worrying about his father," Marheh said, trying to be fair. The thought had crossed her mind on more than one occasion as she struggled to get on top of the job.

"It's probably time we had a bit of a shake up," Jik said. "It doesn't do to become complacent."

"Perhaps the next meeting will be another Great Debate," Marheh said. "New ways of thinking and old traditions revisited."

"What is it, fifty years since the last one?" Kel asked.

"More than that, it was the year Nemle was apprenticed."

"It was eighty two years ago," Jik said. "I think we must have become complacent then too, given what we know of what was happening."

"As I understand it the Great Debate drew attention to the important things, the disciplines and why we practise them." Marheh looked at Kel. "I remember how Sul explained it to us when we were both apprentices."

Kel nodded.

"He was only a third or fourth year apprentice when it happened, but he knew enough to be aware that not all the Silberay were practising them and some were becoming lazy about other things too."

"A bit like now then," Marheh said, rather sadly. She finished her scone and swallowed the last mouthful of sperit. "I think I'll go home to *Day Bringer* and sing," she said. "It might be my last opportunity for a while. I'll need to be in the office tomorrow."

They all stood up. Kel opened the doors to the well deck and gave Marheh a hug. Jik walked with her along the gantry towards *Day Bringer* and *Autumn Wind*.

"I'm proud of you niece," he said before stepping onto his boat.

Marheh continued onto *Day Bringer*, thoughtfully, warmed by his support, and settled herself to practise the discipline of the soul, wanting to offer love and light as best she could.

Monday morning usually meant a larger than usual post bag and this first Monday of the Gathering was no exception. It seemed as if all the Silberay were receiving letters while their friends and family knew they would be at the Harbour to receive them. Marheh separated out the personal mail and put it aside. She would ask her first visitor to distribute it into the pigeon holes. Her time would be better spent dealing with the business mail.

The letters from Hemera were still coming, one or two each week. The one this morning threatened torture in the form of evisceration as well as burning. Whoever he was, he had a very nasty imagination. She tried to ignore it, feeling that she was safe enough while the Silberay were here for the Gathering. When the letters first came she had wondered about the pseudonym the writer had chosen but the very limited number of reference books in the library had not been helpful and she had not pursued it further.

There was also a fairly steady stream of Silberay wanting to pay for things. The mentors had decided not to increase the dues this Gathering but ask those who could afford it to add a little extra and already three or four had done that. Marheh realised she would need to go into Sefton Middle to the bank within the next day or so, and once she had done that she could start writing cheques again. Their creditors would be pleased.

She had just accepted cash from Whin for his blacking paint as well as a cheque for his dues and put both away in her cash box when Leura stalked into the office shutting the door behind her with a bang. Marheh's heart sank. Leura had been the Harbour Master between Jik and Bixa and been the one to set the precedent of using capital to pay for things. Her name had not been mentioned during the meeting but Marheh had fielded a few resentful glances as she spoke and was not really surprised to see her now.

She was not a mentor, which was unusual for someone who had been Harbour Master, but Marheh thought she remembered there had not been any candidates for apprenticeship the year Leura turned seventy. The trouble was that there was a certain status in being a mentor and she was aware that it was not easy for some to accept the lack. It would perhaps be even harder if you had once had the status of Harbour Master.

"I suppose you're pleased with yourself," Leura said, having spent a moment or two staring at Marheh. "Miss Goody Two Shoes."

Marheh shook her head but did not speak. Leura was a tall woman and now she towered over Marheh, still seated at her desk.

"You always did have a good opinion of yourself. The Silberay should have slapped you down more often."

Marheh raised her eyebrows but still did not speak.

"Well, say something. You had plenty to say yesterday."

"What do you want me to say?" Marheh asked. "I can understand that you might feel responsible and I'm sorry. No one blames you or Gilt. We are all to blame for being too complacent."

"We are all to blame for being too complacent." Leura gave her words back, mocking her. "You know all the right words, don't you? What makes you the authority? You pop into the position on a whim, dig up what dirt you can and come out smelling like roses."

Marheh started to laugh then gasped as Leura reached over and slapped her face. There was a frozen moment as they stared at each other then Leura sank into the visitor's chair and covered her face with her hands.

"I'm sorry," she muttered, not looking at Marheh.

"I'm sorry too," Marheh said, one hand held to her smarting cheek. "I shouldn't have laughed, but what you said was so far from the truth."

"What do you mean?" Leura stared at her.

"I never wanted the job. I still don't and I needed so much help. I was just lucky that Jik and Bixa were prepared to be generous with their time and their knowledge."

"Well, I'm sorry I hit you," Leura said. "But you do always seem to fall on your feet and it can be very exasperating at times." She stood up. "Being Harbour Master was not at all what I expected. Jik handed over everything in perfect order but I didn't know how to keep it that way and I was too proud to ask." She opened the door and paused in the doorway. "I suppose I should thank you really."

She disappeared before Marheh could frame a reply, closing the door quietly behind her.

Left alone, Marheh took a deep breath and let it out very slowly. She could understand that the older woman might feel as if she was being targeted, but no names had been mentioned. Jik and Bixa, who had been careful not to spend capital, would have been justified in proclaiming their innocence, but had chosen not to so that no one would be singled out.

She was still worrying over what had happened when there was a light tap on the door. She straightened and took up her pen, wanting to look businesslike.

"Come in."

Bixa opened the door.

"I just met Leura. She said you might need a friend."

She closed the door behind her and looked at Marheh.

"What happened to your face?"

Marheh's light laugh threatened to turn to tears. She stood up.

"It must be lunchtime. Come and eat with me on *Day Bringer* and I'll tell you all about it."

That evening Marheh had supper with Jik and Dom on *Autumn Wind*. Kel was there too. They didn't comment on her bruised cheek and she didn't speak of it. She was tired and left them almost as soon as the meal was over, knowing they would understand. The Gathering was usually a celebration, a time to enjoy. Until now she had never given a thought to the work of the Harbour Master who had to make it happen.

She ought to sing, tiredness was no excuse. She got ready for bed, put on her dressing gown and made herself comfortable in the armchair. In singing she must let go of self and that could only be good for her as well as for the Silberay as a whole and if she fell asleep making the attempt she would be forgiven.

The rest of the week seemed to fly past. There were times when she thought she would never get her head above water and the tasks seemed to overwhelm her. The Silberay had responded generously to the call for ideas and her in tray was flooded with suggestions, some scribbled on scraps of paper, some carefully explained in neat writing, one or two even typed. She read them all before passing them to Nisfa. There would be a meeting of the mentors on Friday, she was informed, and she was expected to attend. Like it or not, she was the Harbour Master.

A trip into Sefton Middle to the bank made a welcome break. She took the bus in, but once she had deposited the money she felt free to walk back through the sunny afternoon, enjoying time to be alone and to think. She wished the mentors would give some thought to appointing a new Harbour Master. Whoever they chose needed to be involved now, while decisions were being made. She had a nasty feeling they were postponing any discussions in the hope that she might continue in the position, though perhaps that was arrogance on her part.

The apprentice classes seemed to be going well and the refitting of the boats was on schedule. She had ordered the tunics for Beuda and Glik now she had their sizes and they were promised in time for the ceremony. She had plenty of volunteers now for the various activities on the open day. Her next job should be to make a roster. You don't need to do everything yourself, she told herself sternly. Let someone else help. Tippa would be good at organising the afternoon tea people and perhaps, if she gave some thought to it, instead of just asking her friends, she could persuade one of those Silberay in their sixties, who might be a potential Harbour Master, to organise the tours. That would just leave the boat rides to her, which made sense since those were the most controversial part of the program.

Nisfa had wanted to meet with her most days, sending Sampi with a summons to attend for sperit on *Cloud Drift*.

"It always feels like a royal command," she told Kel on the Saturday evening at the end of the first week. "I keep thinking I should curtsy, but at least it doesn't feel like being sent to the headmistress any more."

"You would, of course, know how that felt," he teased.

She grinned.

"Oh yes."

They were on *Storm Cloud* eating an early tea and enjoying time together before going back to the meeting hall and the entertainment that was planned for the evening. There would be more singing and some country dancing and normally Marheh would have been looking forward to it, but she was tired and a quiet time with Kel and an early night would have been more appealing. There was no help for it though, as Harbour Master she had to be there and look as if she was enjoying herself.

"Do you think Leura had someone like you to lean on?" she asked suddenly.

"Where did that come from," Kel asked.

"I was just thinking how tired I am and how much you and Jik have done for me. I don't think I could keep going without you."

"I expect you could," Kel said, standing up to remove their empty plates. "But I'm glad I've helped."

Coming back from the sink he eased her out of her seat and into his arms. She leant against him and closed her eyes. Just to be held was such a comfort. Her mind stopped its anxious checking and crosschecking and rested. A few minutes later he settled her in the armchair.

"I'll just take care of the dishes. You have a little sleep if you can. I'll wake you when it's time to go."

It was easy then to close her eyes and let go of everything pertaining to the Harbour Master.

The meeting could easily become another Great Debate, Marheh thought the next afternoon, looking out over the rows of seats. The Silberay were almost all gathered even though proceedings were not due to start for ten more minutes. She had laboriously collated the ideas that had been offered and summarised them on the blackboard that was mounted on an easel behind her.

The mentors' meeting Nisfa had called for on Friday had not offered anything new and Marheh had needed all her patience as the discussion seemed to go round and round without getting anywhere. She was pleased though, that Nisfa had adopted the suggestion she had made to invite Leura to join them. She tried to recognise that everyone needed to come to terms with the position in their own way. She, after all, had had much more time to think about things.

With her customary attention to detail Nisfa opened the meeting at precisely two o'clock, then called on Marheh to read through the list on the blackboard for the sake of those at the back who might find it difficult to see.

"Lots of you gave suggestions," she explained before she began to read. "Some of them were similar so I've tried to group them, but they are in no sort of order, just as they came to hand."

She moved so that she was not blocking anyone's view of the blackboard and read from the duplicate list in her hand.

"Increase the dues," she began. "Sell some of the land on the road, rent out our buildings, register as a charity, rent land for allotments, sell the boats on the hard standing."

There was some muttering when she finished as people took in the reality of the situation. Nisfa gave them a few minutes before calling them to order and offering Marheh the opportunity to comment. She shook her head however, wanting to give others a chance.

Nisfa turned to the meeting.

"We will discuss the ideas separately," she said. "And get an idea of how you feel about each one, but it is unlikely we will reach any decision today."

Marheh was not sure whether the subsequent sense of tension relaxed was a good thing, but there was not much time to wonder, as Nisfa immediately called for discussion on the matter of increasing their dues.

Yes, no, by how much, what about exceptions, why not a sliding scale according to ability to pay – everyone seemed to have an opinion. If they were to spend as much time as this on each point they would be still there at midnight, Marheh thought, trying to note down each new comment.

Selling some land seemed popular at first until someone pointed out that was only a one off possibility and someone else mentioned low interest rates and thus not much return on capital. Marheh took particular note of the woman, called Chanra, who had made that comment. An understanding of finance could point to a potential Harbour Master and she was desperate to find one.

Rent out the buildings had a following, but it seemed to Marheh that no one had given much thought to the logistics of doing that. Register as a charity might or might not be possible and would only help a little. Allotments too might contribute n a small way. The idea of selling the boats on the hard standing appealed to no one and Marheh wondered who had made the suggestion.

No more new ideas came out of the meeting, but at least everyone had had a chance to contribute and to hear all the possibilities.

Before Nisfa closed the meeting Marheh suggested that each afternoon of the coming week could be spent working through the ideas with those interested so that a more detailed plan could be put forward for each one. Afternoons at the Gathering were traditionally free for most of the Silberay so they could catch up with chores or visit friends or just relax, but there seemed to be general approval of this idea. Nisfa announced that two o'clock would be the time and they should check the notice board for topic and location. Marheh understood that it would now be her job to schedule the meetings and rather wished she had held her tongue.

After the meeting she went back to her office with the notes she had taken and tried to put them in some sort of order. She had just finished writing them out in her best hand writing when one of the older Silberay came to the door.

"I saw you taking notes," she said. "I could type them for you if you like."

"Chanra! That would be wonderful. Then I could put them on the notice board and people could actually read them."

Chanra laughed.

"I expect they could read your writing too, but I could do a couple of carbons as well, one for Nisfa and perhaps one in the annex as well as one here."

She took the pages Marheh handed her and scanned them briefly.

"Lovely writing, I won't have any trouble with this. I'll put the copies up for you when I'm done and leave this on your desk, shall I?"

"Are you the fairy godmother?" Marheh asked.

Chanra laughed again.

"Are you feeling you need one? I'm not surprised. You've a lot on your plate."

She disappeared. Marheh sat back in her chair and sighed. One job done. The sensible thing would be to stay a bit longer and work out an agenda for the next couple of meetings. Tomorrow, being Monday, meant the morning's mail would take up most of her time before lunch. She might as well schedule the meetings in the same order as they were discussed today. The apprentices had a class in Silberay law in room two tomorrow afternoon, but room three should be big enough. Not everyone would want to waste the afternoon discussing whether to sell a bit of land.

The idea had some attraction. It seemed like an easy solution to regaining a bit of capital, but it was very short term and could hardly be repeated next time they ran out. It would also, perhaps, bring neighbours too close. She had best make a point of inviting Chanra to the meeting. She would be exceeding her authority if she said anything about the job of Harbour Master to her, but surely it wouldn't hurt to mention her name to Nisfa and maybe sound out Jik and Bixa informally. The next Harbour Master ought to be an integral part of any deliberations about the future and she definitely did not want the job herself.

She was just writing up the notice when she realised that if she were taking things in order she should have begun with the suggestion to increase the dues. Everyone would have an opinion about that and room three would not be big enough. It was inevitable there would be some increase, the issue would be how much and how flexible. If she left that discussion until last perhaps the outcome of the other meetings might help them decide.

Taking up another sheet of paper she began scribbling down questions and ideas. Time passed and she was still in the office when Chanra came back with her notes. She looked up in surprise.

"That was quick!"

"Not really. I'm used to typing for people and yours was not difficult. I didn't expect you would still be here though. Have you had any supper?"

Marheh shook her head.

"I forgot the time. I suppose I'd better eat something though, the concert will be starting soon."

The second Sunday evening of the Gathering was always a concert given mostly by the musicians amongst the Silberay but often including a skit or two. Marheh still remembered the skit she, Tippa and Pon had been encouraged to rehearse when they were second years. It had, she thought, been intended as some kind of exercise in working together and one of the mentors had helped them learn it. Pon had been the heavy father, Tippa the ineffectual governess and she the naughty brat. Sometimes she thought the older Silberay still thought of her as the naughty brat. There would not be second years performing a skit at this Gathering though.

Chanra still stood in the doorway.

"You only have fifteen minutes," she said. "Do you really need to be at the concert? You look tired."

Marheh smiled and stood up.

"I am a bit, but I'll enjoy the concert." She moved around her desk towards the door. "Thank you for doing that."

She closed the door behind her and the two women walked together towards the kitchen.

"I'll be happy to take notes and type them up for all the meetings if it would help," Chanra said.

"You really are a fairy godmother!"

Marheh had been so busy that she had all but forgotten that the Monday was her fifty second birthday. However Jik had not forgotten and he and Kel had been busy turning the evening's program into a little celebration for her. Not many Silberay birthdays fell within the three weeks of the Gathering but Marheh's almost always did and the Silberay remembered and responded. Dom made a big cake, other cooks offered plates of party food and the musicians offered more dance tunes. It seemed the Silberay were glad of an opportunity to acknowledge the work and thought Marheh had put into the job of Harbour Master and she was surprised and touched to be teased and feted. Somehow she still expected a degree of disapproval, especially from her elders.

The daily meetings were well attended and although discussion was sometimes heated it was not acrimonious. Jik and Kel continued to look out for Marheh, making sure she had at least one good meal each day. Plans for the open day seemed to be falling into place. It had seemed a long way off when she first thought of it, but now it was almost upon them. There had not been time to return to the pub since the Gathering started and she wondered whether the people she had met there would visit.

The letters from Hemera appeared daily now and she could not help worrying about them although she tried to pretend they were trivial. She did not speak of them to anyone and hoped those she had told when they first appeared had forgotten about them. Ignoring them was the thing to do. What he wanted was for her to be anxious, fearful even, and she would not give him the satisfaction.

On Friday she gave all her attention to last minute details for the open day. Even the mail was mostly ignored although she did separate out the personal mail and put it aside for delivery by any willing visitor. The last couple of days had been wet and rather chilly but Friday the weather seemed to be clearing which gave her hope that Saturday might be a nice day. It would make things much nicer if the sun shone.

The afternoon was spent carefully lettering some signs indicating locations and activities before taking a tour of inspection with Jik, Bixa and Leura, who had surprised Marheh by suddenly throwing herself into preparations.

Everything looked inviting. The rooms shone with cleanliness. The table by the front door held a pile of copies of Hafa's history and a vase of flowers. The tours would begin there. One of Marheh's signs was mounted on the wall above giving the times. The kitchen already held carefully covered plates of biscuits and small cakes and when they moved into the big meeting room they saw the tables set out ready for the afternoon tea they hoped visitors would enjoy.

Outside along the gantries the boats shone in the sun, brass polished, paintwork washed. Any visitors who took a boat ride would see the harbour at its best. Even the patch where the poisoned grass had been dug over looked fairly healthy, like a newly planted garden bed and they could only hope the effect was similar beneath the waters of the harbour.

Work would continue in the two docks. Visitors could see the boat being worked on in the dry dock and witness the comings and goings in the wet dock although they might find the empty cavern there confusing. However the carpenters would be working and the boat owners available to guide visitors if they wished. The edges of the water dimension were not always clearly defined and Marheh was aware that some would be able to see more than others.

They finished the tour back at the Harbour Master's office. Marheh looked at them all. Four Harbour Masters working together, she thought happily and spoke her thought aloud.

"Why don't we go up to the flat and have sperit," she invited. "There will be room to spread a bit there, and then we can sing."

Back on *Day Bringer* after supper and the evening's program she took up her journal.

Tomorrow, she wrote, *the open day is tomorrow. I can't quite believe it really. If only people come. We've all worked so hard to make everything ready it will be really disappointing if they don't. I'm glad we sang. It seemed like a blessing on the time ahead and I'm sure it was good for Leura to feel like one of us. I hope she can go on being an honorary mentor.*

I talked to Teg and Sula and neither of them can remember a time when our neighbours were invited to visit, which means it hasn't happened in living memory. It is quite a scary thought. I'm very aware that if things go wrong it will be my fault. I wonder what Nemle would be saying to me. I hope she would approve, I think she would.

Next week will be quite an anticlimax, except we still have all the financial things to deal with. At least now I've mentioned Chanra's skills to Nisfa. She has been really useful and supportive at the meetings and I'm sure she would make a good Harbour Master. Jik things so too, but I haven't said anything to Bixa. She is pretty preoccupied. I think Beuda is proving to be rather a challenge.

Marheh put down her journal and sighed. She couldn't warm to Beuda and it made her feel guilty, wondering whether she was being influenced by the fact that Bixa was not as available as she had been. She would just have to try a bit harder to be supportive instead of critical. Obviously her plain speaking at the interview had not endeared her to Beuda and she had not made any effort to redress it. Next week she would do better but now it was time for bed.

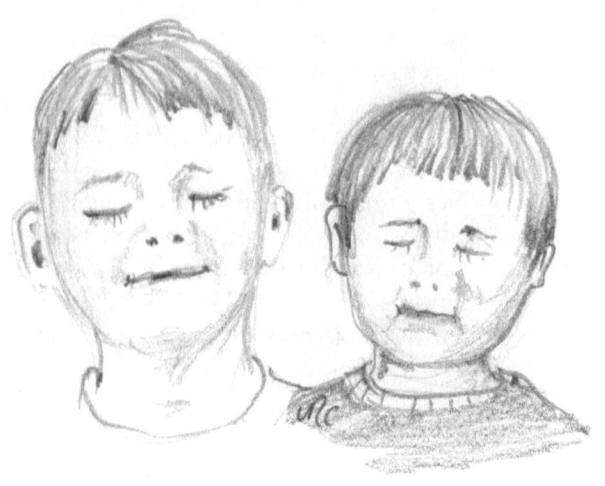

Eyes closed

Chapter Fifteen

Saturday dawned clear and bright, full of promise. Marheh was up very early, anticipating the adventure of the open day. The candle flame that was her portal to the soul song seemed to dance in front of her as she washed and dressed and she spent a few minutes singing before sitting down to her breakfast.

When she had eaten and washed up, sorted her fire and made everything tidy, she did the engine checks and moved *Day Bringer* around to the loading bay. It was too early really, but she was to be the first for the boat rides so it wouldn't matter. No one else was about, but by the time she had finished tying up Kel's tall figure was striding towards her. She looked up, grinning, and he swept her into a hug.

"Do you know what the time is?" he teased as he set her down.

She shook her head.

"Quite early I think."

"Not quite seven o'clock."

She gave a little giggle.

"Oops! I didn't realise."

"I thought perhaps you didn't." Kel's eyes laughed at her although his voice was solemn. "You can't possibly expect a passenger before ten o'clock and there is nothing else you need to do so I think you had better have a second breakfast on *Storm Cloud* with me."

"How do you know it's the second?"

He looked at her and laughed.

"Come on," he said.

He had cooked porridge for them both, making it special by adding honey and cream.

"Sef and Greya must have needed all their patience sometimes when you were a child," he commented as they sat opposite each other at the little table.

Marheh raised her eyebrows and lifted her chin.

"Are you implying that you need patience now?"

He laughed at her again.

"I was just thinking that you probably raised the whole household at four in the morning when it was your birthday."

"Is that a guess, or have you been talking to Mother and Father?"

After breakfast they sang together. Kel's steady rhythm helped Marheh to settle but still allowed her song to dance and, for that, she was grateful.

At nine o'clock she thought she might go to see whether the mail had come. It would be good to get it out of the way before any visitors arrived. She could, at least, get it off the floor in the front hall and sort it in the office, even if there was not time enough to deal with it. The usual letter from Hemera did not come. She was not sure whether to be glad or sorry. What if the omission was a presage of something worse?

At a quarter to ten she shut the office and made her way outside. As she walked towards the entrance she saw several other Silberay out and about. Those who saw her waved cheerfully and she responded happily. Nearing the road she realised that there was a little knot of people standing waiting. Toby and his family were amongst them. She had asked them especially, hoping they would give others confidence to trust themselves to her in order to enter the water dimension. Ellen, from the pub was there too, with her husband. She needed to rack her brain for his name. Luckily it came to her just in time to use it to greet him.

"Dave, Ellen, I'm so glad you came. Meet Toby and Susan, Emily, Jack and Rob." She turned to smile at the others she didn't know. "Come along in all of you. It is near enough to ten o'clock. You are our first visitors."

As they followed her along the drive Jack stepped up beside her.

"Can we go on the boat please?"

"Of course you can. Would you like to do that first? It will only be a short ride today I'm afraid, but perhaps there will be time for a second turn later."

She sensed that Dave and Ellen and the other adults were curious now. Jack's question had been a good introduction.

"Toby and his family have been out on the boat before," she explained, turning to the others. "In fact, they inspired this open day. When they came before though, mine was the only boat in the Harbour, now there are lots."

As they rounded the building Susan stopped to gasp at the shining array, but she was the only visitor who could see them. Marheh remembered how difficult it had been for her at first and stopped to grin at her.

At the loading bay she gathered the visitors around her and began to explain.

"The thing with the water dimension is that only a few see it naturally, some can learn to see it and some never do, but everyone can experience it. Just now, my boat *Day Bringer* is just here at the edge of this terrace, which for us is the loading bay. I would be a bit crowded on board if all of you came at once, but another boat, *Storm Cloud*, is just behind *Day Bringer* ready to take passengers too. The real difficulty is that in order to get on board you will have to trust me and you don't know me so that might be difficult. Luckily Susan can see the water so I'm going to ask her if she would pick up Emily and go onboard and down into the saloon. You will see her disappear into the water dimension."

Faces were sceptical, but Susan picked up Emily and disappeared just as Marheh had said she would. Then she directed their attention towards the further end of the loading bay.

"If you watch, you will see *Storm Cloud*'s owner leave his boat and come to greet you."

As she spoke, Kel came striding towards them. When she had introduced them she told the group that she was just going onboard to check that Susan and Emily were alright. She disappeared to them, just for a minute, then returned.

"I know it is surprising," she told them. "Kel and I find it nearly as surprising to see you intersect with the water dimension unknowingly, but we've had a lifetime to get used to it." She turned to Toby and the boys. "Ready to have some fun?"

"You bet," Jack said and Rob grinned widely.

"Would you like to tell these other people what happens?"

"You have to close your eyes," Jack said importantly. "Then she tells you about the boat and you have to make a picture in your head. Then she holds your hand and tells you where to step. When she says open your eyes, you're there."

"Shall we show them?"

He nodded.

"Me too," Rob said.

"One hand each," Marheh said. "Are you ready with your eyes closed?"

They both turned their faces to show her.

"Good on you. Keep them closed. Make a picture of the boat with the gunnel just in front of you. That's the bit where you step, remember? If you lift one foot and put it down just ahead you might be able to feel it. Can you? Excellent, now take a step, and another one."

They were on board now. She put a hand on a shoulder of each and guided them towards the back steps.

"Remember there are steps now. Feel carefully for each one. Jack, you can go first. Can you do it without me now? You've only one more step."

A moment later both boys were safely on board and hurrying through to find their mother. Marheh went back to the loading bay where Kel and Toby were reassuring the others. She grinned at them.

"Absolutely no pressure," she said. "But I'd love to show you my world?" She looked at Kel. "Obviously I'll take Toby and I've room to take Dave and Ellen if they wish. Are you ready to take any others who want to go?"

"Ready and willing," Kel said, sketching a salute.

He led three of the other visitors along the loading bay to *Storm Cloud*. Two chose to wait and consider. Marheh guided Toby on board and went back for Dave and Ellen.

"Who first?"

"It's crazy," Ellen said.

"It is, isn't it?" Marheh agreed.

Ellen looked at Dave who shrugged.

"Me then," she said.

Marheh took her carefully and left her with Toby in the back cabin then went back for Dave. When they were all on board she guided them through to the saloon, giving them time to take in what they were seeing. Dave was particularly interested in the engine and would have lingered but Ellen was keen to keep moving. Susan and the children were sitting in the well deck so the saloon was not too crowded.

Marheh was aware that it was important not to rush things. Just now there was no pressure of time, but later, perhaps, there might be. She could see it would be much easier if there were two Silberay for each boat, one to explain and remain with the visitors and the other to steer. Would she have time to rearrange the schedule to allow for that, and to make sure everyone involved knew?

After lingering to answer questions and enjoy their amazement she explained that she would go up to the back deck and begin the short ride around the harbour that was all that was possible today. Her visitors were welcome to join her there if they wished but some people preferred to be more enclosed. They could watch through the windows while she loosened the mooring lines and freed *Day Bringer* for her journey.

165

A few minutes later *Day Bringer* set out on a lap of the Harbour. Marheh took her very slowly past the gantries then under the bridge and onto the water road, just getting the stern around before backing up and re-entering the Harbour. As she went under the bridge again she saw Kel leaving the loading dock and recognised *Autumn Wind* moored there with Jik guiding someone on board. It was all happening just as she had hoped. Their neighbours were visiting and getting to know them.

Carefully she steered *Day Bringer* into the space left by *Storm Cloud*'s departure and set about helping her passengers disembark. Already there were others waiting and the happy faces leaving *Day Bringer* were a good advertisement.

"It's like magic," Ellen said. "Hard to believe, but wonderful to see." She looked at Marheh. "I didn't expect the place to feel so ... so beneficent."

"I'm glad you felt it. Part of our work is trying to keep it feeling that way."

She smiled at them all.

"Have a wander around. Toby might show you the dry dock if you're interested. Have a tour perhaps. The guide will tell you more about us and our work."

She smiled farewell and turned to the waiting group and began her explanation again.

By the time she had finished her third trip it was nearly midday and she was feeling rather tired. It was the end of her shift. As she moved *Day Bringer* back to the gantry where she lived Sampi brought *Cloud Drift* in to take her place. Once she had moored and was walking back along the gantry she had time to look around and realise that there were a lot more visitors now. They were lucky in the weather and the day was perfect for wandering and talking as well as enjoying the novelty of the boats. She stepped out more quickly, wanting to be visible so she could continue to make people welcome. She had a couple of hours free now before her stint as tour guide began.

Passing the dry dock she could see four or five visitors peering down at the two apprentices who were blacking the hull. Luff was standing with the spectators explaining what was happening. In the wet dock it was quieter. The two boats being worked on were not visible to the visitors, but Lidy was standing by ready to pass things to the carpenters who were still working on *Evening Star.* Marheh went in to greet her and heard that she had been able to escort a couple of interested visitors on and off.

Out in the sun again she almost danced along the loading dock, smiling at the little groups who were waiting there. Nisfa and Sampi were heading off on their first trip and the passengers who had just disembarked from *Storm Cloud* were busy exclaiming and reassuring those waiting. Kel gave

Marheh a grin and headed back to his mooring as *Autumn Wind* arrived with Dom at the tiller and Peli brought in Afternoon Light to replace *Storm Cloud*. It was not just the visitors who were enjoying themselves, the Silberay were too.

She had just rounded the building and was heading along the drive when she saw Glik running towards her. After his initial cool reaction, Whin had warmed to the open day and was taking a shift at the entrance, welcoming and explaining.

"Can you come?" Glik was panting a little when he reached her. "There are some people at the entrance trying to stop the visitors."

"Of course."

She started to jog with him. Whin would be polite, too polite probably, and his skills with the discipline of the mind had only developed for defence and then only in a limited way. She had a feeling she knew who the protesters would be and, sure enough, it was the cult leader and five of his followers. She looked at the other people, those wanting to visit and smiled at them.

"These people are from The Holy Temple of Light," she explained. "They have fairly extreme views. You might have heard of them. Please go in and make up your own mind."

"Are you really a witch?" one of them asked, responding to the chant that was beginning as the cult leader recognised her.

Marheh shook her head.

"Of course not."

She moved out onto the footpath, stepping between the two groups.

"If you would like to go in I'm sure Glik here will go with you and show you where things are."

Most of the bystanders trickled in and headed down the drive with Glik. Whin fell into conversation with the last couple and strolled away with them. Marheh suddenly found herself alone with a hostile group of men. A moment later she was surrounded.

"Why don't you go in too," she said, trying for lightness. "See for yourselves that there is no magic involved, just a different way of seeing."

She might have been speaking to the stones on the road or the concrete slabs that made up the footpath. The chant continued, low and menacing. She had turned their thoughts before, she thought, standing straighter and trying to focus. Then she felt herself seized from behind.

"Don't touch me," her mind snapped into his.

He sprang away as if burned then shouted.

"She magicked me."

"No"

She spun around, no chance of subtlety now. Someone else grabbed at her and she turned towards him.

Her mind, heightened and alert, was about to respond with a command when an anguished cry reached her from another mind. Bixa was fighting for her life. Forgetting herself Marheh sent her mind to support her. Jik was there too, she found, and both were in combat with several Yareblis minds intent on breaking them. They were struggling, both better at defence than attack.

Yareblis, at the Harbour, how dare they!

A moment for these thoughts to feed her passion and she was there in the midst of it.

Brightness flew around her, flashing like forked lightning. One of the Yareblis minds retreated as if burned but another dodged and struck at her, fire against light. Behind her Jik seemed to rally, but Bixa still struggled and Marheh understood she was shielding another mind.

Without conscious thought she spun around them, enclosing them in a miniature whirlwind that repelled the darts of their attackers. Her whirlwind shrieked around them then raced towards the Yareblis, snatching at the minds and tossing them like blown leaves. A wall rose before her then, rock-like, impervious. The wind whisked upwards then fell like snow, a thick, smothering blanket of cold. The wall crumbled and began to burn but the snow became an icy torrent washing away the embers.

Washing, washing, and the power diminishing, the illusion fading. Who was she now? Not the invisible wind or the melting snow. Lost. Where am I? Lost. Echoing emptiness that waited for her to dissolve into nothing. Who am I? Then a mind she knew, calling her, orienting her, enabling her to consolidate and rebuild.

"I am Marheh."

It was enough. The battle was done and the enemy fled. Kel.

.....

"We're supposed to take off her clothes so he can search her for witch marks."

A woman's voice, sounding troubled, roused Marheh from the exhausted sleep that followed the exercise of her mind's extraordinary power.

"Witch marks! What are they?" another woman's voice asked.

Marheh gave a little sighing breath and tried to ease herself back into sleep. What had witch marks to do with her?

"Helios has been reading about how to identify witches. The devil has branded them. You have to search for the marks."

The woman began to tug at Marheh's tunic, trying to pull it up and over her head. She roused a little, weary and disoriented.

"He said she was in a trance, bewitching the men, but it just looks like sleep to me."

There was the sound of a door and another woman spoke sharply.

"Get on with it. Helios is waiting."

"It doesn't seem right. What if she isn't a witch and we've let the men see her without her clothes on."

"Of course she's a witch. Just get on with it."

"Yes Hemera."

Hemera. The word pierced Marheh's sleepy daze. Hemera. Hemera was a woman! Hemera was here. Where was she? She blinked and struggled to sit, but hands pushed her down and something soft was pulled over her head.

"She's awake. What if she magicks us?"

"Helios is protecting us."

Marheh tried again to sit up, struggled to understand what was happening to her.

"Please," she said, trying to shake off the hands. "Please," she repeated, pulling at the fabric that covered her eyes.

Her tunic was whisked away and she saw that she was enclosed in a very small room with three women, one on either side of the narrow bench where she lay and one at her feet. One of them was already reaching for the buttons on her shirt.

"Don't do that!"

She grabbed at the edges of her shirt, tried to swing her legs off the bench and get up, but the woman at her feet leaned heavily on her ankles and a second woman pulled at her arms. If only she could get her mind to focus. Where was she? How did she get here? Her mind had been engaged hadn't it? Someone had needed her. Bixa had needed her. Memory of the battle nudged. Whin had left her with... with... Bixa had been hurting. She had sent her mind to Bixa but where had she been? Who had defended her body while her mind was engaged?

As memory returned fear came with it. No one had been there to defend her body and now she was here with Hemera.

. . ...

At the Harbour the carefully planned order of the open day had begun to come unravelled. Jik and Marheh had been the first to respond to Bixa's need, but many of the other Silberay had reacted to the Yareblis threat, some by entering the soul song, others by ensuring their own defences were in place. Only Jik and Kel and Jik's apprentice, Dom, had previously experienced the extraordinary nature of Marheh's intervention and its power was confronting to some.

Silberay attention was no longer solely upon their visitors, who found themselves suddenly abandoned. Only those actually on a boat were unaffected since the boats offered a degree of protection to their owners, enabling them to continue as planned.

Jik and Kel, who knew how Marheh's illusion would act on the Yareblis, were quick to take the opportunity to excise the water dimension from the minds of the two or three dazed Yareblis who were still at the Harbour, but they were aware that the Yareblis attack had come from at least half a dozen, perhaps even double that, who had recovered enough to flee.

Bixa, having risked her mind in order to protect her apprentice, was still shaken and in a degree of discomfort, but she, more than anyone, knew what she owned to Marheh. As soon as she could she began to look for her, to thank her and assure her of her wellbeing. It was not until she had failed to find her on *Day Bringer* or in the office or anywhere in between, that she began to feel concerned.

Soon she was asking anyone she met if they had seen her. No one had, but everyone had an opinion about her, amazed, discomforted, concerned, even angry or affronted. It was all her fault, seemed to be the consensus, but they did want to find her and she was nowhere to be seen.

It was Glik who told how she had gone with him to the entrance at Whin's request, how she had encouraged a group of visitors to enter, despite the words of a group of protesters and suggested he show them around.

"Protesters?" Glik was asked.

"Something about witches and magic," he replied.

Bixa looked at him, horrified.

"And she was alone with them?"

"I think so. It was a bit confusing, but I think Whin came behind me with a couple of visitors."

She looked at Whin, who nodded a bit uncomfortably.

"She seemed to be dealing with the protesters."

"But not when she sent her mind to defend me," Bixa said.

She looked around the group of Silberay, but realised that most of them knew nothing of the cult or the letters from Hemera.

"We have to find her."

"Marheh can look after herself," Whin said, and a couple of others nodded their agreement.

"She's had letters," Bixa said. "Threats, from someone accusing her of witchcraft."

She whirled around, then remembered Beuda. She was her responsibility and she was still looking dazed and confused. Rapidly she scanned the faces.

"Juni," she said, seeing the old woman on the edge of the group. She looked sympathetic and strong enough. "Will you?" she asked, indicating her apprentice.

A moment later Juni had taken the girl's hand and begun to speak quietly. Bixa began to run towards the entrance to where Marheh had been last seen.

…..

The woman, Hemera, continued to lean on Marheh's ankles as the other two attempted to remove her shirt. Marheh was holding herself together with difficulty, trying to gather enough strength to use her mind to suggest they stop. She thought perhaps one of the women was uncomfortable about the actions she was taking and wanted to build on that if she could. If she had to resort to mind control it would only confirm their opinion of her and she was so weary from her battle with the Yareblis that she was not even sure whether she could.

She wrapped her arms across her body, trying to keep them from taking her shirt, but Hemera reached forward and slapped her and the other women used the surprise of it to strip the shirt away. She was angry as well as frightened now and the anger was driving out the fear for the moment. Abruptly she pulled her knees up to her chest, taking Hemera by surprise so that she let go her hold. The other two women were still occupied with her shirt and she was able to swing around and propel herself off the bench then turn swiftly to face them.

Hemera opened her mouth to shout for help, but Marheh gathered herself and sent a control to stop her, aware that if once the men were admitted she would be overwhelmed. Here and now was her best chance of escape and there was little point in saving her strength.

With Hemera frozen in place, the other two women backed away from her fearfully. She reached out her hands and spoke gently, unaware of how startling she looked to them, her midriff bare between her trousers and her very plain cotton bra, her arms and shoulders, slim and pale, but revealed to be strong and well muscled from her years of operating locks and her stance poised and ready for action.

"Please don't be frightened," she said. "I don't understand why you are treating me like this. I've never hurt you."

"Helios says you've slept with the devil."

"Helios is wrong." She looked from one to the other. "What have I done to injure you?" she asked.

The women glanced at each other then turned back to her.

"You magicked her son," one of them said. "And now he sees things that aren't there."

"But they are there. I could show them to you too if you like."

Was she getting through to them? Could she persuade them to give her back her tunic and shirt and let her go?

"Helios made his father give him a purge to get rid of the evil. He was so sick, but the evil isn't gone and he's such a little boy."

171

"But why is it evil, just to see differently? The poor little boy, he was so happy and good on the boat."

"But there was no boat," the boy's mother shouted. "And now... now." She began to cry.

Marheh started towards her then swung around as the door behind Hemera burst open.

"What's going on? Why isn't she ready?"

It was the cult leader flanked by several other men. Marheh eyed them warily. She had been able to turn the thoughts of some of the men at their previous encounter but now her mind's strength was still recovering and here on what she supposed was their own ground it would not be so easy.

Hemera was still frozen in place. Her back was to the door so Marheh hoped that her unnatural stillness would pass unnoticed. The threats in her letters took on new power here in her presence and Marheh was almost more afraid of her than of the men who stood staring at her from the doorway.

Without taking her eyes off them, she sent a little request to one of the women, who put her shirt in her outstretched hand.

"This absurdity has gone far enough," she said quietly, trying for words to convince them. "The police have seen the letters Hemera sent. If anything happens to me they will know where to look."

The cult leader drew himself up.

"Helios is above the law and you are outside it."

He took a step towards her, his companions crowding in behind him. One of the women gave a little gasping sob.

"No one is above the law, or outside it."

Marheh held herself steady with difficulty. Taking even a small step back might be enough to encourage them to attack her, but the little room was very crowded now and filled with menace.

She doubted she could talk her way to freedom, but she had to try and every minute gained would give the Silberay time to discover her gone. Bixa knew about the letters and Whin had seen the protesters. Surely they would make the connection.

"You call me a witch," she said carefully. "You believe it, why do you need to prove it?"

"Witches are the devil's whores," Helios spat at her. "We will find his brand on you and cut it out." His face changed. His eyes became sly. "If you confess and repent it will be easier for you."

"Confess what? Repent how?"

"Admit you have slept with the devil, demonstrate your repentance by accepting punishment."

"And if I were to confess?" Marheh asked, still careful. "If I were to repent?"

"You would demonstrate your repentance by requesting punishment."

Some of the faces became avid, but there was, again, a muffled sob from one of the women.

"And what would that be?"

Every word was considered. She must do nothing to provoke them to action. The man, Helios, was watching her, assessing her with his eyes.

"You would be stripped and your devil's mark displayed to the assembly," he said.

It seemed to Marheh that he relished the thought.

"Then you would be whipped until the devil leaves you."

She must not show fear, not for an instant. They would recognise her vulnerability then. Very deliberately, without taking her eyes off the man, she moved so that she could shrug one arm into the sleeve of her shirt. Another, careful swing of the other arm and she had it around her shoulders. Then she was wearing it.

"And if I don't repent?" she asked. "What then?"

In the Holy Temple of Light

Chapter Sixteen

At the entrance to the Harbour Bixa stopped, gasping for breath and scanning the road. There was a couple a little distance away, strolling towards the Harbour and, from the other direction, a man and a woman with a toddler and a pram approached. No sign of Marheh though or any protesters. She took a couple of steps in the direction of Sefton Middle and then a couple more. Marheh would not have left the Harbour of her own accord, not with all the activity of the open day, not with the threat from the Yareblis.

She was anxiously looking around for any signs when a woman eased herself out of a hiding place beneath some shrubbery.

"Are you… are you looking for someone?" she asked.

Bixa swung round eagerly and the woman took a step back. Recognising that she was afraid, Bixa tried to be calm.

"I'm worried about my friend. She's disappeared."

The woman nodded.

"There were men chanting," she said. "I was frightened so I hid. I couldn't make out what they were saying, something about witches."

She paused. Bixa thought she was still shocked and frightened.

"They took the woman. She was talking, welcoming people, then all of a sudden she was still, very still. The leader of the men walked around her and she didn't move. He said something and three of the other men picked her up and she still didn't move. They took her with them."

It must have been Marheh. Bixa went to the woman and put an arm around her.

"You've had a shock. Will you come in with me and have a cup of tea? I'll need you to help me find my friend."

It was all Bixa could do to remain calm and encouraging but she knew she could not act alone. Jik and Kel would be her best hope, but she needed the woman to tell her story to any Silberay who were about, and she knew the woman needed nurturing too.

The woman raised her eyes to scan Bixa's face then seemed to make up her mind. She nodded and allowed Bixa to guide her towards the entrance. Having overcome her fear it seemed she needed to talk.

"She was dressed like you, your friend, but she had a long plait... "

All the way down the drive she went over what she had seen, telling Bixa how Marheh had arrived with a young man, how she had encouraged people to go in with him and the other man.

"I wanted to go in too," she finished. "But I was scared."

"It's lucky for my friend that you stayed to see what happened to her," Bixa said, guiding the woman into the building.

Luff was at the door with his apprentice.

"Marheh's in danger. Can you and Onn round up some help, Jik and Kel, anyone else? I'll be in the meeting room with this lady. She saw what happened." Find Whin too, if you can."

It seemed to Bixa to take far too long for Jik, Kel and Whin to join her. They did not come alone. Nisfa arrived with Sampi and Tippa and Pon hurried in with Toby. He had been chatting with them when Onn told them about Marheh. Dom came from the kitchen with tea and scones for the woman whose name, Bixa had discovered, was Violet. She told her story, a bit shy at first, but gaining confidence as her listeners encouraged her with kind words and gentle questions.

"The policeman told us the cult was called the Holy Temple of Light," Bixa said. "I saw some of the letters she received. They were horrible."

"That's the lot Rob's little friend's parents belong to," Toby said. "They won't let Rob play with him any more."

"I'm afraid for her if they've taken her," Bixa said.

"Surely Marheh can take care of herself. She's very strong," Whin said.

"Not after what she did for me," Bixa said, anxious at the time they were taking. "She will have exhausted herself. Kel, Jik, I think it's urgent we find her."

Toby looked around at the Silberay.

"I do too. They're weird that lot." He turned to Jik, whom he had met.

"I brought Susan and the kids in the car today. I could take a couple of you to the place where they meet if you think it worthwhile."

.....

Marheh was beginning to feel her mind strengthening, but she still hesitated to use it to place a control, knowing it would only confirm their opinion of her. Helios had not yet realised that she had controlled Hemera, but it would not be long. She watched and waited warily for an answer to her question. Keeping him talking was her best hope.

"We will search until we find your devil's mark," he said, and she understood he was enjoying what he saw as his power over her. "And it will be cut out of you."

She remembered Hemera's threat of evisceration and took an involuntary step backwards then wished she hadn't as he moved towards her, bumping into Hemera, still frozen in place.

"What have you done to her?" he shouted, thrusting forward angrily.

"Nothing," Marheh said, backing away.

Her back was against the wall now and there was nowhere she could go. Her mind reacted almost without her willing it. Helios stopped in his tracks, frozen mid stride. The men behind him stopped too and stared at Marheh fearfully.

"What have you done to him?" the boldest one accused her.

"I've stopped him from hurting me," Marheh said. "That's all."

The wall behind her was a support as well as a trap. She looked at the people around her. The two women were closest to her and she no longer felt any threat from them. One of them, she saw, was quietly weeping, but she had nothing now with which to comfort her. Hemera and Helios, both standing in place, frozen by her commands, formed a kind of barrier. The half dozen other men seemed reluctant to pass them, but she doubted that would last, already the boldest one was edging closer.

Taking a deep breath and forcing herself to relax the tension in her arms and shoulders she stepped away from the wall and spoke gently.

"I'm sorry you have been taught to fear me," she said. "I don't bear you any ill will. Helios accused me of being many things. I am none of them."

She paused, watching the faces for any sign that she had reached them.

"What I have done to your leaders was done in self defence and will not harm them. When I am safe I will reverse it."

She thought perhaps one or two of the men might be softening, but not those closest to her.

"I know you call this the Holy Temple of Light, but your hatred makes it seem very dark to me."

Words would not keep them back much longer, she thought. She might perhaps have strength for one more control, but if they were to injure her she may not be able to sustain any of them.

"May I have my tunic please," she said to the woman nearest her. "I'd like to leave now."

The woman jumped as if stung and bent to pick up the tunic from the floor and hand it to her. It was burnt orange, one of her favourites, flame-like against her white shirt. She held it over one arm and took a step forward, then another.

The two women edged back behind her, but no one else moved. She paused for a moment then continued until she was standing just an arm's length from Hemera and Helios. She looked past them to the group of men then back to the two still figures. Whatever she said or did they were unlikely to believe her now when she said she was not a witch. How could they be so closed to something, someone, they did not understand?

Her attention had not moved from the other men for more than a minute, but it was long enough for the two nearest her to act. One lunged at her from between Hemera and Helios while the other went around them to grab her arm, twist it behind her back and pull her against him.

There was a moment of panic when she reached for strength to use her mind, but then she clamped it down and forced herself not to react. Instead she allowed the man to push her ahead of him towards the door. Wait, she cautioned herself, you'll have more chance out there.

Out there was the place where they held their ceremonies she decided. It was about half the size of the big meeting room at the Harbour but it held tiered seating on three sides focusing on the fourth side where an enormous painted sun looked down on a gilded table with a lighted candle at each end. The clear space in the centre held another table, sturdy and plain, with some pieces of rope lying on it. The man was propelling her towards it and she realised suddenly that it had been prepared for her.

The recognition broke her careful self control. With the last of her mind's strength she stopped her captor then wrenched herself clear of him and raced for the only other door she could see. She reached it first and grabbed for the handle, grabbed and twisted fruitlessly, then turned to face the men. Now that she was trapped it seemed they all needed to assert their power over her and many hands gripped as she struggled to free herself. They were taking her to the table and once there ... In desperation she tried again to strike with her mind, but she had no more strength.

Furiously she struggled as she was half carried, half dragged across the room. For a moment she allowed herself to become limp then twisted and writhed again. The shirt she had not had a chance to button was torn from her and the sight of her skin seemed to encourage more rough treatment, more gleeful grasping hands.

They dumped her on the table and held her down. Terror lent her strength and she kicked and punched, scratched, even bit if she could, but she knew she was losing. They had managed to secure a rope around one of her ankles and were attempting to fasten it around one leg of the table when suddenly all action stopped and she was flailing at nothing.

A little sob of thankfulness and Kel was holding her. Trembling with reaction she leant against him while Jik bent to untie the rope and Tippa picked up her shirt and tunic from the floor where they had been discarded. Then she saw Whin standing by as if on guard and finally Toby, who seemed to be scolding the two women who had emerged from the little room.

All the followers of Helios had been controlled and stood around her frozen in place by the commands of the Silberay. Kel felt her shudder as she looked at them, faces still distorted by hatred. She turned her face against his chest for a few moments then looked again at each one, wondering what animated them.

Tippa approached then and held out her shirt.

"Attention seeking again," she said lightly.

"Shocking isn't it," Marheh agreed, attempting to match her tone.

She couldn't seem to move to take the shirt, so Tippa shook it out and threaded one arm into the appropriate sleeve. Kel took over then and finished dressing her, buttoning her shirt while Tippa waited ready with the tunic, then pulling that over her head and straightening it neatly.

All she wanted was to remain in the comfort of Kel's arms and she knew no one would blame her if she stayed there, but nothing was ended, not really. Toby, she thought, looking at him, hovering at a little distance with the two women. Toby had overcome his fear of her to become a friend and he was here. She lifted her head to smile across at him.

"Toby brought us in his car," Jik said quietly. "We would not have been in time without him."

He was approaching her now, with one of the women who obviously needed a little urging.

"This is Jan," he said. "Timmy's mother. You met Timmy. He's Rob's best friend."

"Hello Jan, Marheh said gravely. "You must be very proud of Timmy. He was a very good guest. I'm sorry his outing caused you so much trouble."

"Toby said, Toby said..." Jan was having trouble meeting Marheh's eyes.

"Toby used to think I was evil," Marheh said. "But now we are friends. I'm sure you can trust Toby."

Jan looked at her then.

"I've known Toby and Susan for ages. I would have done better to listen to them than to Helios, but my husband..."

"Aaron has got rather carried away by Helios and his ideas," Toby said bluntly, when it was clear that Jan did not know how to finish. "But I think I can straighten him out now. It will have given him a shock, how he was acting. That Helios has a lot to answer for."

All of them, Marheh thought, all of them will have to be released, but they will be even more fearful, more full of hatred than before. She felt Kel's protective arm tighten a little around her.

"I think Marheh has had nearly as much as she can take," he said.

She shook her head.

"I'm alright."

It was a lie and they all knew it, but they needed to believe it for the moment at least.

"Why don't we release Aaron," Jik said. "So Jan and Toby can talk to him. That will be a beginning."

Toby pointed him and out and Tippa entered his mind since she had been the one to place the control. He completed the action that he had begun before the command then swung around to take in the silently watching Silberay and the unnaturally still figures of the other followers of Helios.

"What... what..."

Anger and fear showed on his face.

"Aaron." Jan took a tentative step towards him. "Aaron."

Dealing with the members of the Temple of Light was not straight forward. Aaron, who at least had wife and friend standing by, nevertheless took some time before he would even deign to listen to their persuasions. He continued to look at Marheh with dislike though he seemed less perturbed by Jik and Kel. He brushed off his wife's concerns rather brusquely and listened to Toby as if on sufferance until Toby told him that he had witnessed what they had been doing to Marheh and made it very clear that he could be prosecuted for his actions.

It all seemed to take forever, but it was no good just leaving the controls to dissipate or just releasing them from a distance. That would not change anything, and change was what was important for the Silberay. Marheh had to be there. She had been the focus of their hatred and fear and must be the focus of their repentance, if any real turning around was to be achieved.

With two or three of the men it was not so difficult. Helios had manipulated them, not like the Yareblis, with a control, but by exploiting their feelings, and with the cessation of action had come the chance to take stock and realise they were glad to have been stopped. The other woman's husband put it into words for all of them when he apologised to Marheh.

"I'm ashamed that he made me think what we were doing was right and good," he said. "I can't believe I was so taken in."

Marheh listened gravely and did her best to respond compassionately. She was dreading the moment when she must release Helios and Hemera.

They were unlikely to be in any way repentant and their hatred of her would only be intensified by the discovery that they had lost at least some of their followers.

Jik would have spared her the confrontation, suggesting that she release them from a distance, but that seemed to her to be a coward's way out. When all the followers had been released and sent on their way she went, with Kel and Jik on either side to support her, back into the little room where Helios and Hemera still stood.

She released Helios first. He was facing away from the three Silberay, but he obviously sensed their presence behind him for he swung around to confront them, stepping back hastily when he realised how Marheh was guarded.

When he felt himself to be at a safe distance he drew himself up importantly.

"She's damned, and so are you if you consort with the devil's whore."

The three Silberay said nothing, just stood looking gravely at him.

"What have you done to Hemera?" he said then, noticing his wife's stillness.

No one answered him, but Marheh eased into Hemera's mind and removed the control. She too spun around to face them then spat at Marheh. Kel took one step towards her and she stepped back but the look of hatred on her face did not alter.

Marheh reached out to touch Kel and he took her hand. Another moment of silence then she spoke slowly, thinking through the words.

"The Holy Temple of Light," she said. "But there is no holiness in hatred, nor any light."

She looked from Hemera to Helios but there was no comprehension in either of them and she turned and let Kel and Jik take her away.

Outside Toby was waiting for them.

"I think we can all squash in," he said, opening the back door of the car.

Tippa was already sitting in the furthest corner making herself small.

"Marheh can sit on my lap," Kel said.

It was not a very long journey back to the Harbour, but long enough for Marheh to begin to collect herself and turn her thoughts to other matters like Bixa and the open day.

"Bixa is fine," Jik reassured her. "You drove off the Yareblis and gave me and Kel the chance to disable a few of them, and Nisfa is well in control of the open day. You've done enough."

She closed here eyes then, suddenly aware of how exhausted she was. By the time they reached the Harbour she was asleep.

Toby drove them all the way to the front door of the administration building. There were still visitors about enjoying the late afternoon sunshine, but it was clear that the Silberay had been on the look out for the return of the car.

Bixa reached it first in time to hug Marheh as she extricated herself from the back seat. She was a bit disoriented from sleeping and glad to cling to her for a few moments. When she looked up again she seemed to be surrounded by Silberay. Then she saw Nisfa, pushing her way through from the back.

"Well," she said as the Silberay parted to let her pass. "That was quite a display. I'll be interested to know how you did it."

It took Marheh a moment to realise that she was referring to the illusion that had scattered the Yareblis. She opened her mouth to try to respond but it was all too difficult.

"But the interrogation can wait," Nisfa continued.

Marheh stood feeling dumb and confused under her scrutiny.

"You look like last week's leftovers." She nodded to Jik and Kel. "You'd best take her and put her to bed."

Marheh staggered a little and clutched Kel's arm. How had she suddenly become a troublesome ten year old?

Nisfa turned to the group that surrounded them and waved her stick at them.

"Leave her be. You can see she's back in one piece. Go and look after our visitors."

A hysterical giggle threatened, but she managed to repress it. The Silberay did as they were told, but not without acknowledging Marheh with a word or a smile. Then, with Jik and Kel supporting her on either side, she made her way down to the moorings and onto *Day Bringer*.

The last hour of the open day passed without her and so did the hour or two of cleaning up after the visitors had left. Perhaps she would have slept until morning, but Kel was aware that she had not eaten since breakfast and took food for them both onto *Day Bringer*. He didn't try to wake her, but moved quietly around the boat bringing in coal, making up the fire, heating the thick vegetable casserole.

She was just stirring when he went in to her. The smell of the food wafted through from the galley and he saw her recognise it, and him. She pushed back the blanket he had put over her and let him help her to stand. She was still dressed, but he had taken off her boots and now she felt for her slippers. He put his arms around her for a few moments then led her through to the food.

Even after she had eaten Kel thought she still looked wan and listless. He insisted she return to bed and let him clear up. He couldn't help worrying about her as he washed up the few dishes they had used. She needed some space and some peace to restore herself. At least the Silberay had experienced something of her strength and her gift now, so perhaps they would not be so critical of her. He let himself out through Marheh's workspace so as not to disturb her. She would not get space or peace here at the Harbour, but how to persuade her that it would be alright to go off for a day or two, that she would not be neglecting her duties.

He set off for *Storm Cloud* still thinking then smiled to himself and changed direction. Nisfa could help and he would talk over his idea with Jik.

Next morning Marheh dragged herself out of bed soon after seven and headed for the office. She had not slept well although she was so tired, but there must be things to attend to after yesterday. There were several letters that she had not had time to open, she remembered, and things to plan for the week ahead. Now that the open day was behind her she could concentrate on the financial problems. There seemed to be quite a bit of coming and going already, but she closed the door against the noise and tried to concentrate. If anyone wanted her they could knock.

She had been working for perhaps half an hour when the door opened without warning and Jik and Kel stood there.

"Will you come with us Marheh please?" Jik said gravely.

She stood up a bit too quickly and steadied herself by holding the back of her chair.

"What's wrong?"

Kel smiled at her.

"Nothing is wrong. Come along."

They walked on either side of her along to the big meeting room which was full of Silberay. Nisfa beckoned from the dais. She was not smiling. Marheh looked uncertainly from Kel to Jik. She felt a bit like a prisoner with a guard on either side. Nisfa was speaking as she approached the dais, still with her two escorts, but she was finding it difficult to concentrate on what was being said.

"And so Marheh," Nisfa's voice sounded stern. "We feel that the only recourse we have is to sentence you to banishment."

Banishment, what did she mean? What had she done that called for banishment? Then she saw smiles and kind looks and understood as Nisfa continued speaking.

"For forty eight hours you must take *Day Bringer* and leave the Harbour. Kel and Jik will make sure that you have all you need and the rest of us will proceed to the loading dock to watch you go."

Forty eight hours, alone on *Day Bringer*, out on the water road, released, after all those weeks and months confined to the office and to duty. She tried to smile, she was smiling, but happy tears ran down her cheeks and dripped off her chin.

The Rook Tree

Chapter Seventeen

Late that afternoon Marheh eased back the throttle and nosed *Day Bringer* into the bank to moor opposite the Rook Tree. The familiar actions had returned as if she had never had the long break, yet there was a new joy in them too.

She had startled herself and worried Jik and Kel by breaking down completely when she reached *Day Bringer* but by the time Jik had emptied her toilet cassette and Kel had filled her water tank she had pulled herself together, washed her face and begun the engine checks. Kel brought her a bag of coal and Jik gave her a casserole and a loaf of bread that Dom had prepared for her.

There were a few more tears as she loosed *Day Bringer*'s lines and moved slowly out under the bridge and into the water road. The Silberay were grouped around the loading dock waving as she went by and still watching as she turned for a last look.

She had been along this section of the water road many times before but somehow today it was all new, even though it held so many memories. The Great Northern. Here she passed the entrance to the WEG where she and Nemle had waited for *Storm Cloud* before continuing to Clanning. Here was the first stage of the journey to Deerford and the pottery.

The Rook Tree was about the furthest point comfortably reached from the Harbour in a day's boating. She and Nemle had usually taken two days over it unless there was a particular reason to hurry. She was always reminded of Nemle when she moored there. They had so often sat together in the well deck after supper watching the rooks fly home and talking quietly together about the new route they had been given, or the new task.

Now she made herself sperit and cut a slice of Dom's loaf and took them out with her journal to sit in the silence and watch and listen and let the peace speak to her in Nemle's voice. Daughter of my heart, Nemle had called her and she could almost feel the feather touch of her hand on her cheek and hear the loving tone of her words.

The Rook Tree stood alone at a little distance across a wide field. It was tall and spreading and she could see the bones of it beneath the haze of soft green that was the new spring growth. No doubt Nemle had told her what type of tree it was, but to her it was always the Rook Tree, one of a kind.

The field was bounded by a small wood that she had just passed and a hedge dividing it from another field just ahead. In the far distance she realised she could see a couple of chimneys as well as the scattering of trees she was used to. Everywhere, it seemed, places were changing, town and villages encroaching on the land she loved. Change and its impact, that was what she had been dealing with these last three months. It couldn't be stopped, not really, shouldn't be stopped, but directed towards growth not the reverse. Had she helped? It was all she had wanted to do really.

The day had been fine, with the gentle sun of early spring lifting her spirits and a soft breeze taking the songs she had sung as she steered and distributing them in the places she had passed. Now though, clouds were coming in as the wind got up. The sun's rays painted golden shafts across the stripes of grey and she shivered a little. This magnificence was unchanging. It had the power to restore her.

Her sperit was ignored, Dom's good bread neglected as she gave herself to contemplation and then, inevitably, to her beckoning portal and the soul song.

Some time later a few spats of rain brought her back from the song. The last rays of the setting sun caught the Rook Tree and cast long shadows across the field. The birds were all home now, she thought, then saw one lone black shape, like an arrow, flashing across the sky. A noisy greeting reached her from within the tree and she smiled as she gathered up her bits and pieces. There was more rain coming. Time to go in.

Quietly she moved around the boat, making up the fire, lighting her lamp, warming up some of Dom's casserole, checking the windows against the rain. It was a steady downpour now and the sound and sight of it against *Day Bringer*'s sturdy sides made her feel safe and enclosed. After she had eaten she picked up her journal.

What a gift they have given me. When Nisfa said I was banished I couldn't understand at first. Banished is such a strong and lonely word, but it was solitude I needed. I think Kel must have been behind it. He knew I wouldn't, couldn't, just take a day off, not during the Gathering, but now I've had one I realise how much I've needed it. The battle with the Yareblis and the encounter with the Holy Temple of Light were the last straw. I think I have been just holding myself together for some time now despite all the help I've been given. I know tears have come too easily and I've struggled for patience and the ability to listen sympathetically.

She put down her pen and gazed at the gently flickering flames she could see through the glass front of her fire. The last three months comprised the longest time she had been land based since she joined the Silberay thirty two years ago and she had not realised just how imprisoned she had felt until now when she was free again.

Free, she wrote, *that is how I feel, though of course I must return. I choose to return. It's as Nemle wrote to me when she retired, 'Freedom is only ever freedom to choose the path you follow, the challenge you accept'. I'm pretty sure that my job is not quite finished. It isn't just that the Gathering is not over. I will need to be sure that the Harbour is safe from the Yareblis. Jik and Kel told me they could not disable all who felt themselves invited.*

She put her journal away then, but continued to sit watching the fire and listening to the rain until a big yawn took her by surprise and she made her way to bed.

Next morning she woke with the sun, but lay drowsing for a while watching the reflected light dancing on the ceiling and thinking about the day ahead, a whole day, all to herself. She would go on for a bit, to the next turning place, or perhaps the one after, then make her way back to the entrance to the WEG to moor for the night. It was close enough to the Harbour that she could get up very early the next morning and be back in a couple of hours.

The sky was overcast and the breeze chilly, but she dressed warmly and revelled in the feeling that she was part of the landscape. It was tempting to go on and on along the Great Northern but she stuck to her plan and turned after about an hour. If she got back to the WEG in good time she could perhaps take a walk if she felt like it. If she felt like it. How long had it been since she had been able to think that?

Day Bringer throbbed beneath her and she thought the boat felt free too. We'll be back doing our proper job soon, she promised her, and wondered what route the mentors would assign her. They would be allocating routes this week. It would be nice if her route included Deerford, but she would be content with what she was given as long as there was a route.

What else would she find when she got back. No doubt Nisfa would catechize her about the illusion she had created to defeat the Yareblis. Perhaps she would not be the only one. Not many of the Silberay had known of her ability and fewer still had experienced it. It was not something she wanted to speak of, it made her too different. The power had frightened her when she first discovered it, but Nemle had impressed upon her the knowledge that with power came responsibility and she had practised making illusions so that she could respond when needed. Never before had she been needed at the Harbour though. Now that it had happened all the Silberay would have experienced it to some extent.

She made a face then shrugged inwardly. She would put it behind her. She might be a nine days wonder, but they would soon forget. Actually, she thought, grinning a little, there would only be six days left for her to be a wonder. The Gathering would be over six days from tomorrow. It would be foolish to waste this day of freedom with thoughts of the Gathering and her responsibilities at the Harbour. Her proper job was to listen to the landscape, and that is what she would do.

The listening, the experiencing had enriched her and the land through which she passed and by the time she reached her planned mooring she felt as if she had been washed with light. No matter that the weather had not improved and she had been washed with rain at times. She felt alive in a way she had not felt since the attack at Egerinton.

She moored just past the entrance to the WEG and made herself a late lunch with a couple of slices of Dom's bread and some cheese. It would have been nice to eat in the well deck, but sitting at her little table gave her something of the same view. This section of the water road was wider than usual to accommodate the sharp turn into the WEG and the expanse of water was home to ducks, swans and moor hens. She had often seen a kingfisher here too, and a heron.

These usual inhabitants did not disappoint her and provided entertainment while she ate her lunch, even the kingfisher darted out and dived for a fish. Then she pulled on her rainproof jacket and set off to walk for a bit. Like so many places along the water road there were memories associated with the path she walked. She had still been an apprentice the first time, and she had walked with Kel, leaving Nemle and Kel's mentor Sul, to talk together. She and Nemle had been on their way to Clanning, but she had not been told what it was there that they were needed for. It had made her angry to have been kept in the dark, but it had not been the custom to discuss routes and tasks with the younger apprentices. Things were a lot more open now.

Her way went uphill, quite steeply, and she had, reluctantly, to admit that the last three months had impacted on her fitness. She had a particular goal in mind however so she pushed on. Back then, twenty two years ago, she realised with rather a shock, she and Kel had come upon a cottage, the tenant of which was being evicted by some bullies. She and Kel had intervened and later linked the action with the job they had been given in Clanning. Now she wondered about the cottage and what had become of the family who had lived there.

The path she walked gave into what had once been a country lane. It had been macadamised now, but was otherwise much the same. Trees and hedges still lined the way and the verges were bright with spring flowers, Queen Anne's lace and rosebay willow herb vying for position in front of the hedges. A car passed her and then another, so that she had to dive for the verge. That had not happened twenty two years ago. It made for less pleasant walking now it was necessary all the time to be alert for traffic.

At last she reached the cottage and stood staring. The small, rather ramshackle dwelling she remembered had been transformed. New paint, a conservatory and a garage, perhaps even some new building, had converted what had been a farm worker's cottage into a gentleman's residence. It stood in a pretty garden behind a low fence.

She gazed at it for a few moments, wondering, then turned to retrace her steps. Change was everywhere, whether you liked it or not. The important thing was to work for good change. Had this been good change for the woman they had met all those years ago? It was doubtful whether the present incarnation of the cottage housed her and her sons, unless her circumstances had changed dramatically.

Briefly she toyed with the idea that the sulky fourteen year old son they had met then, now had a well paying job and a family and had resurrected his childhood home, but it didn't really seem likely and she shrugged, laughed at herself and let it go. Sometimes it was tempting to live in the past, but that was to ignore the challenges of the present and forget that she had a responsibility to the future.

The walk had given her an appetite and it was easy and quick to heat the remains of Dom's casserole and sit at her table to eat and watch as the twilight took over from the day. Then, when night had fallen and she could no longer see the creatures she took herself to the armchair and gave herself to the soul song.

Even after so many years of practice the song could still surprise her. Bubbles of sparkling light danced in the music and joyous laughter lifted her. She bathed in the sounds that carried her up and out. Her own song seemed effortless, happy play amongst happy friends. She was part of the happiness, giving to the joy, emptying herself so the music would swell and grow, filling the place where she was. Dimly she understood there was a limit, there were thin places somewhere beyond, empty places where the song struggled, but these were far off. For now the song blessed her with light and love.

When she finally relinquished the music she emerged refreshed, as if she had swum in a bright, cool spring, or breathed the air after rain. That too surprised her. Most often the song was work and challenge, spinning gold to warm and heal dark places. Then she would leave only to drown in sleep. Instead, this time, she stood up and made her way out to the back deck. The clouds had gone and the night sky was bright with stars. She reached back for her cloak and swung it around her then stood watching, a still, quiet figure, absorbing the silent, starry night.

The night had blessed her, she thought sleepily, as she finally made her way down to her bed.

Next morning she was up and on her way back to the Harbour at first light. It was only seven o'clock when she eased *Day Bringer* into her mooring just ahead of *Autumn Wind*. Jik popped his head out to smile and invite her to breakfast.

"Forty eight hours isn't up yet," he teased. "You'll be sent away again if you appear in the office."

"Breakfast would be lovely," she said.

She could relax with Jik and Dom. They would not be wanting to quiz her about the illusion she had made to drive away the Yareblis. She finished coiling her lines, stowed the tiller arm and went down to turn the stern tube greaser. They would let her talk or be silent. They would fill her in about what had been happening here at the Harbour. They would cherish and nourish her.

At nine o'clock she thanked them and hugged them and made her way to the office. There would be mail to deal with, meetings to schedule and plans to consider for the graduation ceremony next Sunday. It was important for the apprentices that their progress was suitably acknowledged and for the retiring mentors to know they were loved and valued. She gave a little skip. She could do this now, last the distance, give herself to the task.

There was a boat in the dry dock and she stopped a moment to greet Yarla who was already at work on her blacking. In the wet dock, *Cloudburst* and *Evening Star* waited quietly. Work should be about finished on these two, she thought. Her office door was closed and she hesitated for a moment before opening it. What would she find? There was a neat pile of mail on one corner of her desk and in the centre an envelope with her name on it.

She held it for a moment before slipping a finger under the flap.

Dear Marheh, it read. *Welcome home. We hope you feel refreshed by your break.*

Thank you for spending yourself in our service. We have sorted the mail and distributed that which was personal. Chanra is coming to help you with the rest of it. She is considering our request that she take over as Harbour Master. We think we understand a little better now why it is not your job.

It was signed by all fifteen of the mentors. Marheh held it a moment feeling a little flush of warmth at this recognition, then she tucked it back carefully into the envelope and put it away in her desk. It would be something to keep and she would take it to *Day Bringer* and put it in the little box Kel had made her, many years ago, that held her special treasures.

She had not been working for more than ten minutes when Chanra appeared at the door.

"You're early on the job. Did you have a good break?"

"Lovely. Just what I needed. I hear they've asked you to take over."

"Yes, I'm still considering. Are you sure you don't want to continue? You've done a good job."

"Quite sure – and sure that you will do a better job."

Chanra pulled up the visitor's chair to the desk and began to help open the mail.

"I doubt that, but I would, at least, have a year or more before I had to plan a Gathering. That would be a big advantage." She looked at the document she had taken from the first envelope. "How do you want to work this? Shall we sort into piles – invoices, receipts and other? Would that work?"

Marheh smiled and nodded and indicated the couple of letters she had already opened.

"Those are both receipts. It is so nice to have been able to pay our creditors."

They had not been working long when they heard footsteps in the passageway. Not young footsteps, Marheh thought, looking up. A moment later Nisfa appeared in the doorway.

"Nisfa." Marheh stood up to greet her.

"I won't stay," she said, leaning heavily on her stick. "I expect you on *Cloud Drift* for lunch. Twelve o'clock."

She didn't stop to hear Marheh's reply but turned and stumped away again.

Chanra looked up, raised her eyebrows.

"A royal command?"

Marheh grinned.

"I always wonder whether I should curtsy, but she's very kind."

They bent to their work again. Chanra was easy to work with, and seemed to grasp what was needed in the office very quickly.

"You've worked in an office before, haven't you?" she asked, when the mail was all opened and dealt with.

Chanra nodded.

"I've been temping for most of my working life."

"Temping?"

"Filling in, doing secretarial work when someone was on holiday or when an office was extra busy. It was something I could do and still move about the water road."

"No wonder you know what you're doing. I felt so inadequate at first and because I thought it was only for six weeks I didn't properly take in the things Gilt was telling me about the job. I don't know what I would have done if I had not had Teg to ask, and Jik and Bixa too. They were so generous."

Chanra smiled.

"But maybe the fact that you felt inadequate meant that you dug deeper, tried harder."

"Perhaps," Marheh agreed after a moment of thought. "Are we being unfair, to ask you to take on more office work? I suggested you to the mentors, but perhaps you hate the idea."

"Certainly not unfair," Chanra replied quickly. "I can always say no." She paused then, considering. "I think it is a job I can do and the Silberay need someone with my skills to do it. I don't much like the idea of being anchored here for three or four years but," she paused again then looked at Marheh. "I think you will understand if I say that I see it as my gift and service to the Silberay."

Marheh nodded. She did understand that.

"There are some good things," she said. "Fylan and the old ones, helping work the dry dock, being a contact for the Silberay, the library and even the laundry and the bathrooms, but sometimes it can be quite boring."

Chanra smiled.

"Nisfa hinted that you had some suggestions about the job and I'm sure they won't be boring. She told me you were adamant that whoever took on the job should be involved now in any planning."

Marheh's eyes widened.

"Nisfa said that!"

Chanra laughed.

"Isn't it true?"

"Yes, but…"

Chanra laughed again.

"You keep thinking she will disapprove of you. I think you will have to learn to accept her approval instead."

When they had finished with the mail, including that morning's delivery, Marheh suggested she show Chanra the flat.

"We could have sperit and you could look around. I didn't use it, but you might enjoy the space if you decide to take on the job."

After sperit and time to talk and explore the flat, they went back downstairs and across to visit the old ones and Fylan.

Marheh could not help noticing that she was getting odd looks from some of the Silberay who were out and about and wondered briefly what she had done to attract those, but she put it out of her mind once they reached the house and concentrated on introducing Chanra to Fylan.

Teg was in the sitting room with Lild, his former apprentice, and they stayed to chat with them for a few minutes, but both Marheh and Chanra were very much aware of how precious such meetings were so they did not stay long. There was every chance that, by the time of the next Gathering,

Teg would no longer be with them.

As they walked back towards the office Marheh suggested that Chanra go and visit the chandlery and the docks.

"Those are an interesting part of the job," she said. "At least I think so. I'd best go back to the office and make sure I know what should be happening between now and the graduation ceremony, just in case Nisfa starts quizzing me."

The planning was all but done, she realised, when she reached her desk. Apprentice classes were all timetabled, bookings for the two docks seemed to be proceeding as scheduled and the last couple of meetings to discuss ways of funding the Harbour had been advertised. Her last big responsibility as Harbour Master was the graduation ceremony and she was determined to make it memorable for the new apprentices, the new graduates and the retiring mentors. They were the ones who mattered.

She was at her desk thinking over past graduations and jotting down ideas when Kel appeared in the doorway. She stood up and went around the desk to give him a hug.

"Thank you, thank you, thank you," she said, leaning back a little to look at him.

"You had a good break then," he said.

"I didn't know how much I needed it."

"That's what I observed," he teased.

"Was I so awful?"

He shook his head and drew her close for a few moments more.

"I'm always surprised to see you behind a desk," he commented later when she had returned to her seat and he had commandeered the visitor's chair.

She laughed.

"Not half as surprised as I am to find myself here. Not for much longer though."

"You're sure you don't want to continue?"

"What do you think? I can't wait to get back on the water road."

He smiled at her.

"I suppose I had better let you get on with it now then." He got up to go. "Lunch?" he asked from the doorway.

She made a face.

"I'm commanded to appear on *Cloud Drift*."

"Dinner then."

For a while after he had gone she sat gazing at her notes without taking them in. The warmth of Kel's hug, his loving presence, lingered and she was reluctant to relinquish them. She had done nothing more than pick up her pencil and make a couple of little doodles when Bixa arrived at the door. Marheh greeted her with a hug and offered the visitor's chair. She looked tired Marheh thought, and seemed to have lost the serenity that had been so much a part of her.

"Is it Beuda?" she asked, after the first polite exchanges had been made.

"Is it so obvious?" Bixa said with a wry smile.

Marheh reached out to her across the desk.

"It's just that you look tired."

"I don't think I'm cut out for a mentor. I can't seem to get through to her on any level."

"Doesn't she understand that you were ready to sacrifice your mind, even your life, to protect her?"

"If she does it doesn't seem to have made any difference. I thought she might have been confused, perhaps frightened, but all she has said is that she doesn't know what the fuss was about, a few people had come from her work, that's all."

Marheh closed her eyes for a moment, struggling to contain a sudden rush of anger.

"If she worked with Yareblis is there any chance she has a dormant control?"

Bixa shook her head.

"It's possible I suppose. I haven't had much chance to get near her for that kind of communication. She goes to her classes, but the rest of the time she spends pursuing poor Myl."

"She doesn't seem to listen to any information that doesn't suit her. I did notice that, but surely when Gilt interviewed her he must have made clear some things about the Silberay and the way we choose to live."

"All she seems to have taken in is that she might make a good Harbour Master one day."

Bixa covered her face for a moment then looked up.

"She seems to think that her apprenticeship will last three years at most. By then she will have learnt all there is to know. She then plans to take over one of the boats on the hard standing for perhaps another three years, after which she will be ready to take on the job of Harbour Master. She explained all that to me, very kindly, when I tried to share something of our philosophy with her."

"Yet she can see the water," Marheh said slowly. "There must be something within her that, that has the potential to respond to the values of the water dimension. She hasn't been recruited by the Yareblis. I'm sure we could tell if that was the case."

She picked up her pencil and drew a question mark which she then proceeded to turn into a rough portrait of Beuda.

"Do you want me to ask her if I can enter her mind?" she said at last. "Perhaps she does have some kind of control."

Bixa did not answer at once. Marheh added a torso to her doodle and dressed it with a neatly buttoned shirt.

"I don't think it would be good for her to know that such a thing is possible," Bixa said. "I can imagine her expecting to be able to do it and thinking it unnecessary to ask for permission."

Marheh nodded.

"And you won't have been able to introduce her to the soul song. That might help, but you need quiet and discipline for that."

She screwed up the paper with her drawing and tossed it into the waste paper basket.

"Would it help if I talked to her? Officially, as it were?"

"It might," Bixa said. "I know she thinks I'm too old to be much use, but I think she respects you as much as she can respect anyone."

Marheh looked at Bixa and gave her a little grin.

"It seems all wrong for me to be instructing anyone in how to behave. I will have to pretend that I'm the Apprentice Master and quiz her very sternly about what she has been learning during the Gathering."

Bixa laughed and stood up.

"I'll tell her she has an appointment to discuss her progress with you. Would tomorrow morning suit?"

"Nine o'clock," Marheh said, standing up too. "And now I'm due on *Cloud Drift*."

Sperit and Biscuits

Chapter Eighteen

Nisfa welcomed Marheh very graciously although Marheh knew that it was Sampi who had prepared their lunch. She had made something she called a quiche, a pastry case with egg and cheese and bacon and served it with a small salad. Marheh's lack of interest in culinary matters meant that her experience was limited mostly to the dishes in the rather stained and tattered recipe book that had been Nemle's. She found the quiche delicious and told Sampi so. Nisfa expressed mild surprise that Marheh had not tasted one before and allowed her to finish eating before pinning her down with questions about the illusion she had used to rout the Yareblis.

"Can the skill be learnt?" she asked. "Can you teach it?"

Marheh had a sudden vision of a room full of sixth year apprentices taking earnest notes about how to make an illusion. She shook her head.

"I don't know. I expect some of us could learn, since it is something the Yareblis can do, but with me it was something that happened first when I was under attack. It was the year I graduated and I was afraid at first that I was breaking the law. It isn't very easy to talk about and makes me different, so I don't. I suppose that changes now most of the Silberay have experienced the results of what I did."

Nisfa studied her across the table.

"Nemle never actually boasted about you, but she left the mentors in no doubt that you had exceptional talent."

Marheh looked down at her empty plate and made a small task out of folding her napkin. It was hard to know whether Nisfa was accusing her or praising her, but she didn't want either.

"I think you should consider how the skill might be taught. Next Gathering we might offer the opportunity for selected Silberay to learn from you."

Marheh hoped her horror at this suggestion was not reflected on her face, but Nisfa's next words disillusioned her.

"I can see you don't like the idea, but I think it is your duty and if others learn how to do it you won't feel so different."

Would that be true, she wondered. Did her reluctance indicate a kind of pride in her difference? She didn't know how to answer Nisfa and felt as awkward and rebellious as she had as a schoolgirl sent to the head for discipline.

Marheh the Great came to her rescue in the end. She straightened and lifted her chin.

"I will certainly give the idea some thought," she said. "But now I think we should talk about something else. Have the mentors made any decisions about routes as yet?"

Nisfa seemed a bit taken aback by this bluntness, but behind her, at the sink, Sampi gave Marheh a sympathetic grin.

"Or perhaps I could help Sampi with the dishes," she added. "It was a lovely lunch thank you."

"I'm glad you enjoyed it," Nisfa said, gracious in defeat. "We've had a few conversations, but nothing is definitely decided. The Harbour Master is expected to have an input since she is in a position to know of problems that need addressing and Silberay with appropriate skills."

It was pay back of a kind, Marheh thought. Nisfa was putting her on the spot despite knowing she had had comparatively little time in the job. Marheh the Great was still in occupation however so she smiled, equally gracious, and said she would do her best.

Sampi's splutter of laughter at this elegant exchange earned her a frown from Nisfa, but it was quickly changed to an apology.

"I've been unpardonably intrusive," she said. "As Sampi has just indicated. Please forgive me. There is nothing like a good apprentice for reminding one of one's faults."

Marheh laughed.

"Then perhaps I had better get one as soon as possible."

Talk turned to routes for a while then Marheh raised the issue of the Yareblis who had been at the Harbour.

"It may be necessary to take action against them," she said. "I believe there are still some who feel themselves invited. "It could be disastrous if they were to attack the Harbour once the Gathering is over and most of us gone,"

"You don't think the song of the old ones will be enough to keep them at bay?" Nisfa asked.

"I don't know how many there are," Marheh said, thinking, but not saying, that it was Nisfa who had pointed out the problem when the open day was first mooted.

"Normally it would not be a problem, it was the invitation to the open day that gave them entry."

"But the open day is over," Sampi said. "Doesn't that mean the invitation is no longer valid?"

"It would be nice to think so," Marheh replied, wondering why she had not considered that.

"Of course it does," Nisfa said briskly. "You needn't give it another thought."

Marheh could not feel quite so confident, but she saw that there was no point in pursuing the possibility. She stood up.

"It was a lovely lunch," she said again. "Thank you. Now I had best go and prepare for this afternoon's meetings."

She said goodbye and walked back to the office feeling angry and unsettled. Nisfa took too much on herself. She had no right to tell her what to do or how to think. She didn't understand what she was asking. By the time she was sitting behind her desk again though she had remembered Nisfa's quick apology and her support and her anger turned to self reproach. However she soon realised that that, too, was an indulgence she had not time to permit and gave herself to study of the activity reports from the past two years travels and Chanra's notes of the fund raising discussions.

She thought she had acquitted herself reasonably well at both meetings and said as much to Kel as they sat over cheese and biscuits and sperit after the meal they had shared.

"I'm struggling to keep on top of things though," she said.

"You're too hard on yourself, Kel said. "You don't have to do everything."

"I feel as if I do. Nisfa means well but she is really pressuring me. I nearly lost my temper with her at lunch."

"But you didn't."

Kel smiled and put a hand over hers where it lay on the table.

"There are times when I feel as if I'm the only one to see things, then I feel guilty because that seems so arrogant."

"No point in feeling guilty. I think sometimes you are. That is one of your particular gifts. What is it that we are not seeing just now?"

She took his hand and lifted it to her cheek for a moment then laid it back on the table.

"The open day. There was no point in holding it if we don't plan to follow up the good parts and address the less good. The routes. I'm beginning to see a pattern in the reports, but it isn't clear and no one wants to believe me. The finances. Now that people have paid their dues and the immediate pressure is off people seem to have lost interest. And the Yareblis. I don't think we've seen the last of them here at the Harbour."

"Not very much really then," Kel teased.

She laughed ruefully.

"Am I over-reacting?"

Kel took both her hands in his.

"Probably not, but you really don't have to do everything yourself and it doesn't have to be done yesterday whatever you might think."

He gave her a moment to digest this advice then continued.

"Now, what do you see as the first priority?"

"The voice of commonsense," she said lightly. "The routes, I suppose, they really need to be settled before the Gathering ends."

"And what is it particularly about the routes that bothers you? Have too many people made conflicting requests? Are there known challenges that need special skills?"

She looked at him gratefully. Just hearing him articulate what she had been unable to put into words helped her to discover what troubled her.

"There are a lot of people wanting to go south. I suppose it's only natural. The northern routes had dreadful weather all last year." She smiled suddenly. "And I've just thought how I can solve two problems at once. If the next Harbour Master is happy about it, that is."

Kel looked at her questioningly.

"Can you tell me, or do you want to talk to Chanra first?"

"The thing is," she said slowly. "If we want to encourage the neighbours to use our resources the Harbour Master will need some support, especially at first. The southern route is quite limited compared with the northern routes but if those who want that route were also expected to spend time here working with the Harbour Master … though it would still need the right people."

She stood up.

"Let's get the dishes out of the way, then I think I might have an early night since there's no formal entertainment tonight."

While she washed dishes and Kel dried them they talked about the routes they would like for themselves. Marheh hoped her route might include

Deerford so that she could visit her parents. They both preferred northern routes and each knew that the other wished for some time when their paths would cross or overlap. Kel strolled back to *Day Bringer* with her and hugged her warmly as they said goodnight.

Marheh woke early again next morning. She was not looking forward to her interview with Beuda and wanted to prepare carefully. Singing, and especially holding Beuda in the song, was part of that preparation and did not come easily since it required her to love this difficult young woman whom she found it hard even to like.

Beuda presented herself at the office at precisely nine o'clock. Marheh smiled and invited her to sit.

"The Gathering will be over in a few days," she began. "So this is a good time to have a talk about what you've learnt over the last two and a half weeks, and what you expect from the Silberay as well as what you hope to learn in the two years between now and the next Gathering."

"Well, I'm assuming I will be taught some practical things. As far as I'm concerned the classes I've been expected to attend so far have been pretty useless."

"Oh?" Marheh's inflection made the single syllable a question.

"I can't really see the point of theory. I suppose a bit of history is reasonable but the philosophy classes were just a waste of time."

"In what way?" Marheh asked, wondering just why Beuda had even considered becoming a Silberay apprentice.

"It's all so old fashioned," Beuda said. "Humility, obedience, discipline – what's the point? I thought the Silberay were about helping people. Humility never helped anyone."

"Did you discuss any of this with Jik?" Marheh asked, remembering who had been responsible for the first year philosophy classes."

"Why bother? Glik was falling over himself to get attention. I just wanted the whole business over with."

"What do you think of when you consider the idea of humility?"

"Oh you know, cringing, sucking up."

"I see," Marheh said slowly. "And those are very negative words, but I doubt that anything Jik tried to teach you involved cringing or sucking up. The Silberay idea of humility is more about not putting yourself first, taking yourself out of your listening so that you really hear. I don't believe you have even tried to do that. Jik is one of the wisest men I know, but you have learnt nothing from him. You can learn practical things from anyone who can do them if you want to, but to learn the kind of compassion the Silberay must have to do their job properly you must learn the humility to recognise that you are not the centre of the universe."

Beuda looked scornful.

"I know that of course, but I think it is important to have a sense of my own worth as well. What's the point of saying I can't do something when I know I can?"

"No point at all," Marheh agreed. "And no one wants you to do that, but perhaps your way of doing something is not the Silberay way. If, once you've tried, really tried, both ways then hopefully we might have the humility to learn from you if you still think your way is best, but you have not even begun to consider that our way might have merit."

Beuda continued to look sceptical.

"Is that all? Can I go now?"

Marheh took a deep breath and bit back an angry reply. Had she been as difficult as this? She knew she had tried Nemle to the limit during the first weeks of her apprenticeship, but she had never wanted to fight the ideals embedded in the Silberay promise. What was wrong with the girl? Woman, she corrected herself. Perhaps that was it. Perhaps her age was against her, but she could see the water and had chosen to be apprenticed. If the Silberay refused her would she turn to the Yareblis?

She had been silent for several minutes and Beuda had begun to fidget. Marheh smiled at her.

"I'm sorry I've kept you. I've been thinking. You know, Bixa is a very special person, wise and kind as well as practical. She was a great Harbour Master. You couldn't do better than learn from her if you want to be our Harbour Master in the future. It isn't the practical things, though, that are important. It is the other things that make her special. In a few days you will be making your commitment to the Silberay and to Bixa. Do you think you could put aside your own ideas for a while at least and try to experience what Bixa can teach you before you make up your mind that you know best?"

It was a long speech and Marheh was not sure that Beuda had really listened, but she muttered a response that suggested a kind of agreement and took herself off.

Once the door had closed behind her Marheh stood up and began to pace. There was something wrong. It didn't make sense that Beuda would give up a secure job to become a Silberay apprentice when she was so reluctant to consider Silberay values. She was pursuing Myl, but surely she must realise that Myl's commitment was to the Silberay first.

If she had been working alongside Yareblis she could have a control, especially if she had told her fellow workers that she was leaving to join the Silberay, and she had of course. She had broadcast the fact by distributing invitations to the open day. Marheh stopped her pacing and stood by the window looking out over the harbour with its array of bright boats. She agreed with Bixa that it was too early to draw Beuda's attention to the idea of control, but it seemed to be a distinct possibility that the Yareblis had infiltrated Bueda's mind. Marheh would be breaking the law if she went in to check without asking, but the Yareblis had a purpose for everything they did and their purpose often meant trouble for the Silberay, or even, specifically, for Marheh, whose ability to upset their plans had made her a target before this.

She sighed and continued her pacing. She would have liked to discuss it with Jik or Kel but it didn't seem fair to make them accomplices. Next time she arrived at the window she stopped again, her decision made. If Beuda had unwittingly brought a Yareblis control with her it had been placed in order to cause trouble. It was a question of safety. She had to take action. If she was careful Beuda would never know and nor would anyone else.

That settled, she went back to her desk and attacked the mail, still plenty coming for individuals, but not so much for her to deal with since creditors had been paid. Chanra arrived to help followed closely by Tippa who perched on the end of the desk as if she was planning to stay a while.

"Marheh got you working for her now, has she?" she began.

Chanra raised her eyebrows, obviously not sure about Tippa's brand of humour. Marheh just laughed.

"She can't make excuses about being too busy then."

"Too busy for what?" Marheh asked suspiciously.

"Well…" she paused dramatically. "You know the entertainment on Saturday night?"

Another pause until Marheh nodded, still suspicious.

"It's traditional for the Harbour Master to perform."

Marheh's jaw dropped. Was it? Had she not noticed? Chanra's lips twitched, aware that there was no such tradition.

"I'm organising the program," Tippa went on airily. "What are you planning to do?"

Marheh stared at her for a moment then saw Chanra's face.

"Nothing," she said firmly. "What kind of friend are you, giving me such a fright!"

Tippa laughed.

"Admit, you almost fell for it. Wouldn't you like to start a new tradition?"

"No I wouldn't."

"Who would have thought that Marheh the Great would grow up to be so boring," Tippa teased.

Marheh started. How did Tippa know her family nickname?

"I kept my ears open that evening I had dinner with you and your parents." She answered Marheh's unspoken question. "I was up in the library looking for stuff, and guess what I found? The book with that skit we did in second year. Pon's up for it."

"You're serious aren't you?" Marheh said.

"I offered to organise the program, but I didn't think people would be so hard to persuade. The musicians are all prepared but we need some variety." Tippa grinned at her. "Go on. With us the age we are it will be funnier now than it was then. The Silberay will love it."

"It's all very well for you," Marheh grumbled. "Couldn't you find someone younger?"

"No," Tippa said firmly. "It has to be you. Can we rehearse in the flat after this afternoon's meeting?"

That was all she needed, Marheh thought, when Tippa had gone. She was much too old and too busy to be playing a naughty schoolgirl. Chanra looked at her sympathetically.

"Have I remembered correctly? Did I see this proposed entertainment something like thirty years ago?"

"I'm afraid so."

"Then Tippa is right. The Silberay will love it." She smiled at Marheh. "Go on. Go away and let me do the office work now. You can manage the important things, the final decisions about routes, the last couple of meetings and the graduation ceremony."

And Beuda, Marheh thought, as she thanked Chanra and departed for *Day Bringer*. What would Beuda think about the Harbour Master acting the part of a naughty child? Probably that it was beneath her dignity. Perhaps that made a reason of sorts for doing it. She stepped into the well deck and let herself into her workspace still struggling with herself. Had she become too self-important? Beuda had a very good opinion of herself. It was important to be able to laugh at yourself. She had a tendency to take herself too seriously and Beuda seemed the same. No doubt it would do her good to be laughed at and perhaps it might encourage Beuda to see life a bit differently.

She made herself an early lunch and sat thinking about Beuda. It would not be easy to find a time to enter her mind. It would be too obvious if she tried while Beuda was with Myl, or any of the other apprentices who were kindly putting up with her. If there was no control she could be in and out in a minute, but if it was a question of removing one it would take much more time. She would just need to be ready to act if an opportunity arose.

The afternoon meeting had finalised most of the routes and given Chanra the opportunity to select helpers from those who wanted to go south. Marheh was given a roving commission in the north. It was not very usual, but the mentors had agreed that there was a sense of unease that seemed to emanate from the furthest reaches of the water road and needed her skills to identify. It would be a challenge, but one she was comfortable with, one she felt would use her ability and test her just enough.

The rehearsal in the flat proceeded amid gales of laughter and Marheh realised that it had been good for her. Most of the lines came back without too much effort and it was the sort of silliness that called for improvisation of both words and actions.

She was still smiling as she went to the big kitchen where she had arranged to have her evening meal. Dom was cooking with Sampi's help and she went to greet them before finding a place at the table where half a dozen others were already waiting. She knew them all better now than she had and was glad she had made the effort. It was not as restful as a meal on *Day Bringer* or *Storm Cloud* but a good way to engage with those Silberay with whom she did not normally associate. It had been Dom's idea to offer his cooking skills to facilitate shared meals and there had been no shortage of customers, or helpers wanting to learn from him.

Her fellow diners had plenty to say so all she needed to do was listen sympathetically. Most of the talk was about routes, now that these had been allocated, and it was interesting to hear what others had experienced. She had travelled all over the water road during her years with the Silberay, but still there were places that had revealed other aspects than those she had seen or felt.

Jik and Nisfa were at the table, but the half dozen other diners were not mentors or apprentices. Yarla was there, looking rather tired, and she remembered to ask how her blacking was going.

"Finished, thank goodness," Yarla said. "I've just got back to my mooring. Things took a bit longer than I expected, but at least I haven't over run my time."

"I've been spoilt this year," Marheh said. "Jik and Kel docked *Day Bringer* for me when I was in hospital. It's always a bit of a scramble doing it on your own."

"I did have help," Yarla assured her.

"I didn't manage to book a spot during the Gathering." Another diner joined the conversation. "My own fault, I kept putting off ringing."

Marheh racked her brains for his name. Nin, that was it.

"Neither did I," his companion said. "Best we book together and share the work."

That was Briz, Marheh remembered. She knew him a little. He had been apprenticed at the same time as Kel and they were casual friends.

She smiled and listened and ate Dom's vegetable pie and thought how glad she was to be coming to the end of her time as Harbour Master. She had to acknowledge though, that it had been good for her to have to tackle something uncongenial.

Sampi moved around the table offering seconds and then collecting empty plates. There was no formal entertainment that evening so no one was in a hurry to leave. Marheh began to relax. Sperit and biscuits were offered and accepted. The sound of voices and laughter came from the big meeting room and then faded as a door was closed.

"We were apprentices once," Yarla said indulgently.

Marheh smiled, remembering the Gatherings when she had joined in the laughter and the games with the apprentices. She had needed Kel's encouragement though, especially after the time she had been found guilty of misusing the discipline of the mind and publicly beaten for it. That had coloured her relationship with the Silberay long after she had been exonerated.

She had been foolish to let it, she thought now. Most of them had forgotten and none of the current apprentices even knew it had happened. The memory still popped up to plague her occasionally and appeared in her dreams if she was particularly tired or stressed. Jik had believed in her and supported her through it all. He was looking at her now, a question in his eyes.

She smiled at him. "This was a great idea of Dom's. Are we allowed to help with the dishes?"

She was not sorry when her offer was politely, but firmly refused. An early night would set her up nicely for the last few days. She had just stood and was starting on her goodnights when the door was opened with rather more than necessary vigour.

"Those apprentices are a lot of immature idiots," Beuda announced.

The eye of all the other diners looked to her in surprise.

"Oh?" Jik said mildly.

Beuda turned on him.

"What else can you expect when they're kept apprentices for so long? It's no wonder they haven't grown up yet."

Marheh opened her mouth to speak then shut it again. Jik would do a better job of answering than she would and she could just slip into Beuda's mind, just to check, even if she could not do more right now. She hesitated, needing to prepare herself, then Rima came to the door and the moment was gone.

"I'm sorry if we offended you Beuda," she said to the room in general. "But you're making life really difficult for Myl and we were just getting our own back."

"I don't know what you're talking about," Beuda snapped and marched out of the kitchen.

Rima shrugged and looked apologetically at the observers and followed her out, closing the door carefully behind her.

"Well," Nisfa said, after a moment of silence. "I don't envy Bixa that young woman. I don't know what Gilt was thinking when he accepted her."

There was no easy answer and no one attempted one. Instead the others followed Marheh's example, said goodnight and moved out of the kitchen.

Marheh found Jik beside her as she made her way towards her mooring.

"Something troubling you niece?" he asked.

She turned to him, grateful for his concern.

"I'm thinking of breaking the law," she said. "And it made me remember what happened when the Silberay thought I had."

"Do you want to tell me?"

"Yes, very much, but it wouldn't be right to make you an accomplice."

Jik laughed.

"I don't see how discussing a possible action with your uncle could make him an accomplice. It's to do with that new apprentice isn't it?"

"She's the one who brought the Yareblis to the open day. Apparently they are work colleagues, or so she said. I think she probably has a control, just waiting, to make her cause more trouble. I want to check and remove it, but I don't want to ask her first. The knowledge of what is possible would not be good for her right now."

They walked a few steps in silence, the twilight soft around them.

"It needs to be done," Jik said when they reached *Day Bringer*. "Law or no law, and you are the best person to do it." He gave her a goodnight hug. "I'll watch out for you," he said and continued on to *Autumn Wind*.

It was still early enough to take time to sing before she slept and Marheh made a special point of holding Beuda in the music. It had been a struggle, but a worthwhile one, she thought, as she put herself to bed.

"Lucy"

Chapter Nineteen

Resolving to act was all very well, but she still needed an opportunity and none seemed to present itself. Chanra had taken over the office work completely, so in theory the morning was her own, but Beuda was in class, or off chasing Myl and Marheh herself had only to appear from *Day Bringer* to be greeted with questions and problems or invitations to chat over a cup of sperit. She had never felt herself popular in the past, but this Gathering she had been more visible than usual and people she hardly knew seemed keen to make friends.

There were still afternoon meetings, not for everyone, but Marheh was expected to attend and was happy to, given their purpose.

There was a committee planning the follow up to the open day and, now that the routes had been finalised, another group made up of her and Chanra and those Silberay on southern routes. These were scheduling the necessary help and working out the kind of tasks that would need doing.

The financial situation, though not quite as strong as the Silberay would have liked, had been partly addressed by a rise in the dues and partly by some generous donations from a few Silberay whose income permitted this. They were hoping too, that their plans for sharing the Harbour with their neighbours might ease the burden of the increase in the rates resulting from the re-zoning.

Tippa insisted on rehearsing their skit once the meetings were over. It seemed to Marheh to be getting more ridiculous by the minute but she had to admit that she was having fun. She tried to put out of her mind the idea of actually performing it for the Silberay. That prospect was still rather daunting.

Thursday and Friday went by in this way without any opportunity or indeed any sight of Beuda. Marheh even began to wonder whether she was actually avoiding her. By Saturday the last of the meetings was over and the afternoon was spent in preparations for the evening's entertainment and in finalising the details of the next day's ceremonies. The unlikely combination of Dom and Leura had the final meal under control. Leura had canvassed the Silberay for contributions and together she and Dom planned and cooked party food in the big kitchen, while others made use of their own galleys to add to the feast.

Marheh had not offered to cook anything, being well aware of her culinary limitations, but put her name down for washing dishes.

By the advertised start of the entertainment the Silberay were all present in the big meeting room. Good humoured talk, some laughter and the sound of instruments tuning established the atmosphere. Tippa was compering the first half of the program and she was doing a good job of it. Marheh was conscious of feeling very nervous about her own contribution to the evening. She had, at one time, thought she might enter Beuda's mind while she was watching the entertainment, but there were too many distractions.

The program opened with a lively duet between two violins, then a singer, a flautist and a recitation. Marheh dutifully applauded and smiled at Tippa's jokes and felt more and more nervous about her own part in the event. The violins came back for another turn and then it was interval. Marheh slipped away to one of the small meeting rooms where she was to change. Tippa joined her and then Pon and together they went to meet Yog, who was to compere the second half. He was such a quiet man that Marheh was a bit surprised at this, but then she remembered the dry sense of humour he had revealed.

After a grin at the sight of them in costume and a brief word of encouragement, Yog slipped back into the meeting room. Through the crack in the door they could hear him joke with the audience then tell them to close their eyes so a surprise could be prepared for them. A minute later he beckoned them in and onto the dais.

When the audience was invited to open their eyes there was a moment of silence then a burst of laughter and applause. Marheh, looking impossibly young, her hair in bunches above each ear, wearing a gym tunic that revealed not just lots of leg, but the lower edge of one leg of her bloomers, got up from the table where she sat scribbling earnestly. Tippa, drably clad in a tired looking brown dress, brown stockings and a moth eaten fur tippet, turned towards her.

"Lucy," she said. "Your arithmetic homework is deficient. Your father is very displeased and requires that you repeat it correctly."

"Yes Miss Tinker," replied Marheh, allowing the words to run together. "Sorry Miss Tinker."

It was not great comedy, but the Silberay laughed, jeered and applauded as 'Lucy' tormented poor Miss Tinker and her father and finally seemed about to receive her comeuppance across her father's knee.

"It serves you right!" Miss Tinker shrieked as father raised his hand to strike.

At that interesting moment however Yog switched off the lights. When he switched them on again, the three actors were standing in a row taking their bows. As Marheh looked out over the rows of laughing, clapping Silberay she saw one notable exception to the universal approval. Beuda's face wore an expression of the utmost disdain and she was not clapping.

Poor Beuda, checking for a control had better be a top priority. Surely common politeness would normally have her applauding even if she had not enjoyed the performance.

"Lucy!" Miss Tinker said sharply. Marheh jumped, skipped sideways to avoid Pon's swipe at her rear, put her tongue out at the audience and ran off the dais and out the door, closely followed by Tippa and Pon.

Applause followed them, then they heard Yog's voice introducing the next item. They grinned at each other.

"They loved it," Tippa said. "I knew they would."

Marheh laughed.

"Come on, let's get changed. The violins are going to be on again and I don't want to miss them."

The evening concluded with sperit and scones. Tippa had prevailed upon a half dozen Silberay who were not performing to provide these. Marheh came in for a lot of teasing about her performance but she felt the affection behind it and was warmed by the knowledge that she was cared for.

It was not a late night. The ceremonies tomorrow were the climax of the Gathering and she had an important part to play. There would be Silberay who partied until late, taking a last opportunity to enjoy the company of friends, but not this time for her. At about half past nine she put down her empty mug and said goodnight to the friends around her. Kel gave her a hug and a grin that told her he was remembering Lucy. Jik said it was his bed time and walked with her out into the still, starry night.

They reached the loading dock and paused to look out over the water. A few of the boats showed a glimpse of light, but most were dark. Moonlight laid a path across the Harbour and was reflected off the bits of polished brass that decorated the boats. After a few moments of silence Jik spoke quietly.

"I'm really proud of you niece. You've given yourself to a job you didn't want and done the Silberay proud."

"I've tried," Marheh said, continuing to look out. "I'll be glad when tomorrow is over though." She turned to look at him then. "Except I haven't managed to check Beuda's mind yet, and I'm concerned for Bixa."

"I am too," Jik said. "You know Bixa is my soul friend?"

"I hoped she might be. She couldn't have anyone better."

Jik smiled down at her and gave her plait a gentle tug.

"I'm fortunate in my friend and my niece."

They began to walk again.

"I doubt I will have a chance tomorrow, but perhaps on Monday before they head out. Will you suggest it to Bixa?"

Jik nodded, then, as they reached *Day Bringer*, he stopped to give Marheh a hug.

"Don't worry too much. Bixa is strong and she will cope. It's important you get a good sleep tonight."

He waited while she stepped on board and opened the doors to the back cabin then she turned back to him.

"Goodnight Jik, and thank you."

"Sleep well niece."

Jik's hug made her feel safe and loved, Marheh thought, going down the steps and moving through to the saloon. She wouldn't go to bed quite yet, but sing first, for Beuda and Bixa, for Lidy and Zinda, for Glik and Whin, Juni and Vey. After tomorrow their lives would change irrevocably. She checked the fire then settled herself in the armchair. The moonlight through her windows and the glow from her stove meant that she did not need to light her lamp. A few moment of quiet breathing helped her to centre herself and then she reached for her portal.

Entering the song proved to be unexpectedly challenging but having decided to sing she was determined not to give up. Having finally entered however she found herself drowning in the song of the old ones. Their music lapped around her, enveloping her in sound. Although she had intended to sing for the others it seemed that the old ones wanted to sing for her. For a time she rested, floating in the music. Even when she tried to swim, to add her own tune, her own purpose, the other singers gently restrained her, insisting she be held and cosseted.

What did they know that she did not, Marheh wondered, when the song ended. It felt as if they were preparing her for something unknown. She ought, perhaps, to be fearful, but the safety and the nurturing of the song still held her and she fell into a dreamless sleep.

Next morning she washed and dressed with more care than usual. Today she owed it to the Silberay and the ceremonies to look her best to honour them. Her best trousers were black and with them she wore a dark green tunic over a black shirt. Her tunic was embroidered with a fall of golden leaves over her left shoulder that glowed against the darkness of her other garments. She took extra care with her plait and fastened it with a gold clip at the nape of her neck as well as the usual dark band it its end.

It was still the same face though, that looked back at her from the little mirror in her bathroom. Not much she could do about that.

The first ceremony was the decommissioning of the boats. It was due to begin at half past ten. She had time to sing first. It was a good way to prepare for the day and had the additional advantage of being something she could do without getting dirty, a propensity she had never really outgrown.

The song had been different to that of the previous evening. She realised that many of the older Silberay had been there along with the old ones and the music had been a celebration. She allowed herself to linger in the joy for a few minutes before getting up to go to the hard standing where the ceremony would take place. Juni had been granted her wish to continue living on Summer Breeze so it was only Vey's boat that would be taken from the water. She had checked the winch and the rollers two days ago and confirmed which Silberay Vey had wanted to assist him.

She took up the beautiful, ceremonial cloak that had been given to her on her graduation and swung it around her then made her way along the gantry, poised and feeling very much like Marheh the Great.

Other Silberay were also about, dressed in their best and heading for the hard standing. She went first to the loading dock where Vey waited on his boat Thunder. She had already been emptied and Vey's possessions taken to his room in the house. She was riding high in the water since her tanks had been emptied and only enough diesel left for the short journey to where the winch was waiting. There was a sadness in the knowledge and Marheh was not surprised at Vey's sombre face. She greeted him gently and shook his hand. Her part here was simply to play the apprentice and loosen the moorings for this last voyage.

She waited quietly while he went below to start the engine. Vey was not someone she knew well and she was aware that he had some health problems. It would be a wrench for him to leave Thunder though. The engine noise reached her and then Vey appeared from the back cabin. He was very slow and a bit shaky and Marheh thought perhaps he might have shed a few tears, but he stood straight as he grasped the tiller for the last time.

Marheh felt close to tears herself as she waited for his signal.

"Ready lass," he said at last.

Marheh bent to the back line, her cloak swirling gracefully around her. She coiled it neatly and placed it on the back deck then went to the front to repeat these actions. Finally she gave the bow a gentle push that sent Thunder on her last voyage into the main basin of the Harbour and on to the ramp, the rollers and the winch.

She raised her hand in salute as he passed and he acknowledged her with a formal dip of his head. She watched for a few moments then set off to walk to the hard standing. This ceremony was something she could give Vey, something that might ease his sadness at this relinquishing of what had been his life. It was important that she gave herself to making it fitting. During the short walk she rehearsed her words and actions in her mind, putting aside everything else.

A few other Silberay walked behind her, but most were already waiting at the hard standing. Rima and Myl, both wearing high rubber boots, were standing in the water on either side of the rollers. Myl held the winch cable ready to hook onto Thunder's prow. Briz stood at the winch itself. Marheh walked quietly to her place, a dais erected near the winch. She mounted and looked out to where Thunder was making the turn to enter this quiet arm of the harbour. Slower and slower she approached the ramp. Marheh could see Vey over the roof, grim faced but standing tall. Then she touched the lowest roller. Myl and Rima reached for the bow, guiding her and keeping her square as Myl attached the cable. Marheh lifted her hands for silence.

"Thunder, Vey, welcome home to well earned rest."

As she lowered her hands a flute sounded a single long note then the Silberay began to sing words of greeting, of thanks and affection as the cable tightened and the process began.

As Thunder moved slowly past the dais Marheh helped Juni to mount beside her, then held her hand out to Vey, helping him to step off Thunder's back deck. A moment before, at the tiller, he had stood strong and tall, but now he was a frail old man with tears on his cheeks. Marheh had tears of her own as she embraced him and then Juni. Together they watched until Thunder reached her final resting place, then the words of the song came again, clearer now that the noise of the boat's moving had ended.

When the last note died away Marheh spoke again, her voice clear and strong.

"Juni, Vey, Summer Breeze and Thunder, the Silberay acknowledge and thank you for the life you have lived in our service."

The words seemed to her inadequate, but she did her best to put her heart into them. One day this could be *Day Bringer* if she did not have an apprentice.

Jik and Peli came forward to help Juni and Vey down from the dais, the Silberay applauding softly as they did so. Marheh bowed to Thunder and then to the two old Silberay before she too descended.

The Consigning Ceremony for *Evening Star*, for Zinda and for Lidy, was next and took place back at the loading dock. Marheh led the Silberay as they walked, keeping her pace slow so that Juni and Vey, walking immediately behind her, would have no trouble keeping up. As she went she could not help remembering the Consigning Ceremony when she had graduated and *Day Bringer* became wholly hers. It had been both sadness and celebration, but Nemle had been tired and glad to relinquish *Day Bringer* into her care. It was a very different occasion when the boat continued to be loved and lived in.

Once they reached the loading dock the Silberay ranged themselves around her. Chairs had been placed for Juni and Vey and for Teg and Sula. Fylan stood behind them, already keeping them in her care. They all kept a little apart from Marheh, giving her space, acknowledging her ceremonial role.

Evening Star emerged from the wet dock, Zinda at the tiller, Lidy at the prow, ready with the centre line. As they approached there was a little burst of applause then Marheh raised her arms for silence. The gentle throbbing of *Evening Star*'s engine spoke. This was her moment too, time for her to acknowledge Zinda's care and ownership. Marheh's words gave her a voice.

"*Evening Star* offers gratitude to Zinda of the Silberay. Her life has been enriched because she has lived with her and loved her."

The boat slid gently into place beside the dock and Lidy stepped off, handing her line to Chanra.

Alone on the back deck Zinda reached forward to brush *Evening Star*'s roof with one gentle finger, then she turned to remove the tiller arm, taking it in both hands and offering it to Lidy with some quiet words. Lidy stepped on board to take and fit it once again. Then apprentice and mentor embraced before Zinda stepped off *Evening Star* for the last time.

Again Marheh spoke.

"Zinda, the Silberay acknowledge and thank you for the life you have lived in our service."

She bowed, then moved to embrace her before leading her to Fylan and the empty chair that waited for her.

Lidy stood quietly on *Evening Star*'s back deck as the Silberay sang for the old ones.

> *You are the old, our wisdom, our strength*
> *As you pass let our love wrap you well.*
> *Let it nourish and warm as you journey ahead*
> *To enrich all the stories we tell.*

As the song ended Marheh took the line from Chanra and coiled it carefully, then, when Lidy nodded, she placed it neatly on *Evening Star*'s roof where Lidy could reach it and went to give the bow a gentle push as she had for Vey. *Evening Star* moved slowly past and away to make a lap of the Harbour.

Marheh stood watching on the edge of the dock, ready to welcome Lidy after her short journey.

She was thinking of Lidy and how she must be feeling, remembering the mingled sorrow and delight she had felt twelve years ago and barely noticed quick steps behind her. Then hands thrust hard against her back and she was falling towards the water.

There were seconds in which she recognised the inevitability of a wetting and then a powerful attack on her mind challenged her, demanding all her attention.

The Silberay, stunned by the unexpected interruption to their ceremony, took a moment to react.

Beuda was sobbing "I didn't want to, I didn't want to," over and over.

She was a distraction for some, but Kel had eyes only for Marheh. Her cloak was spread, half floating, over the surface of the water, but she was still submerged. The water was not deep. She could stand on the bottom. He knew she could swim. A moment later he was in the Harbour, reaching for the cloak, then lifting her head from the water. Her eyes were closed, her face very pale against the darkness of her clothes and her wet hair.

Drawing her through the water, half carrying her, he stumbled back to the loading dock where Jik and Dom were already crouched to receive her. As they rolled her onto the floor of the dock her body seemed to convulse and water ran from her nose and mouth. Fylan ran to kneel with Jik, to touch her throat and feel her head for injury. She was, at least, breathing. Carefully they rolled her onto her side, not knowing what else to do for her.

Kel put his hands on the dock, about to pull himself up and out, when he felt her urgent need. Almost before he had time to prepare, her mind had jumped to safety within his. The Silberay saw him stop and turn inward. Just once before, when she was still an apprentice, he had experienced Marheh's mind in his. She and Nemle had both been under attack and needed respite, but for her to need him here at the Harbour was a shock. How had the Yareblis managed it? There was no real chance of speculating, all he had was given to shielding Marheh's mind. He was conscious only of her.

She did not stay with him long. The initial attack had come like a huge boulder rolling downhill to crush her. She had become the wind and flowed around it, but she had been unable to manage the physical self that was near to drowning as well as the mental challengers who seemed intent on destroying her. The wind she had become threatened to dissipate and go beyond her strength to control and in desperation she had gathered herself to leap, trusting him to catch her.

As soon as she felt her strength returning though, she left him again. She would not risk bringing him to the attention of her attackers. The weight of the boulder had been made up of many minds that now had split into a rain of sharp stones that sought to bruise and batter her into submission. She spun into flame, faster and faster, white hot, so that the stones shattered in the heat only to reinvent themselves as an avalanche of snow, intent on dowsing the fire.

The flame rose on golden wings, a phoenix soaring above the snow, chased by a shower of dark arrows that fell short as she flew towards the sun trailing wisps of steam. Then the sun became a ball of fire and she was too near. The phoenix was falling, her feathers scorched and useless. Her scream echoed, the sound diminishing to become a sigh as she was caught and held in a soft cloud that took and hid her.

Needing a Bath

Chapter Twenty

As Jik and Fylan crouched beside Marheh and Kel emerged from his trance to hoist himself out of the water it was Teg who grasped what was happening.

"Sing!" he shouted. "We must sing!" His voice gained strength with each repetition. "Sing!"

Some of the younger apprentices misunderstood and waited open-mouthed for a starting note, but the old Silberay understood immediately and set the example, entering the soul song with determination and skill honed by long practice.

Soon all those who were capable of it had entered the discipline of the soul, building a raft of music that stretched over the Harbour. Only Jik, Kel and Fylan remained outside the song. Kel because he was holding his mind ready should Marheh need him again, Jik and Fylan because they were caring for Marheh's physical self, lying damp and unconscious on the loading dock.

.....

Hiding in a cloud was never a long term solution, but Marheh's mind understood this was respite and recognised that she was being given strength from somewhere. When she entered the battle again it was not to fight illusion with illusion but as herself, Marheh, shining warrior princess, with an army at her back.

Dark minds, harsh and malevolent, flung themselves against her but were consumed by her light. More and more darkness surged around her and fell back transformed as it touched the glow from her mind. Gradually the waves of attacking darkness paled. Still Marheh's light shone out. Weariness and fear were irrelevant since she understood there was no possibility of retreat. Only when there was no more darkness was she permitted to fade and allow her mind to rest.

．．...

For Jik, Kel and Fylan the only signs that things had changed were a little sigh and a small easing of her body as if she was seeking a more comfortable bed.

"I think she is back with us now," Jik said.

Fylan nodded.

"Then we had better get her out of those wet clothes and into somewhere warm."

She looked so small, Kel thought, bending to gather her into his arms, when, just a little time earlier she had been tall enough to draw all eyes. Jik helped him to stand and Fylan hurried ahead of him to open doors.

"Bring her to the house. I'll run a bath," she said. "And one for you too Kel."

"Don't worry about me," Kel said, panting a little with the effort. "I'll use the annex, but I'm afraid we'll drip on your floor."

"I'll mop the floor," Jik said, following behind.

The house was always kept warm since the old ones tended to feel the cold. Fylan led the way to the bathroom while Jik choked off Blin who had declined to attend the ceremonies, but was now all agog to observe a possible disaster involving Marheh.

With the door firmly closed against him, Fylan and Kel stripped Marheh of her wet clothes and Kel lowered her gently into the warm water. She seemed peacefully unaware. Fylan knelt by the bath and supported her carefully then looked up at Kel.

"I'll be as quick as I can," he said. "Jik will stay if you need help."

Fylan nodded. Neither of them mentioned what they most feared, that her mind might have been broken.

"Will you organise someone to bring dry clothes?" Fylan asked.

Kel nodded, then knelt for a moment beside her, took one of Marheh's hands in his and spoke her name. A faint hint of movement shimmered across her face and her eyes opened for a brief moment. He and Fylan looked at each other. It was a good sign.

"I'll be as quick as I can," Kel said again, getting to his feet and disappearing through the door.

He took a moment to report to Jik, still standing guard outside the door, then headed out across the grass towards the annex. Some of the Silberay stood around the loading dock and appeared to be still immersed in the soul song, others, tired after the effort this involved, drowsed on the grass in the sun. Bixa, her face grey with anxiety, held Beuda, who had stopped her wailing, but sat, staring at nothing. Kel paused for a moment and met Bixa's eyes. He could see her conflict and her question, but had nothing really to give her. Tippa stopped him just before he reached the annex and offered to go for Marheh's dry clothes. Her eyes too held questions he could not answer.

Ten minutes later Tippa was outside the bathroom door, a bundle of dry clothes in her arms. Jik still waited there. He was aware that Marheh's mind might need time to recover since he had been with her on other occasions when she had fought the Yareblis.

"Dry clothes," Tippa said when he had greeted her.

He nodded and opened the door for her.

"Fylan will probably need help to get her out of the bath. She won't have much control over her actions yet."

"She'll be alright though?"

"I hope so."

Tippa looked up at him, a bit disconcerted by his answer, then, as Blin approached again, whisked through the door and into the bathroom.

"Oh good," Fylan greeted her. "Dry clothes."

She was still kneeling by the bath making sure Marheh did not slip under the water. She had already washed off the mud of the water road and undone Marheh's plait to rinse her hair.

"Come on my lovely," she said to Marheh's apparently unconscious form. "Time to get you out."

Tippa went to help her as she pulled out the plug to let the water drain away then the two women bent to haul Marheh up and onto the edge of the bath. As they moved her, her eyes opened and this time stayed open. Then she made a small noise that sound for all the world like a little giggle.

Fylan and Tippa looked at each and then at Marheh.

"Jik said she won't have control over her actions yet," Tippa said.

Another sound, definitely a giggle came from the limp, rag doll Marheh had become. It was contagious. Tippa gave a grin and a little snort of laughter.

"Here, I'll hold her while you grab a towel."

By the time Tippa and Fylan had extricated Marheh from the bath, wrapped her in a towel and sat her on the seat of the toilet all three were laughing. Marheh still could not speak or tell her limbs how they should move, but she was beginning to be able to hold her head up.

"You're a fraud," Tippa said, holding her steady while Fylan rubbed at her hair with another towel.

Getting her dried and dressed became a hilarious game that celebrated the knowledge that she had been victorious and was recovering from her mind's exertions. By the time she was fully clad she could just about stand with support and smile at Jik and Kel when Fylan opened the door. Kel swept her into a hug as she tried to wobble towards him.

"I'd say all you need now is a good sleep," Jik said, hugging her in his turn.

…..

It was not until the next morning that the Silberay learned the whole story. No one had wanted to continue the ceremonies without Marheh so once she had been left to sleep on *Day Bringer*, Nisfa gathered the mentors and tried to make sense of what had happened. It soon became clear that Beuda had a Yareblis control and as Bixa and Jik questioned her they began to understand that this had been aimed specifically at Marheh.

"They know she is the one to be reckoned with," Jik said. "She has got in the way of their schemes often enough."

Without making an issue of it, he supported Bixa while she entered Beuda's mind to remove the control. It was not a skill she had practised, but with Jik to guide her she managed without causing Beuda too much discomfort. Beuda was still inclined to be petulant, but the knowledge that she had been controlled for the purpose of harming Marheh was a shock to her. She kept saying that it wasn't her fault, that she couldn't help it, but did appear to be listening when Bixa suggested that she had not perhaps tried very hard to resist.

Once Nisfa had made the announcement that Marheh was recovering and the final ceremonies would be held over until the next day matters were left to be taken up again in the morning. There seemed to be an atmosphere of sober thought about the Harbour that evening and Dom ventured to suggest to Jik that for many of the Silberay the whole incident had awakened them to new awareness of their purpose.

. . . . . .

Marheh woke early having slept for something like fourteen hours. She lay looking at the play of light reflected from the water onto the ceiling and testing her ability to control her movement by stretching and relaxing all each of her muscles. Even when she was confident that all was well she still lay thinking about her experience. There were so many questions. Beuda must have had a control, but how did the Yareblis controller know the perfect moment for the attack? Could she have drowned? Was that the intention? Were her best clothes completely spoiled? This last caused her a rueful smile and she stretched again and swung her legs out from the covers.

As she dressed she thought back to how Fylan and Tippa had cared for her. How she would have hated the vulnerability, the naked helplessness, when she was younger. At least now she had grown up a bit and even learned to laugh at herself. It had been funny, she thought, remembering their struggles with her heavy, slippery, inert limbs.

She was very hungry and made herself a big helping of porridge, glad to be safe on *Day Bringer* and doing something so ordinary. What next? Had they finished the ceremonies? Could she head out today? What had happened to Beuda?

It was foolish to think she could go today. There were goodbyes to be said, people to thank for their care of her, loose ends that needed tying off.

No one else seemed to feel the need to be away either, she thought, looking through the window at the quiet Harbour as she washed her few dishes. Life would be so much easier if she could just slip away, but of course she couldn't and not just because it would be rude and ungrateful. She had done very little preparation for the travels to come. All her focus had been on making things right for the others. She had not laid in her usual supplies, flour, oats and tins of tomatoes that could be stored for those times when provisions were hard to come by. Perhaps she could go into Sefton Middle today. She should pick up some coal too.

She was about to head out for the coal store when a little tap on *Day Bringer*'s roof and the movement of the boat signalled the arrival of a visitor.

"Jik!"

She met him as he descended the steps into her cabin. He gave her a hug them held her at arm's length for a few moments.

"You look a bit more the thing," he said. "Sleep well?"

"Very well. Would you like sperit? The kettle is hot."

He followed her through to the galley and sat at the table, allowing her to wait on him.

"So what have I missed?" she asked when the two steaming mugs had been prepared and she was sitting opposite him.

"Not very much," Jik said, saluting her with his drink. "The Gathering has been extended and the rest of the ceremonies will be held today. No one wanted to proceed without you."

"Oh." She flushed, pleased and surprised.

He told her about the meeting Nisfa had called and about the control he and Bixa had removed from Beuda. She told him about the battle she had fought. He told her how Kel had been so quick to understand that she needed help. She told him how she had escaped into Kel's mind when the initial attack threatened to overwhelm her.

They were still talking when there were footsteps on the gantry, another little tap on the roof and Tippa's face, sideways on, appearing in the window of the saloon.

"Come on in."

Marheh went through her work space to open the doors to the well deck. Tippa was carrying a bundle of folded clothes and Marheh's cloak over one arm. She handed the bundle to Marheh before stepping over the gunnel and into the well deck.

"The cloak is not quite dry," she said. "Another hour or so in the warm should take care of that though. Everything else has come up alright."

Marheh looked at her, unable to find words. The tunic had been Nemle's last gift to her. Despite the pain of her arthritic hands she had painstakingly embroidered the golden leaves and given it to her the last Gathering before she died. Marheh had worn it to honour her at the ceremonies of leave taking and at every special ceremony since.

"You're a magician," she said at last. "I was afraid they would be spoiled."

"I'm good with fabric," Tippa said. "Go and hang up the cloak. I'll make my own sperit."

She grinned at Jik and moved into the galley as Marheh hurried through to her cabin with the clothes.

Kel was the next visitor. Jik and Tippa stayed long enough to greet him then departed tactfully. Marheh went into his arms and rested there for a long time. There was no need for words between them. Kel had sheltered her mind in his and she was closer to him than anyone else in the world. There had been a time when she longed for the physical intimacy of love making, but it was not the Silberay way and perhaps the conscious relinquishing had enabled this other closeness. She didn't often think of it now, but the feel of his arms around her was as safe, as comforting as the warmth and shelter *Day Bringer* provided.

After a while he moved with her to the armchair and settled her on his lap so they could sing together.

The shining joy of the music stayed with her when the song had ended. She had not known that she needed healing until healing had happened with the song. Kel kissed her gently as he left. She watched him striding along the gantries back to *Storm Cloud*. Don't go, she wanted to cry, don't go. Perhaps the strength of her longing reached him because he turned to look at her across the roof tops before disappearing onto *Storm Cloud*.

It seemed a bit late now to be going for coal. She should perhaps go along to the office for what she hoped would be the last time. Probably Chanra would have everything under control, but she could check and it would help her to remember that she was still the Harbour Master with just these final ceremonies to preside over.

Sampi waylaid her as she made her way along the gantry. Nisfa wanted to speak to her, she was told, rather apologetically. Marheh smiled at Sampi.

"Now?"

"If you've time."

It was not a long visit, just time enough for Nisfa to quiz her about her experience of the previous day. She didn't really want to hear the question that Marheh thought most important, how did the Yareblis manage to time their attack so precisely, but expected Marheh to explain what she had done and how she had done it.

"I never really know," Marheh told her. "Unexpected things happen when I care enough."

It was clearly not what Nisfa wanted to hear, but she ceased her inquisition and instead told Marheh what had been planned for the remainder of the day.

She would have been welcome to lunch on *Cloud Drift*, but she refused the invitation politely and instead made her way along to the annex hoping to catch Bixa and Beuda. It seemed to her important that she connect with them both. She knew Bixa would have been concerned for her, perhaps was still, but Beuda was her responsibility and she would have made her a priority.

Although the work on *Spring Song* was finished it was not customary for the apprentice to move on board before the ceremony of initiation when promises were made and indentures signed. When she entered the little sitting room Bixa was already there sitting by the fire. She seemed to be staring at the flames and did not look up when Marheh came in.

"Bixa."

She swung around then sprang to her feet.

"Marheh."

They hugged then stepped back, each to study the other.

"How are you?" they asked in unison.

They laughed a little but quickly sobered, each concerned for the other.

"It was Beuda, wasn't it? Jik told me you removed a control."

Bixa nodded.

"I'd never done it before but Jik guided me."

"But you're still worried for her," Marheh said.

Again she nodded.

"For her and for me. She just doesn't seem to understand any of our values and I don't know how to help her."

Marheh looked sympathetically at her friend and was about to speak when they heard footsteps on the stairs and Beuda clattered into the room. She stopped abruptly when she saw Marheh and looked as if she wished she was somewhere else.

Marheh smiled at her but did not speak.

"It wasn't my fault," Beuda blurted into the silence. "I couldn't help it."

"I know that," Marheh said gently. "But nevertheless you might perhaps be sorry that it happened."

Beuda reddened.

"I am of course."

"And you might," Marheh went on inexorably. "Stop to consider that learning and practising Silberay values can help you to resist the demands of a control like that. I certainly don't hold you responsible for what happened to me, but I would like to think you could learn from it, and from Bixa, who has already given something of herself to care for you."

Beuda's face continued to redden and she looked from side to side as if wanting to find a way to shake off Marheh's words. Marheh held out a hand to her.

"Think about what I've said, remember that you are not the centre of the universe and things will go better."

She looked at Bixa then and laughed.

"I've needed to tell myself that so many times. My brothers don't call me Marheh the Great as a compliment."

Beuda looked from Marheh to Bixa then back to Marheh. Her face appeared more thoughtful than Marheh had ever seen it.

"I'll try to understand," she said at last.

"Good. That's all anyone can ask. Now, why don't we see if we can find some lunch?"

. . . . .

The party that evening did not seem to have suffered too much for being postponed for a day and it seemed to Marheh as if there was a new spirit of rejoicing amongst the Silberay. Everyone seemed to want to speak with her, to assure themselves of her wellbeing and sometimes even to thank her for reminding them of their purpose.

Ten minutes before the formal part of the evening was to commence she took herself off to the office for a few quiet moments. None of what was to follow was about her and she needed to remember that, but if she didn't play her part properly it would not be the enriching and affirming experience it ought to be for the apprentices.

She brought each one to mind for a moment, picturing them and what she knew of them, glad she had made an effort to learn a little about each. The ceremony would begin with Glik and Beuda and end with Lidy and these she held in her mind for longer. Then she picked up the list that would remind her of the correct order and went back to the meeting hall.

The last of the tables was being cleared to the edges of the room and the last rows of chairs put in place facing the dais. She saw that Chanra was directing operations with the help of some of the younger Silberay. This was one occasion when the apprentices were not expected to help. Instead they were already lining up in order of seniority, youngest first. Nisfa seemed to have that under control. Several of the other mentors were already sitting in the front row, each with an empty seat beside them.

Marheh was whisked back in time to her own apprenticeship and Nemle, loving and anxious for her to succeed. The new tunics were waiting, folded, on a table, a different colour for each level until the need for classes had passed. Lidy's cloak was draped over a chair. It was a tradition for the mentor to provide this, sometimes to make it, as Nemle had for her, sometimes to purchase it and sometimes to pass on their own.

The time had come, she thought, as the last few chairs were slid into place and sat on by the helpers. Taking a deep breath she stepped up onto the dais.

She had prepared a little speech of introduction, congratulating the apprentices, but as she stood there looking out over the assembly it seemed too formal, too contrived. As the room quietened she smiled.

"I doubt that anyone who knew me as a young apprentice would have expected to see me in this position, but I'm grateful to you all for the opportunity. Thank you for waiting for me and welcome to this most important event in the life of the Silberay."

She reached out to touch the little pile of new tunics.

"A different colour for each year to mark learning and progress, but really there should be a rainbow pile with enough colours for us all to mark our learning, because we never really stop. It's a mark of who we are. Sometimes it seems hard, I know, sometimes we want to rest, but if we follow the example of our elders, of Zinda, Juni and Vey, who have earned the right to rest, we will, I think, begin to understand that continual learning is required for a rich, fulfilling life."

She paused and looked towards the line of apprentices.

"In a moment, two new apprentices will promise themselves to the Silberay and choose for their lives the active pursuit of goodness and beauty. It is a choice we have all made, but perhaps when we made it we didn't understand that learning to identify goodness and beauty would be a life's work, the best work a life can undertake."

She called the apprentices then, each by name, beginning with Beuda.

She looked softer somehow, Marheh thought, and spoke her promise thoughtfully, as if she was considering its meaning. The gold coloured tunic was pulled over her head and Bixa came forward to sign the indentures then lead Beuda to the seat beside her while the Silberay applauded to welcome her.

Glik and Whin came next followed by the other apprentices. Then it was Lidy's turn. Marheh swung the cloak around her and embraced her before taking her hand and presenting her to the Silberay.

When the applause for Lidy had died down and she had found her seat amongst the Silberay, Marheh nodded towards the little group of musicians. The ceremony always ended the same way with a song for the young. Nothing happened however and before she could make a stronger signal Nisfa had stood and begun to mount the dais. Surprised, Marheh reached down to steady her on the steps. Still holding Marheh's arm she turned towards the assembly and, a moment later, Marheh found herself being thanked, not just for her work as Harbour Master, but for the example of what Nisfa described as her dedication to the Silberay.

It was too much, she neither expected nor wanted special treatment. She shook her head, but the Silberay were all applauding and it would have been churlish to run away. She felt herself become warm and knew that she was blushing, but she stood and smiled and allowed Nisfa to give the signal for the song.

> *You are the young, our heartbeat, our hope*
> *As you dance let our love partner you*
> *Let it lift and support as you leap into life,*
> *To dare, to become and to do.*

It was for the apprentices really, but she supposed that for Nisfa she too was one of the young.

As the song ended she raised her hands.

"The Gathering is ended. Hold to your promise. Travel safely into the future."

"Travel safely into the future," the Silberay responded as they did each Gathering.

There was a brief moment of silence and then the noise of departure, of voices exchanging goodbyes, promise of meeting, words of encouragement or advice. There was laughter and the sound of the chairs being collected and returned to their places.

Marheh stood, suddenly drained of the energy that had sustained her through the ceremony. Then Nisfa gave her a little shake and she saw Jik and Kel coming towards her, smiling.

…..

Three days later, moored behind *Storm Cloud* at the mouth of the WEG, she took out her journal to try to make sense of her feelings.

I had expected to be away the next morning, but of course that was not possible. For one thing, I was not properly prepared, but more importantly there were things still being asked of me. Bixa and Beuda came to talk because Beuda wanted to say thank you. That was a surprise. Chanra and I had some loose ends to discuss. I think she will do a great job and also have some help with implementing the changes we have planned. Lots of people wanted to say goodbye. That was a surprise too. I suppose that, in the past, I have headed out so early that I didn't give them the opportunity.

Nemle would have asked "What have you learned?"

Dear Nemle, I have learned that people care, that there are good things about making the effort to get to know them. I've learned that there are rewards in doing what is asked of you even if it is not congenial. I've learned to be more than ever grateful for your careful, loving teaching, and for the love of Kel and Jik and for my life on Day Bringer. Thank you.

ABOUT THE AUTHOR

Rosalind, like many Australians, loves to travel. She fell in love with the canals of England during her first visit there and this has remained a life-long passion. She spent nearly three years living and traveling aboard a 37ft narrowboat and this experience has informed her writing so that although the stories are fantasy the boating experience is authentic.

When not writing she enjoys walking her dog, practicing her violin, painting watercolours, choral singing, reading and of course traveling.

Marheh can be contacted at Marheh@gmail.com

Or keep up to date with Rosalind's writing at https://rosalindkentwell.net/

www.ingramcontent.com/pod-product-compliance
Lightning Source LLC
Chambersburg PA
CBHW030920120626

46554CB00001B/212